Enduring *you*

To Kelley,
Enjoy!
S Heller

S.T. Heller

Visit my website at www.shellerauthor.com
Cover Designer: Sarah Hansen, Okay Creations,
www.okaycreations.com
Editor and Interior Designer: Jovana Shirley, Unforeseen
Editing, www.unforeseenediting.com

This book is a work of fiction. Names, characters, places,
and incidents either are products of the author's
imagination or are used fictitiously. Any resemblance to
actual persons, living or dead, events, or locales is entirely
coincidental.

ISBN-13: 978-0-9972630-1-5

This book is dedicated to those living with the diagnosis of meningioma, the most common type of primary brain tumors.

Prologue

Wedding Day, Take 1—Thirteen Years Ago
Keegan

"And here we were, afraid it would be a rainy, chilly fall day. Instead, it is sunny and ninety-four degrees in October," my mother says to no one in particular while the limo driver explains to my father why the car is so hot.

It appears the air-conditioning system is low on refrigerant, making it feel like a boiler room inside the vehicle.

I'm not going to stress today, I'm not going to stress today, is my continued mantra, going over and over in my head.

Asking for assistance, I hold my comfy shoes for the reception in one hand and my wedding bouquet in the other. My top and only priority is getting married to my happily ever after, Will Henderson. It won't be long until I'm at the altar, staring into his beautiful eyes and reciting our vows.

Wedding Day, Take 2–Two Years Ago
Will

I look up at the clock tower atop the courthouse entrance, watching the minute hand creep closer to two o'clock. As the time of my impending nuptials near, the debate within me grows louder in my head.

I'm getting a second chance.

But what if I have to bail like I did the last time?

This isn't fair to Keegan or Kyle.

God help me, what am I doing here?

Do I skip out?

Do I try to explain to her about the past and what could possibly happen in the future?

Would she understand why I did it?

Could she ever forgive me for putting our family in danger?

No, I've got her back, and I'm not losing her again. I'm going into this courthouse and making her mine forever.

/

Present Day
Keegan

"**S**hit, shit, shit! I cannot believe this is happening to me again!" I mutter under my breath with a few additional colorful expletives, hitting the steering wheel to emphasize each one. I slowly pull the rental truck up the drive to my parents' house and strategically park it for unloading.

Like so many women these days, I am moving back to my childhood home after separating from my husband. I, Keegan Brigid Fitzgerald Henderson, an intelligent thirty-four-year-old college graduate with an MBA and a mother of one, cannot believe this is happening for the second time in thirteen years. I divorced and naively remarried the same man, thinking it was forever, only to end up right back where I was five years ago. What is the saying? *Fool me once, shame on you. Fool me twice, shame on me.* That is exactly what I'm feeling—shame, hopelessness, and a lot of heartache.

"Keegan! Welcome home! Where's Kyle?" Mom asks without giving me a chance to even get out of the truck.

"Mom, I told you, Kyle's spending the weekend with Will's mom while we finish clearing out the house. He doesn't need to witness the dismantling of his home for the second time."

"Honey, please stop being so melodramatic! This is just a little bump in the road. You'll regroup in no time and be back on your feet before you know it. You did it before, and you can do it again."

"Save it, Mom. I don't need one of your pick-yourself-up, start-all-over-again, rah-rah speeches right now. Please, just allow me some time to wallow in a little self-pity. I think I've earned it. Why did I ever think I could make it work with Will a second time?"

"Keegan, do I really have to tell you how this happened? Will and you started going down memory lane, reminiscing about all the good things in your first marriage. He charmed the pants off of you, and—ram, bam, thank you, ma'am—you guys got back together. Before we knew it, 'Here Comes the Bride' was happening for the second time."

"Mom, I believe it's *wham*, bam, thank you, ma'am." I can't believe I am correcting her backhanded comment.

"Whatever." She waves me off with her hand. "I think *ram*, bam is more accurate," she mutters under her breath, walking away.

I shout in her direction, "Gee, thanks so much for the lovely synopsis of my life and times with Will Henderson!"

William Kyle Henderson, known to all as Will, is my soon-to-be ex-husband for the second time and the father of our only child. At thirty-six years old and standing not quite at six feet tall, Will still has the hot body of his college days, six-pack and all. His light-brown hair with natural blond highlights and green eyes make him look as if he should be surfing somewhere off the coast of California. Instead, he works in the Criminal Investigation Bureau of the state police.

Enduring *you*

Our son, William Kyle Henderson II—whom we call Kyle—was born during our first marriage that lasted eight years. After being separated and divorced for a total of three years, we remarried for the second time, only for it to now end two short years later.

Although charming, Will has many personality flaws that override any redeeming qualities. He has become a stranger to me. No longer the caring man I fell in love with in college, he is now a demanding and, at times, an irrational person. In the past year, he has developed a short fuse toward me but, fortunately, not toward Kyle. He verbally attacked me whenever our son was out of sight and hearing range. I hated to be alone with Will, knowing an explosion could happen at any time. I suggested counseling, but was told, by him, that none was needed. He had no desire to salvage our marriage.

During my college years, I was described in a write-up in the school paper as a "high-spirited redhead." I lost that girl somewhere along the way, and I desperately want to find her again. My auburn hair and blue eyes are from my dad and the Irish side of our family. Some mistake my confidence as stubbornness and are occasionally offended by my outspoken ways. I embrace my Irish heritage, believe passionately in women's rights, and have as many male friends as female ones.

When we started dating in college, Will said it was love at first sight, the moment he laid eyes on my sexy curves and met my carefree sass. We got married after graduation, and he'd started his law enforcement career as a state trooper. The following year, I gave birth to our son, Kyle. For about seven years, we were happy, living the American dream in our new home and having successful careers. Then in the eighth year of our marriage, something snapped within Will, changing him into someone I barely knew anymore. Once divorced, I met another man, only for that relationship to end a year later. Will was there to help me pick up the pieces and convinced me he was a changed man who had never stopped loving me. We remarried and were happy the first year, and then the second one turned into a nightmare.

The toughest thing for me to deal with were his short temper and accusations of imaginary hook-ups and affairs. I was truly devoted to both of our marriages and never understood why he couldn't see it. There was something different about him during our second marriage. It was as if he had a mountain of secrets being kept close to the vest, never allowing me in. I could write it off as being a part of his job, but when pressed about it, he would turn into a man I no longer recognized. As each day passed, the trust in our marriage eroded, leaving me no choice but to end it for a second time.

When we decided to separate, Will agreed to move back to his mother's while Kyle and I continued to stay in our house until it sold. We never expected to find a buyer so quickly, making us move much sooner than we had originally planned.

Normally, I would take the bull by the horns and find a place of my own. I can easily afford one, being a part of the management team at one of the corporate offices of a global financial company. Recently, the company announced a reorganization plan that could abolish my position and many others in management within the upcoming year. Not knowing if and when this might happen, I lack the confidence to take on the financial risk of a mortgage or lease.

My life, at the ripe old age of thirty-four, is now crumbling down around me. With my world spinning out of control, I feel like such a loser, and I hate the thought of running back home to Mommy and Daddy.

My parents, Mitch and Sandy Fitzgerald, live in a neighborhood by a lake in the suburbs of Maryland, located approximately forty-five minutes outside of Baltimore and Washington, D.C. Both are retired civil service employees—Dad, a fire chief in the federal fire service, and Mom, a government contract specialist. Dad now works at the local community college as an instructor for fire rescue and paramedic courses. Mom stays home, doing all the things she never had time to do while working. My parents live comfortably in a spacious lakefront home that has an in-ground pool with a built-in hot tub, dock, and boat. There is plenty of room in their four-bedroom house for Kyle and me. I will take over the walkout ground level, which is private from the rest of the house.

Anyone looking from the outside would think I had hit the jackpot, having such dream accommodations at no cost. Herein lies the problem. There is a cost. The cost is my privacy. Next to Kyle, my privacy is the most important thing in my life. Although we will all have our own space, being under the same roof with my parents brings them into my business—my own private, personal business. It makes me feel as if I am back in high school— not a kid anymore, but not quite an adult on her own. I should be more appreciative of my parents coming to help me in my hour of need, but instead, I am frustrated and full of resentment.

"Where's your father and brother?" Mom inquires.

"They should be pulling up at any second. I left them at the storage unit to unload Dad's truck."

Ryan, my brother and our father's namesake, is helping with the move. As Kyle does, Ryan goes by his middle name, so not to be constantly confused with Dad. There is a three-year age difference between him and me. We have the typical love-hate sibling relationship with Ryan being the older, wiser brother and me being the irresponsible baby of the family. We are critical of each other and feel neither does anything right, but when needed, we are always there for each other. I love him to pieces and don't ever want to find out what my life would be like without him in it.

Ryan was the only one in the family honest enough to voice his doubts when I announced my reconciliation with Will. He tried to talk me out of it to the point of threatening not to attend the civil ceremony. In the end, he was there for me, knowing I was making a mistake.

My brother always makes life look so easy. It seems he has proverbial sunshine shoved up his butt. Sometimes, the aura of happiness glows so brilliantly from him that you need to wear shades when in his presence. Okay, I might be exaggerating a bit, but his life does appear to be drama-free in comparison to mine.

After graduating from college, Ryan fell into his dream job and married his longtime college girlfriend, Liz. They have two awesome children, whom I love to death.

At times, I find myself resenting their happiness. Don't get me wrong; I'm beyond thrilled for my brother's good fortune. I just wish some of their happiness would rub off on me. I don't understand how two children raised by the same levelheaded, loving parents, with no traumatic childhood experiences, could turn out so completely different.

Hopping down from the driver's seat of the truck, I stretch, grab my cigarettes, and head down to the lake to take a break for a few minutes. I have the rest of the day to empty the truck and settle in.

I can't help but notice the show of color the leaves are putting on this October day. With my parents living on a lake, one would think that summer was my favorite time of the year, but I've always been partial to fall. That was why I got married both times in this season. The weather is still warm, the colors are phenomenal, and the seasonal food is delicious. I can almost taste the roasted turkey, dressing, and pumpkin pie that will be served next month Thanksgiving. These last few warm days are an added bonus.

Kicking off my shoes before plopping down on the edge of the dock, I dangle my toes in the cold water, remembering simpler times. My left foot slowly moves in a circular motion, creating a small rippling effect in the water. I can almost hear the motor of the boat as it dragged Ryan and me across the water, tubing, during our younger years. Our screams would quickly turn to laughter as Dad jerked the boat back and forth, and our tubes skipped across the lake. For a short time, my thoughts provide an escape, but it soon ends when Ryan walks up behind me.

"I always know where to find you, sis. Come on, I don't have all day to get you settled in. Liz is waiting for me to get back, so she can go shopping with her mom."

Leave it to Ryan to ruin the moment and bring me back to reality.

Slipping my shoes back on, I exhale and crush out my partially smoked cigarette. "Thanks for your help today."

"Well, if you had listened to me two years ago, we wouldn't be doing this today."

"You know, Ryan, I don't need your I-told-you-so bullshit right now," I snap back before stomping away.

Ryan knows he messed up and quickly caught up to make amends. Grabbing my arm, he says, "Hey, sis, I'm sorry."

I look away to avoid the hurt in his eyes. "I know. Let's finish unloading the truck, so you can get home to Liz and the kids."

Reaching the truck, I see Dad is already busy unpacking it. "Dad, Ryan and I can do this," I tell him.

"No, I can tell you have one of your headaches. Go inside, and lie down on the couch while we empty the truck. When we're finished, I'll come get you, so we can return it before the rental place closes."

I give Dad a hug. "Thanks, Dad. I love you."

"Love you, too, princess," he says, giving me a tight squeeze.

I know it won't take them long. Being an overly organized freak, I packed the truck in the order I wanted it unpacked. What's being unloaded now are boxes and items, such as bikes and a portable basketball hoop that Kyle insisted on bringing here.

Later in the evening, after the truck has been returned, I empty a few boxes and shower. Afterward, I crash downstairs in my bedroom, exhausted and still dealing with my migraine. I am the lucky one of the family who inherited my grandmother's headaches. I've gone to the doctor numerous times. One visit was particularly scary when I lost feeling on the right side of my face and down my arm. Tests and scans were done, and I received the good news that I not only had a brain, but all was normal. I try never to leave home without my over-the-counter meds, and I have been popping them all day to take the edge off my current headache. I have prescriptions that are much stronger, but I only take them when I have the luxury of staying home.

Once comfy in bed, I pull my laptop out of the leather messenger bag Will gave me for Christmas. As it powers up, a picture of Kyle on my parents' boat appears. This picture was taken during happier times when our family and Mom and Dad were enjoying a day out on the lake. I immediately begin to feel better by looking at my son's smile.

I check my social media accounts to see what is happening. Yes, I admit it. I'm a social-media junkie on both social and business sites. I update my status and post a picture of the filled rental truck taken earlier today.

> *The deed is done. All moved back in at my parents'. Now trying to get rid of a headache.*

Immediately, my male BFF, Seth, responds.

> *Seth: Been thinking about you all day. Sorry I couldn't help.*

Marcy: Sorry I couldn't help out either. In need of a night out soon.

Bill: Let us know your new address.

Chrissy: It will be better soon. Hang in there.

Me: Seth and Marcy, totally understand. It's all cool. Seth, how was the beach? Any new hotties?

Seth: Hell yeah!

I notice there are already ten Likes on my post. Although I've been on these sites for years, the instant response one receives from posts still amazes me. All of a sudden, I feel disappointment toward my friends.

Are they clueless? What in the hell is there to like about a thirty-four-year-old woman with a preteen son moving back in with her parents because of a failed marriage? Okay, time to shut down the machine and take a step back. My friends are simply trying to show their support during this sucky time in my life. For God's sake, get a grip, Keegan!

When I shut down my laptop, my thoughts drift to my BFFs, Marcy and Seth, who have been there for me through thick and thin since first grade. I think back to meeting them on the first day of school while we waited in line for our turns on the slide. An immediate bond was formed that continues today.

Marcy and her husband, Roger Bennett, are going through their own difficult times. Still childless after several years of trying, they are struggling with the reality of possibly never conceiving. Even though Marcy is dealing with her own personal heartache, she has been there to hold my hand through mine.

As for Seth, one word sums him up—man-whore. He wrote the book, has the movie rights, and literally owns the T-shirt stating this claim to fame. A bad breakup in college has kept him from pursuing any sort of a serious relationship. He breaks out in hives if his name and the word *commitment* are ever used in the same sentence. Watching my comedy of errors hasn't helped matters.

Lying in bed, I try to give myself a pep talk by repeating the words Kyle has heard more than once from me during the past few months, "Tomorrow is a new day filled with new opportunities."

Finding little comfort in those words tonight, I lean over to turn off my bedside lamp. With tears streaming down my face, I whisper into the empty darkness, "Home again, home again, jiggity-jig."

2

Will

Sitting in a half-furnished condo, I look at the picture of the rental truck and read the comments in Keegan's post while taking another sip of whiskey from my glass. It burns on its way down, and I could easily blame it for the tears welling up in my eyes.

Damn it! How did I let this happen again?

My selfishness should never have made me reach out to Keegan the second time, causing this heartache for everyone. I knew better but couldn't stay away.

God, I hate the pain I've caused her. My family means everything to me, but their safety takes top priority. It doesn't matter what kind of an ass Keegan thinks I am. Knowing the real truth and protecting her from it—either until my death or the threat is gone forever—is my only concern.

My family thinks I'm moving back to my mom's house. Today, I moved clothes, pictures, and other valued possessions over there. Work knows I'm leasing this condo located right off of the expressway before Baltimore's city line because of my undercover assignment.

It's a short drive to both work and my family. More importantly, it's not far from the bowels of the city where the scum lives and where my work often takes me. I only took the bare necessities from the house to furnish my new secret home. I don't want Keegan or Kyle to have any knowledge of this place, so there will be no chance of them showing up here. I refer to it as my storage unit, so Keegan doesn't question me about where I'm taking my portion of the furnishings.

I will stay at the condo when Kyle is with Keegan. He is at my mother's tonight as I sit here grieving the loss of Keegan in private with a bottle of whiskey. I made up some lame excuse—cleaning the carpets in the house—to explain my absence to Mom, and I'll do the same again on nights when I stay here. None of the people I care about will ever know about this place, except for one person— Brittany.

My burner cell rings, and I see her number appear on the screen. "Yeah?" I answer.

"I talked with Hugo today during our session, and I think he took the bait," she responds.

"That's good news. How long do you think it's going to take for it to go up the ladder to his dealer?" I ask.

"No idea. You never know how this stuff is going to pan out," she replies.

"God, I hope this idea works. If anything gets screwed up now…"

"Cool your jets, babe. It'll be fine. Talk to you later."

I hate the lies. This is not who I am. Or is it?

It seems, as each day passes, I'm finding it easier to live the lie. It's the only way to keep the most important people to me—my family—safe and away from harm.

Bile rises up my throat as panic overtakes me.

Who would have guessed the stupid shit I did as a teen would follow me to this day?

I'm constantly looking over my shoulder, making sure my past never meets my present.

I've got to think this through.

What if everything blows up in my face?

I need to come up with some way to let Keegan know why we couldn't be together in case something happens to me.

A letter.

With paper and pen, I begin to write.

> *Keegan,*
>
> *I don't know where to begin, other than to say I love you. As you read this letter, please remember this. Everything I did was because of my love for you and Kyle...*

Feeling much better once the letter is finished, I slide it in an envelope that is addressed to Keegan with the date in the upper right corner. Getting another envelope out, I enclose some information printed off from my computer along with a key for the federal agent who is working on the case with me. On my way to work in the morning, I will drop both envelopes off at my attorney's office to put with other personal papers he's holding for me in his safe.

Calling it a night, I start toward the bedroom when my phone rings.

I see it's Brittany. Hopefully, she has some good news.

"Yeah, did you find out anything?"

"Well, hello. I love you, too, babe."

"Get to the point."

"He took the bait. You can go ahead and say it. I'm wonderful!"

"Thanks. I owe you. When all of this is over, I'll make it up to you, I promise."

"Babe, I can think of a million and one ways for you to show your appreciation to me."

"Never gonna happen."

"Haven't you learned never to say never to me?" She giggles. "See ya later."

And our conversation ends once more with no good-byes.

After settling in bed, I think about the woman behind the voice.

Brittany Peters is a beautiful blonde with a body that gave me lots of pleasure during my college days before I met Keegan. She's a social worker turned informant, who grew up in one of the rougher areas of the city and worked hard for her master's in social work. Brittany takes her job seriously and gets angry when the drug dealers and gangs of the city cause problems with her clients.

Years ago, Brittany contacted me regarding a boy in foster care, who she was desperately trying to keep from becoming a member of a local gang. She now gets information for me about the drug deals in the city. Brittany knows all too well how dangerous it is, risking both her job and life.

Our arrangement became even more complicated after my first divorce when I had an affair with her. Although Brittany was furious when I went back to Keegan, to my surprise, she continued serving as my informant.

God, I'm getting hard from just thinking about some of our past fun. The longer I lie in bed, remembering our prior hook-ups, the harder I get. We know each other's bodies intimately, bringing ultimate pleasure to both of us. In college, we would go at it all night and sleep in the next day, exhausted and not caring about missing our classes.

The whiskey isn't cutting it tonight, and I know who can make me forget about the pain. Reaching for my phone, I start dialing the all-too-familiar number.

"Hey, handsome! For some reason, I knew you would eventually call me back. I just didn't figure it would be so soon," Brittany answers in that sexy low voice of hers.

"Hey, what are you doing?"

"You?"

"You know where to meet."

"I love a guy who gets to the point. See you in an hour?"

"Okay, see you soon."

"Will, I'm glad you called. I've missed you, babe. One more thing," she continues.

"Yeah, what's that?"

"I refuse to be used again. If your head isn't in the right place this time, don't bother showing up. You understand?"

"Yeah, I understand. Britt, I can't make any promises about our future, but I swear, Keegan and I are never getting back together."

"I can work with that. See you soon."

3

Keegan

Six months have passed since Will and I separated. Christmas and Easter are behind us, and it is now late April.

Mom's favorite topic of conversation these days is either about her garden or summer vacation at the beach. Dad has contacted the marina, where he stores our boat, to arrange a time for pickup. Everyone seems to have fallen into a comfortable routine with the new living arrangements and fifty-fifty custody of Kyle. For some reason, Will appears to be more amicable this time about the terms of our separation and pending divorce, or maybe it's just easier the second time around.

To maintain consistency with established routines, Will and I felt it was important for Kyle to remain in his current school. Since Will's mom, Joyce Henderson, lives in the school's attendance area, Kyle rides the school bus back and forth from her house.

I am packing up my messenger bag at the end of the workday when a text comes over my phone from Mom.

Mom: FYI, Kyle was in a funk this afternoon when I picked him up from Joyce's.

> *Me: I'll text Will and see if he knows anything.*
>
> *Me to Will: Anything going on with Kyle that I should know about?*

Will: Not that I'm aware of. Why?

> *Me: Mom said he was in a funk when she picked him up. I'll talk to him and let you know what's going on.*

Will: Okay.

> *Me to Mom: Will doesn't know of anything. I'll talk to Kyle when I get home.*

Mom: Okay.

I find Kyle waiting for me in my bedroom. He's stretched out on my queen-size bed, staring up at the ceiling, with his foot nervously wiggling back and forth.

Before I can put my purse down, Kyle jumps off the bed and yells, "Mom, you need to tell Grandma Henderson that my name is Kyle, not *Little Willy*!"

Mustering all of my self-control not to laugh, I tell him, "Calm down and explain to me, in detail, what happened."

"Today she called me Little Willy! I refuse to be called Little Willy! Seriously! Who calls a twelve-year-old that? Is she flippin' clueless as to what she's calling me?"

"Did you try to explain this to Grandma?" I ask calmly.

"Yeah, sure I have. She says it's just a harmless nickname that she used to call Dad. No wonder Dad is such a dick sometimes."

"Kyle! Watch your language! I will not tolerate you disrespecting your father like that!" I correct him.

"Mom, you need to do something, or I'm not going back there. I don't care what you and Dad agreed to." Stomping out of my bedroom, Kyle slams the door behind him to put an exclamation point on his anger.

A few minutes pass. Then, Mom taps on the door and enters my room at the same time. "So, what's going on with Kyle?"

"It would appear that Joyce is calling Kyle by the name of Little Willy."

"Seriously? Is she clueless?"

"Interesting. Those were Kyle's exact words. Joyce told Kyle she called his father Little Willy, and I guess since he's named after his dad—"

"God, I don't know which one is the bigger pain in the ass—Will or Joyce."

"Mom! Stop! Kyle might hear you!"

"Oh, give me a break! By the way, dinner is ready."

After dinner, I decide it's time to face the music and call Will about Kyle's issue with his grandmother. Conversations like this never go well with Will.

"Hello?" he answers on the first ring.

"Will, it's me."

"I kind of figured it was when I saw the number. You do know I'm in the Criminal Investigation Bureau for a good reason."

"Oh, for Christ's sake, can you please stop with the sarcasm? I'm really getting sick of it."

"What's going on with Kyle?"

"Your mom called him Little Willy today, and he's very upset over it. Can you please speak to her?"

"About what?"

"About her calling Kyle by the name he prefers—Kyle. If she doesn't, he's threatening not to go back over there."

"So, what's this really about? I can't believe Kyle is making this big of a deal out of Mom calling him Little Willy. Why do I get the feeling his threat is not from him but you? Is this your way of trying to get sole custody? If it is, you can forget that ever happening, no matter how you try to manipulate him!"

"What? Are you serious?"

"Yeah, I'll make goddamn sure you never see him again if you continue to push this shit!"

"All I'm asking is for Joyce to call Kyle, Kyle!" I cry into the phone.

"Cut the fucking waterworks, Keegan. It doesn't work on me. Mom isn't doing anything wrong. She takes good care of our son, and I refuse to let you make her the bad guy. Tell Kyle to deal with it."

"You know, Will…you're…you're…you're such a *dick*!" I scream into the phone while emphasizing the words with a stomp of my left foot, like a petulant child.

Will hangs up on me, ending both the call and our argument.

I start pacing back and forth in my bedroom, muttering under my breath, "That asshole did not just hang up on me. I can't believe he did that to me."

I really hate talking to Will. I wish our conversations were civil and ended with us calmly resolving the issue at hand, especially when it's about our son. We both love him and have his best interests at heart.

Why can't our love for Kyle be a common ground for us to forge a new relationship during our divorce?

I know why this can't happen.

Because Will is a dick!

My factory-installed ringtone plays loudly on my phone. No, I don't have the time nor am I clever enough to come up with cutesy ringtones for each of my close contacts. Life is too damn short to waste time on such nonsense.

My first thought when I hear my phone is that Will is calling back to apologize. He will tell me how immature he has been about everything. My fantasy continues with Will granting me all of my wishes, the first being to burn his mother at the stake.

Okay, maybe that last thought is a little uncalled for and not nice.

Glancing at the screen, I see Marcy's number. "Hey, Marcy. What's up?"

"Hey, girlie. I was just going to ask you the same thing! Are things still going well at your parents'? Or has your Mom turned into a crazy woman, demanding no more wire hangers?" Marcy asks.

"God, does being a smart-ass come naturally, or do you practice that crap?"

"Sorry, Keegan. If I didn't tease a little bit, you would think I was sick or something. You sound a little testy tonight. Everything okay?"

"Yeah, things are fine with Mom and Dad."

"So, why are you so bitchy tonight?"

I proceed to share with Marcy all the details of the day and my phone call with Will.

"She did not call Kyle Little Willy, and Will did not defend her! God, he's such a dick!" Marcy exclaims, getting no argument from me. "You need a night out. How about this Saturday? Kyle is with his dad. Roger has plans for golf and dinner with his buddies. It's a perfect night for us to take a cab to Donnelly's to unwind with a few Black and Tans, and come back here to crash. Maybe Seth could even meet up with us. How does that sound?"

She said the magic words, *Black and Tans*. It's a heavenly concoction of two ales, one light and the other dark, being drawn perfectly from the tap into a pint glass.

I haven't had the time or desire to go out. I miss hanging out with Marcy and Seth.

In high school, we were constantly together. After we graduated, Seth and I went to the same local state college while Marcy went to a private one nearby. The three of us remained close during those years and still are today. I remember when my roommate broke Seth's heart and how he leaned on me to get through his heartache. Both he and Marcy are now here for me as I work through my second divorce.

"That sounds like exactly what I need. See you Saturday."

Ending my call with Marcy, I am feeling much better, looking forward to an evening of good times with my best friends. I can forget about the crazy in my life for one night and relax.

Marcy and I find Donnelly's in full party mode as we enter the Irish pub on Saturday night. It is wall-to-wall people with a soccer game between Manchester and Liverpool playing on the flat screen above the bar. A dart match is about to begin in the alcove off to the side, and a local band, The Express, is getting ready to start their next set.

Seth is already here and sitting at a high-top off to the far side of the bar. When we reach him, he stands, pulling me into a hug. "How are you doing? Are you all settled at your parents'?"

"So far, so good," I reply back.

"Hey, Seth, are you up for a match tonight?" Colin, a friend of his, yells from the alcove.

"Excuse me, ladies." Seth takes his drink and heads over to play darts.

Donnelly's is one of my favorite places on earth. I embrace my Irish heritage, appreciating the history of my ancestors, who hail from Dublin, to a properly drawn pint of ale. When it comes to holidays, St. Patrick's Day ranks number one, with Christmas following close behind. Although Will never quite got my love of all things Irish, he would be a good sport and join in.

Watching the bartender draw ale into our pint glasses, I glance across the bar to find a set of piercing blue eyes gazing back at me. I notice those baby blues belong to a gorgeous guy who has the sexiest smile. Gathering my wits, I head back over to our high-top with drinks in hand.

"OMG, Marcy, you will never believe what I saw over at the bar!"

"A sexy guy with blue eyes who's about six feet tall?"

"Yeah. Did you see him, too?"

"Yeah, he's standing right behind you." She motions with her head toward me.

"What? Oh God…do you think he heard what I said?"

"Yep, pretty sure he heard every word." Marcy nods.

"Shit!"

"I heard that, too." He laughs from behind me.

Turning in my chair to face him, his blue eyes now meet mine.

"Hi, I'm Cameron. May I join you?"

"Sure," I squeak out.

God, what is different about this guy? He makes me feel so off-kilter. I'm acting like a silly fangirl, and I need to get a grip. Guys normally don't faze me like this, no matter how hot they are.

When Will and I met for the first time, our chemistry was off the charts. I not only held my own, but I also had him chasing after me, begging, before the night ended. Eventually, I had my way with Will, but it was in my own sweet time and on my terms.

My plan has never been to declare celibacy during my separation, but a hook-up isn't at the top of the agenda. It's got to be the booze or the twinkle in those damn blue eyes or his kissable lips and sexy smile or his six-foot-tall chiseled body outlined with that black tee he's wearing. Or maybe I'm just horny as hell. Let's face it; the whole combo is making me a mess. It's dangerous.

"So, you know my name. What's yours?" inquires Cameron.

Marcy speaks up, "Hi, I'm Marcy and happily married. This is my best friend, Keegan."

Focusing his attention on me, he says, "I have two questions. Are you married? And, depending on your answer, can I be your friend?"

"I'm sorry. I am married," I say, trying to act apologetic.

"I'm confused. Are you telling me you regret being married? If so, there's a solution to that problem. Or you're sorry that you're not available?" Before I can answer, Cameron points to my left hand. "I see your hand is missing bling, so I'm going with, you regret being married, and you're in the process of doing something about it."

I take a moment to catch my breath. I stare deep into his eyes. "You are an observant man. Yes, I'm separated from my husband, and if you're lucky, you could possibly be a friend."

"I have to fess up. I'm not all that observant. I'm going through a divorce, too. How long has it been for you?"

"I'm halfway through my year of separation before I can file. And you?"

"My wife and I have been separated for over a year, and we're still not divorced."

Marcy pipes up, "Yeah, Keegan not only got mar—ouch!"

She quickly bends over and rubs the shin I just kicked, maybe a little too hard, as a signal to stop talking. I give Marcy my best get-lost look.

"Oh, I see Morgan over at the bar. I think I'll go say hi and see what's new with her."

"What was she saying about you?" Cameron asks, watching Marcy limp away.

"God only knows." I wave my hand, as if I'm batting a fly away.

Cameron orders me another drink as we continue to get to know each other.

During the evening, I find out his full name is Cameron Justin Holloway. He lives about half an hour away and is a mid-Atlantic zone manager for a flooring manufacturer. His marriage lasted almost ten years, and he shares custody of his two girls, ages nine and seven, with their mother.

Cameron asks, "How long were you married?"

"Thirteen years." Since I already shared that Kyle is twelve, I don't bother to clarify the time includes two marriages and the three years in between them.

Cameron is easy to talk to and has a wild sense of humor.

Marcy and Seth return to join in on the conversation, and by the end of the evening, we all have a nice buzz going. Life is great.

Before leaving, Cameron pulls out his cell and asks for my phone number. He punches in the digits on his, and my phone rings. "Now, you have my number, too. I'll talk to you soon. Night, Keegan." And he leaves the bar.

Once Marcy and I are at her house, I settle in bed as memories of my first divorce come to mind.

Six months after separating, I met and fell in love with Alex Parker. After dating for six more months and when my divorce was final, we moved in together. Kyle was eight years old and became attached to Alex.

I foolishly thought my happily ever after had finally arrived. My life with Alex came to an end almost a year later when a former girlfriend contacted him. He swore to me that nothing was going on between the two of them. Ten months after moving in with Alex, I found he'd been secretly texting her. With feelings of betrayal consuming me, I couldn't move out fast enough, only to shatter the bond Kyle had made with Alex.

Once again, with my second marriage ending, Kyle is working through the heartache of missing and not seeing his Dad every day. Bringing another man into his life at this time would be heartless. Not to mention, I have trust issues over previously failed relationships, which is a whole other story.

I'm awoken the next morning by a ding from my cell phone, signaling a text.

> *Cam: Good morning.*

> *Me: Is it?*

> *Cam: Are you always this happy in the morning?*

> *Me: You woke me up. What time is it?*

> *Cam: 7:30 a.m.*

> *Me: Seriously? WTF?*

> *Cam: What?*

> *Me: It's too damn early for me to be up, much less all cute and witty!*

Cam: Guess you don't want to go for a run this a.m. with me?

     Me: Nope. Going back to sleep.

Cam: A little hungover, are we?

     Me: Go away, and come back at a decent hour. Say around noon?

Cam: How about breakfast?

     Me: How about late lunch?

Cam: How late?

     Me: 1?

Cam: How about an early one at 11?

     Me: Seriously?

Cam: ☺

     Me: Did you just emoji me?

Cam: ☺

     Me: This could be a deal-breaker.

Cam: Was a deal brokered last night?

     Me: Negotiations were possibly opened.

Cam: Negotiate this. Both of us are kid-free today. Don't waste it on sleep. Come out and play with me today.

     Me: I need to recover from last night.

Cam: I have a remedy.

   Me: What?

Cam: Me.

   Me: A little sure of yourself?

Cam: No, just want to see you.

   Me: What do you have in mind?

Cam: Not sure if you're ready to hear what I have in mind.

   Me: Negotiations just closed.

Cam: Seriously, it's a beautiful fall day. Perfect for a ride on my bike.

   Me: As in, motorcycle or the kind you have to pedal?

Cam: Motorcycle.

   Me: You had me at ride on my bike.

Cam: Come pick you up?

   Me: I'll meet you somewhere.

Cam: Do you know where Joe's Diner is, off of 70?

   Me: I'll find it.

Cam: Be there at 11?

   Me: Or whenever I get there.

I look at the time on my phone. I still need to get out of here, go home, and get ready, so I text Cameron back.

Me: I can't get there before noon.

After gathering my things, I find Marcy and Roger at the table in the dining area with their preferred sections of the Sunday paper and morning cups of coffee. On the surface, no one would ever guess they were dealing with the heartache of being childless. They truly are an amazing couple and would make awesome parents.

"Morning," I greet both while getting a mug out of the kitchen cabinet for some coffee.

Marcy answers back, "Good morning! I wasn't expecting to see you up and ready to go so early this morning. I thought we could hang out at the mall today and see if there were any good buys."

"And where in the hell are you going to put any more stuff? Our walk-in is already overflowing," comments Roger.

Ignoring him, Marcy continues, "What do you say, Keegan? Do you feel up to some girl time at the mall?"

"Sorry, I already have plans for today. Maybe we can go shopping the next time Will has Kyle." I hope Marcy doesn't ask for further details regarding my afternoon plans.

"Ah, could your plans have something to do with your new friend?"

Damn it! Knowing I wouldn't be allowed out of the house without sharing some little morsel of information, I respond, "Mmm…maybe…maybe not. Meeting for a bite to eat, and I'll see where things go from there. You know, sober-in-daylight kind of thing."

Successfully escaping further interrogation from her, I say my good-byes, and I drive home with a heavy foot on the gas. Glancing in my rearview mirror, I see lights flashing. A ticket is the last thing I need this morning while hungover and rushing home to get ready for a date. I see an unmarked car is pulling me over. As if things couldn't get any worse, I look in the rearview mirror and see Will casually strolling up to my car.

"In a little bit of a rush this morning?" he asks, peering over his sunglasses at me.

"Sorry. Didn't realize how fast I was going."

"Good thing our son isn't with you."

"Get to the point. Why the pull-over?"

"Kyle's fever broke last night. This morning, his temperature was normal. So far today, he has been able to keep food down."

"I know. I read your texts from last night and this morning. Didn't you get my texts? Why in the hell are you even in your state car? I thought you were spending the day with Kyle."

"I had to run into the office this morning for a few minutes. I guess the music at Donnelly's was a little too loud for you to hear your phone last night."

"How…are you—what the hell? Are you having me followed?"

"No. Call it a lucky guess. After being married to you twice, I know when you're hungover, and your favorite place to go is Donnelly's. Since we are on the subject of tying one on at Donnelly's…"

"Didn't know we were," I mutter under my breath.

"Do you really think drinking alone at a bar is safe behavior? How many times do I need to tell you the risks? I don't want to pull up to a crime scene and find you're the victim. It would kill me, never mind what it would do to Kyle. God, Keegan! How can you be so fucking selfish, not thinking about Kyle and your family or even me? If something happened to you, it would be…it would…"

I jump in my seat as Will slams his fist on my car's convertible top.

He reins in his anger and continues, "It would be bad for all of us, damn it!"

"I wasn't alone. I was with Marcy and Seth, and we used a cab. You no longer have a say as to whom I see, what I do, or where I go. Now, if there's nothing else, I would like to leave and go home."

"Well, you might think I no longer have a say in who you see, what you do, or where you go, but the day we had our son was the day I was given the right. I especially have the right when your irresponsibility could have a long-term effect on Kyle. Bottom line, I will always be in your life, no matter how many times we get divorced!" Will stomps off to his car, pulls out into traffic, and speeds away.

Dropping my head to the steering wheel, I try to hold the tears back. I wonder if we will ever get to a point in our relationship when there will be no more shouting and tears. What happened to our love? We created a beautiful son out of it. How could something so beautiful turn so ugly?

Pulling myself together from my encounter with Will, I drive home to find Mom and Dad working in the flower beds.

"Morning, sweetie. Or is it afternoon?" Mom questions, looking up at me from under her wide-brimmed straw hat.

"It's still morning, Mom. Making a quick pit stop to hop in the shower and freshen up. I'm meeting a friend for lunch."

"A friend?" Dad suspiciously asks as he pauses from raking the mulch.

"Yeah, someone I met last night."

"Care to share any details with us?" Mom says, standing and walking closer to me.

"It's just a guy I met last night. He seems very nice and asked if I would like to meet him for lunch today. It's really no big deal," I say, trying to downplay things in front of Dad.

It appears I've succeeded because he leaves to get something out of the garage. I'm not as lucky with Mom.

"Keegan, don't you think it's a little soon? All I can think about is what happened between you and Alex. Maybe it's unfair for me to bring him up, but I'm your mom, and I worry about you."

"It's only lunch. I'm not moving in with the guy, for God's sake!"

Mom studies me for a moment and sighs with a smile. "Okay. Sorry for sticking my nose where it doesn't belong."

I acknowledge Mom's apology with a quick nod then leave before she makes any further comment.

I pull into the diner's parking lot and see my car is one of the few here. There must be every type of motorcycle imaginable parked in the lot.

Cameron's baby blues spot me the moment I enter the diner. As I walk up to the booth, he stands and gives me a hug. I'm definitely getting the message that he wants to give me more than a ride on his bike. Honestly, it's something I want, too, once the terms are sorted out in my head.

No sooner do we sit down than the waitress places a plate of greasy fried eggs and bacon in front of Cameron. "I hope you don't mind that I went ahead and ordered. I was starving."

"Breakfast for lunch?"

"Love it, especially on a lazy Sunday!"

I decide on a plain bagel with jelly and a cup of coffee. Between the fun banter we share and the food, my hangover is quickly forgotten.

After we pay our tab, we go outside to Cameron's bike, which is one sweet-looking ride with its custom chrome sparkling against the black paint. He turns on his bike to warm it up. After putting his helmet on, he takes a brain bucket–style one out of his sidesaddle for me to wear.

He pulls me close and tugs hard on the strap to tighten the helmet while saying in my ear, "Are you ready for the ride of your life?"

Chills go down my spine with excitement shooting to my core, which I have not experienced for a long time.

Throwing his leg over his bike, Cameron mounts it, bringing it fully upright to kick up the kickstand with the heel of his biker boot. He then brings down the back pegs for me to use. I hold on to his shoulders as I climb on the bike behind him. Once on, I scoot up, firmly wrapping my inner thighs and arms around him, and I snuggle into his leather jacket.

Chuckling, he yells back to me, "Are you ready?"

I yell back, "Yeah, let's go!"

Twisting the throttle on the handlebar a few times, Cameron revs up the motorcycle. He puts it in gear and slowly rolls out of the parking lot. Once on the main thoroughfare, he starts popping the clutch, making the bike take off like a rocket. I find it exhilarating and squeeze Cameron a little tighter from the thrill of it all.

We head toward the mountains on this beautiful spring day with budding trees bursting out in bloom. Feeling alive and free of life's trappings, I get lost in the kaleidoscope of colors flashing by me.

A few minutes into the ride, Cameron reaches down with his left hand and gently rubs my outer thigh. It is such a possessive, sensual touch, and I love how it feels.

After an hour of riding, Cameron pulls into a gravel lot off the side of the road. We dismount and stretch.

He asks, "Are you up for going on a little hike?" He nods to a path leading into the woods. "There's a view up there that I would love to show you."

"Sure." I wonder if it is wise to be so trusting in such a short amount of time.

I keep hearing Will's words echoing in my ear. *"I don't want to pull up to a crime scene and find you're the victim."*

I shake his words from my thoughts and take Cameron's hand as we head up the trail.

It isn't long until we reach an outcropping of rocks looking out over a breathtaking view. A farm surrounded by a patchwork of fields and a beautiful stone church are off in the distance. The beauty overwhelms me, and a couple of tears stream down my face.

"Hey, what's wrong?" Cameron asks.

"Nothing. Absolutely nothing. It's perfect. You're right. It's beautiful. Thank you for bringing me here today."

I wrap my arms around Cameron's waist and hug him tight.

How did he know this was exactly what I needed?

He looks down at me and kisses the top of my head. As I gaze up, he bends down further to kiss me. It starts as a soft kiss but soon deepens with me parting my lips, inviting him in. He takes full advantage of it, and soon, our kissing takes on a level of unexpected passion, leaving us both breathless.

Cameron then says to me, "I want you, Keegan. God, I hope you feel the same way. Come home with me."

I nod, smiling. "Okay. Let's go before I change my mind."

4

Will

It's after ten p.m., and Keegan's vehicle is the only one left in the parking lot. *Where in the hell is she?*

Around four this afternoon, a fellow trooper contacted me as Kyle and I were watching a movie on TV. He'd spotted Keegan's car at a popular biker hangout during a routine traffic stop in front of the place. I told him to cruise by occasionally and let me know when it was gone. I contacted my mother-in-law, Sandy, only to be told that Keegan had lunch with a friend.

And here I am, six hours later, worried sick about her.

Six years ago, after receiving a photo of Keegan and Kyle with what looked like blood splattered on it, all I have thought about is my family's safety. The intended message of the photo was loud and clear, and I started to come up with ways to keep an eye on them. One way was to ask troopers I knew personally to watch out for Keegan's vehicle during their shifts and to notify me of anything that looked suspicious. They probably thought I suspected her of cheating or that I was keeping my wife on a short leash. Let them think whatever they want. It's easier than explaining my past, which is full of secrets that I'd rather not share with others.

When I entered the state police academy, I passed the background check because my juvenile records had been wiped clean. I was one of the lucky ones with loving parents who had deep pockets to save me from my rebellious youth and the temptations of the inner city.

While I'm checking Keegan's car for signs of foul play, a motorcycle comes roaring into the parking lot, stopping on the other side. God, I hate motorcycles.

I can't believe the scene transpiring in front of me. It takes me only seconds to see it's Keegan glued to some guy, riding on the back of his bike. I have no idea who he is or if there's a connection between him and my current work or past.

Sizing up the situation, I decide, if he gets off the bike, I'll cuff him to contain any possible threat. I hear Keegan tell him to sit tight as she climbs off the bike. Ignoring her instructions, he dismounts, removes his helmet, and then takes a stance, as if daring me to make a move. Under the circumstances, that's all the excuse I need to justify cuffing him, and I proceed to do exactly that.

Keegan shouts, "What the hell, Will? Get those cuffs off of him!"

"Not until you tell me this asshole's name and where the hell you've been!"

"What? Are you kidding me? Why in the hell are you even here?" she shrieks back at me.

Fighting the cuffs and trying to get out of my grip, the guy yells over his shoulder to Keegan, "Who is this joker? What the hell's going on?"

It doesn't help matters that I'm in street clothes and driving my personal vehicle. I reach into my pocket, pull out my badge, and flip it up in his face. "State Police. Now, shut up while I talk to my wife!"

"Will, take the cuffs off now, or I swear, you will never see Kyle again! I mean it, Will. Take them off now!"

As the guy puts two and two together, he continues to mouth off while I take off the cuffs.

"What? Is this your ex, Keegan? He's a state cop? What the fuck?"

"Hey, asshole, we're not divorced yet, and I can put the cuffs back on if you don't shut up," I respond back. "Show me your license."

He reaches into his back pocket. "Can I ask why I was cuffed and am now showing ID? Did I do something illegal while coming into the parking lot? Or is it because Keegan was up against me, enjoying the ride?"

"Watch it, fucker," I warn him.

"Do they know at headquarters that you do this kind of shit?" he asks me.

While I'm noting his name and address, Keegan says, "Enough, Will! Give Cam his license back. Cam, stay put while I take Will over there and find out what the hell is going on."

Reading his name off his license, I say, "Well, Mr. Cameron Justin Holloway, here's your license, and you can take off now. I'll make sure Keegan gets home safely instead of being dropped off in a vacant parking lot in the middle of the night."

He looks over at Keegan. "You okay?"

"Yeah, go on, Cam. It's fine. I'll talk to you later."

My stomach turns as I watch this guy take Keegan into his arms. He plants a long good-bye kiss on her lips. "Thanks for a great day. I'll call you later, okay?"

Keegan gives him a nervous smile and nods.

Son of a bitch!

No husband should ever have to watch something like this while trying to maintain a look of indifference on his face.

After he peels out of the parking lot, Keegan mutters under her breath, "Damn it!" She quickly turns on her heel and gets up in my face. "What is your problem? Why do you feel the need to hound me every second of my life?

Why is it so hard to understand that what I do is no longer your business? How the hell did you even know my car was here?"

I get right back in her face. "You know, Keegan, you drive a pretty hot-looking black sports convertible, which all my trooper friends notice and envy a little bit. When one of them spots it in a parking lot at a joint like this, it's noted. When the same trooper drives by the parking lot a few hours later and the car is still there, it's noted even more. That trooper makes a courtesy phone call to me, wondering if I should be concerned that your car has been sitting here for over three hours. I call your cell but no answer. I call your parents, and all they know is that you left before noon to meet a friend for lunch. I'm notified again when the fucking car is still here once the place closes. I come by to check it out myself to see if there are any signs of foul play because something is definitely wrong. Christ, then you come pulling up on a motorcycle, no less, with some guy I've never seen before. So, yes, now, I'm totally pissed off. Did you fuck him, too?"

Keegan, ignoring my question, responds, "What? You called my parents, like I'm sixteen years old? Damn it! Why did you do that? Now, there will be a lot of questions when I get home. Just because you're with the state police, it doesn't give you the right to do this to me. We are over, Will!"

"We will never be over because of our son. I will always be in your life, like it or not. You never answered my question. Did you fuck him?"

"Yes, I did! It was the best I ever had! Do you want to know how many times? Sorry, I can't tell you because I lost count. Do you have any other questions?"

I am speechless. I start to walk toward my SUV. I stop and take a deep breath to calm down. I turn around and walk back to her. "Keegan, even though we didn't work out, remember only one thing. I will always care about what happens to you. Maybe I'm a dick at times, but your and Kyle's safety will always be my top priority. Now, get in the damn car, and go home. I'll follow since the asshole left you here with no clue as to what might happen between us."

"I don't need to be followed home like a child."

"Keegan, if you don't want to be treated like a child, I suggest you stop acting like one. Now, get in the fucking car!"

As I follow Keegan home, I make a mental note to run a check on Holloway to see if he has any priors or questionable connections. I'm still not convinced it was an innocent date, and I fear Keegan is being used as a pawn to get to me.

Once I see Keegan turning into her parents' neighborhood, I speed off with my adrenaline still pumping through me, and I'm in need of an outlet. Before I know it, I'm calling Brittany.

She answers the phone, "Hey, babe. I thought you were hanging out with your son tonight. Are you at work?"

"I was called out on a special case."

"Do you want to get together before heading back home?" she asks me.

"All depends on what you have in mind," I respond.

"Anything you want, babe."

"Meet you at our place?"

"Okay. See you soon. Bye," Brittany says before hanging up.

Our place is whatever room is available at a hotel we use that's located in the northern part of the county. We park in the back, and whoever arrives first gets a room, using an alias. Once checked in, the room number is texted to the other.

My phone buzzes, and I see room 204 is the place to go this evening.

Brittany greets me at the door, wearing a sheer black lace push-up corset with matching thongs. Handcuffs are dangling from her manicured fingers.

God, she's hot!

I greet her by asking, "So, you want to play rough tonight?"

She nods and gives me one of her mischievous smiles.

Brittany wastes no time in stripping me out of my clothes. I push her down onto the bed and then rip off her corset and thongs. Brittany has a gorgeous body, and I take in every detail of it as my hand caresses and plays with her breast. Taking both of Brittany's wrists in my hands, I yank them above her head to cuff.

Once she's cuffed, I tell her, "Don't move your arms. Open your legs wide, so I can see all of you."

"Just one question. Do I get to cuff you afterward and have my way?"

"Hell yeah!"

Starting with her full red lips, I devour her luscious body with my mouth. She's so responsive to my touch, moaning softly as her first orgasm hits. I am only getting started. Flipping Brittany over to her hands and knees, I take a moment to admire her glorious ass, and then I smack it hard. Grabbing ahold of her hips, I start pounding into her from behind. Each time is a little harder and deeper than the last. It isn't long until we are both coming, screaming out in pleasure.

Afterward, I collapse beside her on the bed and take off the cuffs.

Before I know it, she's cuffing me, and with the sexiest smile on her face, she says, "My turn now."

5

Keegan

I sit in my car for a few minutes, trying to get my tears of frustration under control before going inside the house. I need a cigarette, so I head to the dock.

How am I ever going to face Cameron and explain what happened tonight?

After crushing out my cigarette, I head to the house. Using my private entrance, I enter, undetected. I soon hear footsteps coming down the stairs, and I know Mom is on her way to question me.

"Mom, now really isn't a good time. Can we do this later?" I ask as she reaches the bottom of the stairs.

She stands in the open doorway to my bedroom. "No, Keegan, I don't think we can. The call from Will had us worried since your text earlier today didn't say much, other than you would be home later tonight. I think we're owed an explanation. You can either talk to me or your father. Pick your poison," Mom responds.

Although I love them both dearly, Mom and Dad are two entirely different types of people when it comes to communication. My dad is a man of few words and has little middle ground in his life. He is decisive and says his piece, and often, it is not what you want to hear. Then, he leaves, signaling the conversation is over. It comes from his years of being a fire chief, barking out orders and directing emergency incidents. Mom, on the other hand, loves to talk, and she's a woman of many words, playing the roles of negotiator and peacemaker in our family. This is a no-brainer. I pick Mom.

I wave her into my bedroom before walking over and flopping down onto the bed. Mom stands quietly, waiting for me to speak. She soon understands that I'm not going to offer any information. If this is an inquisition, so be it. I'm not volunteering any details. I will only answer her questions.

"So, since you're not talking, can I assume you've been with your 'friend,' the same one from last night?" she asks, using annoying air quotes to emphasize the word *friend*.

"Yes."

"Can I assume since Will called, inquiring about your whereabouts, he knew you were with this guy?"

"He knows now."

"And, from your whole demeanor, can I also assume that there was a confrontation between you, Will, and this guy?"

"Yes."

"Was blood shed?"

I jerk my head up at Mom. "Of course not! Only cuffs."

"What? Did Will arrest your 'friend'?"

"Just stop with the air quotes, Mom. It's irritating!"

"Well, since I don't have a name for your 'friend,' I have no choice."

Mom and I are now in a stare-down contest.

Damn it! I lost by blinking first, so I look away.

"His name is Cameron," I mutter in a voice that's barely audible.

"You didn't answer my question. Did Will arrest Cameron?"

"No. He was just being a bully. It was his version of a pissing contest."

"Up to that point, did you have fun today?"

A smile comes over my face. "Yeah."

"I'm glad you had fun. I'm sorry Will ruined it. Just do one thing for me, and be careful. Okay?"

"Okay, Mom. Good night."

Mom walks over to the bed and motions for me to get up. We hug as she softly says in my ear, "Good night, sweetie. Love you bunches."

She leaves my bedroom as tears come over me. Those were the same words she used when tucking me in as a child. God, I needed to hear them tonight.

The next morning, I wake up and stretch. I smile, recalling my perfect day with Cameron yesterday. My anger over Will's earlier pull-over disappeared once I met up with Cameron for lunch. It felt good, having my legs hugging him tight during our ride on the bike. The vibration of the bike made our connection all the more intense, and it was a total turn-on.

I giggle as images of us in bed yesterday fill my thoughts. We were two people desperately filling each other's sexual needs numerous times. Once more, I felt like the sensuous woman, who had disappeared during the last year of my marriage.

As we lay naked and exposed, following our afternoon romp in bed, we spoke of living in the moment with no promises for the future. There was talk of schedules and times when we would be kid-free at the same time. We agreed to keep it easy and fun with no demands, other than being monogamous.

It's the perfect kind of relationship for two people in the middle of dealing with their divorces.

I remember feeling relaxed and sated while nestled against Cameron during the ride back to the diner. As we pulled into the diner's lot, life could not have been more complete until I saw Will's SUV parked beside my car. I knew my perfect evening was coming to a screeching halt.

Grabbing my phone from the charger on the bedside stand, I text Cameron.

> *Me: I'm so sorry about last night. Can we talk?*
>
> *Cam: Now is not a good time.*

Surprised he is up so early and responded right away, I text back.

> *Me: When would be a good time?*
>
> *Cam: I'll let you know.*
>
> *Me: Why do I get the feeling I'm never going to get a chance to explain?*
>
> *Cam: TTYL.*

Disappointed we can't talk and clear the air, I get up to get ready for work. Hopefully, I will hear back from him later and get the opportunity to explain and apologize in person.

It's been a long day at work, filled with meetings and talk about the reorganization. The day was very depressing and even more so with no further texts from Cameron, making me feel ten-stories-below-the-gutter kind of low.

Thinking back to Will's words from last night, I decide some ground rules regarding our social lives need to be set between us. While I'm lost in thought, my phone signals a text.

Cam: Are you free for drinks?

Me: When?

Cam: Tonight.

Me: I was scared I wouldn't hear back from you.

Cam: I want to see you again.

Me: Seriously? After last night?

Cam: What can I say?

A smile slowly spreads across my face as I remember the multiple orgasms he gave me.

Me: Where?

Cam: My place?

Me: Can you behave long enough for me to tell you how sorry I am about what happened with Will?

Cam: I'll behave.

Me: Time?

Cam: How about coming over when you get off work? I'll order pizza. What do you like?

Me: Cheese and mushrooms.

Cam: Not a lover of meat? I mean, on the pizza.

Me: Watch it, or I won't come.

Cam: Both of us know that's a lie. See you soon.

With a new spring in my step, I call Mom to let her know that I will be out late tonight. I then go to the restroom to freshen up before leaving for my date.

Nervously, I walk up to Cameron's door and ring the doorbell to his townhouse. He opens the door, wraps his arms around me, and softly kisses me.

"God, I couldn't stop thinking about you all day," Cameron says, holding me in his arms.

"Me, too. After our texts this morning, I was worried I might not get a chance to explain," I say, cuddling into his chest.

"Come on in."

The pizza arrives minutes later.

Armed with pizza and cold beer, we get comfortable on the couch as Cameron says to me, "Okay, explain to me what the hell happened last night and why I ended up in cuffs."

"I'm sorry. Will can be a little overly protective of me at times. I should have warned you. I had no idea an APB had been put out on me because my car was left at the diner after closing."

"How did he even know it was there?"

"A trooper who knows my car contacted Will after seeing it had been parked there all day and after closing. Will was checking the car since I hadn't answered my cell.

I'm sorry you got in the middle of it all. I wish we could have cleared it up this morning. Did you have to head into work early?"

"No, I was in the middle of a discussion with my ex about seeing the kids. She can be, uh…what word should I use? *Difficult* probably would be the nicest way to put it," he says with a smirk.

"You mean, a bitch? It's a terminal condition ex-wives suffer from. On numerous occasions, Will has told me that I have the same condition."

"I can't believe that. All I see is a woman whom I'm having a hard time"—he looks at me with a grin—"keeping my hands off of tonight."

Laughing, I place our pizza on the coffee table and straddle him. "Just how hard is it?"

In no time at all, Cameron is carrying me off to his bedroom. This time, our interaction with each other is more affectionate and playful than last night. Cameron takes his time caressing and exploring my body as I do the same with him.

His mouth travels down my body, feathering me with soft kisses and caressing my breast. Soon, he has me wanting and begging him for more. The night culminates in mind-blowing orgasms, leaving us both shattered.

I leave Cameron's home with a feeling of contentment, which has been missing from my life. My lost confidence is returning, and I no longer feel the need to cower to Will's verbal assaults or demands. During the drive home, I make the conscious choice to take back control of my life that I so easily handed over to Will. I find this liberating, and the tension I've been carrying around slowly releases from my neck and shoulders.

The next day, I call Will.

He answers his phone on the first ring by shouting, "Seriously, Keegan? We only separated six months ago, and you're already fucking other guys! Is he your next Alex Parker? What about Kyle?"

Instead of shouting back at him, I decide to respond to his outburst in a calm, even tone, "Will, we need to talk about the other night. I thought by giving you a day to cool down, we would be able to discuss this without yelling at each other. I will not allow you to disrespect me with your verbal assaults anymore. They stop today. Can we discuss this like two adults? Please?"

At first, there is silence, and then he asks angrily but without shouting this time, "What do you want?"

"Will, you know we're toxic together. All we do is fight. We need to stop. You're right about always being in my life. Honestly, I wouldn't want it any other way. Can we try to find the friendship we used to share? I miss it."

"So, what do you want, Keegan? Us to be BFFs? Not sure if I can pull that one off."

"No, I want us to be civil and to stay out of each other's business. Also, when we discuss Kyle, we shouldn't use him as a weapon to hurt each other. Do you think we can do that?"

Again, there's silence on his end for a moment or two. Then, he says, "All I can promise is that I'll try, but don't expect any miracles to happen overnight. Just remember, although we can't be together, I will always care about you. I miss my friend, too."

"Will, one of these days we're both going to meet people, and we'll want to introduce them to Kyle. There will be special occasions—like birthday parties, graduation, and weddings—we'll want them to attend. We need to be able to—"

Will interrupts me mid-sentence, "Stop right there, and don't say another word. I don't want that guy at *any* family functions we both need to attend—*ever*! You might have your rose-colored glasses on, but I'm not there yet! Do you understand me?"

"Yeah, I understand. Maybe we just need to take this in baby steps and work on being civil to each other. We can worry about the rest later."

"I'm warning you, Keegan. Don't test me on this one. I will never accept another man being a father to my son. I still remember what happened with Kyle when you broke up with Alex. I agree, we have stuff to work on, but this other shit is never happening! Anything else on your mind?"

"No, other than I'm seeing Cameron, and I would appreciate you backing off. I don't want a repeat of the other night."

"I would appreciate it if you kept your new boy toy away from our son," Will replies back sarcastically.

Refusing to become defensive with Will, I simply say, "I have no intention of introducing Cameron to Kyle."

"That's good to hear. At this point, all I can agree to now is, I'll try to stay out of your personal life. But you need to know, if I see anything I think is out of line, all bets are off."

Giving up on our conversation, I end it by saying, "Good night, Will."

"Night, Keegan."

6

Will

I pour a glass of whiskey as I stew over my conversation with Keegan. I might not be with my family, but I'll be damned if I'm going to be replaced.

I made some stupid choices in my life back when I was just a year older than Kyle. Never could I have imagined the dumb decisions of a thirteen-year-old could have such a lasting impact on my family and me. I'll do whatever it takes to keep my son safe and prevent him from doing anything half as stupid as I did at his age.

As I sit with my drink, my thoughts go back to the day I met Troy Martin, skateboarding in a park close to where I lived.

I was thirteen years old and in middle school. I thought I was hot shit because a sixteen-year-old high school guy was giving me the time of day. Being maturer and taller than most kids my age, I would often be mistaken for being much older. Troy and I liked the same things—skateboarding, rap music, and cool clothes. We wanted to be the two most badass skaters on the streets of the city. Like me, Troy came from a nice home with parents who were pillars of the community.

All to soon, he became my worst nightmare, and I ended up immersed in the violence of the city's drug scene. I was no longer only listening to lyrics in rap music. I was living them by helping Troy run drugs for a local dealer to bankroll my own escalating habit. It was exciting and thrilling. At times, it was some of the scariest shit I had ever done. Working for a dealer provided an adrenaline rush as addictive as the drugs we pushed.

To this day, it's a miracle I survived those few years. Fortunately, I escaped but not without a price.

That time in my life not just affected me, but also my parents. They might have saved their only child, but they sacrificed their marriage to do it. When the shit hit the fan with me, the stress was too much for them to handle.

Believing in the sacrament of marriage, Mom and Dad never divorced. A distance developed between them, and they lived separately under the same roof.

Dad passed away from a heart attack during my junior year in college. Mom never remarried, and to this day, she continues to make me her primary focus in life.

Going into law enforcement was a way, I thought, to pay my debt back to my parents for the hell I'd put them through. I could also help make the streets safer for other teens facing the same kinds of temptations I'd had at their age. Instead, it only brought the problem I'd thought was long-forgotten to the forefront of my life.

I remember the day well. It was during my first marriage to Keegan, and Kyle was six years old. A local news crew interviewed me about a shooting I was investigating. Afterward, I received an envelope with no return address at the state police barracks. A photo of Keegan and Kyle fell out when I opened it. There was something red splattered all over their faces.

A note was attached, stating that I needed to run interference with investigations involving the sender's

drug-trafficking. The note was simply signed, *Skate On,
Bro*—something Troy and I used to say in jest to each
other.

I sent the envelope along with its contents to
forensics, knowing nothing would come of it. With no
identifying prints or any other hard evidence, there was no
way to link Troy to the delivery. The red splatters were ink,
not blood as I had feared. I knew this was a scare tactic to
get me to do what Troy wanted, and it was working.

My past was finally catching up with me. This was the
first time I ever felt my work could put Keegan and Kyle
in jeopardy. The only way I could think of to protect them
was to distance myself from them by ending my marriage.
I knew exactly how far to push Keegan, and it didn't take
long for me to make her life so miserable that she left with
Kyle. I figured Keegan would probably move in with her
parents until she got back on her feet. I could still be in
their lives as the estranged husband with my family safely
tucked away in the suburbs.

What I hadn't figured on was Alex Parker, and luckily
for me, he wasn't around for very long. Due to my bruised
ego, I had become distant during the time Keegan was
with him, and as a result, Kyle and Alex became close.

A part of me wants Keegan to find happiness with
someone else, but I will never allow another man to
become a father to my son.

I bolt up in my chair, spilling my whiskey, when Kyle
stumbles in half-asleep.

"Hey, Dad."

"Christ, you scared me! What are you doing up?"

Kyle laughs. "I had to go to the bathroom. I came
down for a drink of water."

"You need to get back to bed, or I'll never be able to
get you up in the morning for school. I'm surprised your
grandmother isn't down here, giving us both hell for being
up."

We head upstairs to bed after Kyle gets his water, and I turn off the lights. Reaching the top of the stairs, I stop Kyle to hug him before he enters his bedroom.

"I love you, son."

"Love you, too, Dad."

The next morning, my schedule allows me to take Kyle to school. This is a treat for both of us because this doesn't happen very often. We stop along the way at our favorite greasy spoon diner to get some breakfast. I love these special moments with him, and I will do whatever it takes to continue to have them.

On my way to work after dropping Kyle off at school, I hear a song over the radio that makes me think of Brittany. I met her in college during freshman orientation, and we dated until my senior year. We were both from the Baltimore area but from different sides of the tracks. My parents were always a little standoffish toward her but tolerated our relationship.

One weekend, during a college football game, I noticed Keegan sitting several rows down in front of us. Brittany saw how I couldn't stop looking at her and became upset with me. We broke up a couple of weeks later.

After our breakup, I actively started to pursue Keegan. I still remember approaching her in the library while she was checking out a book. She was stunning with her beautiful auburn hair and crystal-blue eyes. I thought it was as good a time as any to talk to Keegan, so I asked her some stupid question about the book she was holding. We began dating shortly after that, and as they say, the rest is history.

I didn't hear from or see Brittany until years later when she contacted me about one of her clients. It was around the same time I'd received the photo from Troy. I found Brittany knew more about the drug scene than I could ever have imagined, and she slowly took on the role of an informant. I needed to keep her identity a secret, so we started meeting at the hotel to exchange information. Our relationship turned into a sexual one after Keegan and I'd officially separated the first time.

It's funny how history seems to be repeating itself.

Does this make me an asshole?

Possibly.

Does it bother me?

Maybe a little, but I've been called a lot worse.

7

Keegan

School is out for the summer, and I can't believe the Fourth of July has come and gone. I've dodged being laid off from my job, and I'm thinking about renting a house in the fall. After all, who could pass up on having access to a lake, pool, and hot tub during the summer?

My relationship with Cameron is an interesting one. We're lucky to see each other more than once a week due to his job and our children's sporting events. Later in August, he is scheduled to visit showrooms along the Eastern Shore. Locals often refer to this area as the Delmarva Peninsula, home to some of my favorite beaches, and the plan is for me to join him. Timing for this trip couldn't have worked out better because it falls during Will's vacation time with Kyle. Cameron is taking care of all the arrangements. I hope the week doesn't end up with me sitting, alone, on the beach all day while he works.

Cameron travels a lot with his job, but we seem to find ways to keep in touch. We speak of our kids meeting in the abstract, but we haven't taken any steps to make it a reality. Love is never mentioned by either of us, but talk of the future is often a part of our conversations. I'm hesitant to change the dynamics of this relationship with Cameron. Something is telling me to just keep the status quo with him for the time being.

Like many migraine sufferers, I have learned how to push through the pain to lead a productive life. I refuse to allow the headache to win and incapacitate me. Between my boredom and the migraine that is slowly building, I decide to text Marcy.

> *Me: Help! I'm bored. No kid, and a migraine is brewing. Are you busy?*

> *Marcy: Nope. Come on over.*

> *Me: On my way.*

Marcy meets me at her front door with a bottle of water for me.

"Seriously? You don't have anything stronger than bottled water?"

"You mentioned the word *migraine* in your text. I'm guessing you have popped some of your meds, and booze is probably not the best thing for you right now."

I stare at Marcy. "When in the hell did you become my mother?"

"On the playground back in elementary school."

The afternoon is just what the doctor ordered. It's full of girl talk as we spend it in the family room, pigging out on junk food, with old chick flicks playing in the background. The conversation becomes emotional as I begin to tearfully spew out every pent-up frustration and stress experienced during my separation with Will. I tell

Marcy that my relationship with Cameron has been one of the few bright spots for me.

Sitting beside me on the couch, Marcy reaches for the remote and turns off the TV. While listening, she rubs my back and occasionally gives a sympathetic nod.

When I finish, Marcy chooses her words carefully, "I'm sorry you're going through all of this with Will, but this isn't your first rodeo at divorce. Let's face it; if you and Will got along, you would still be together. The end of a marriage has stages of grief, just like any other death. Sweetie, you won't feel like this forever, I promise."

Nodding in agreement, I wipe my nose with the back of my hand, like a five-year-old. "You're telling me to suck it up, buttercup."

"That's your line, not mine. But, yeah, I guess I am...in a nice way." She smiles sweetly, handing me a box of tissues from the nearby end table.

"I know, I know. I'm so lucky to have you, Seth, Kyle, and Cam to help get me through all of this. Cam and I have been each other's sounding boards. His wife is putting him through the ringer about seeing his kids. I wish I could do more for him. I was thinking maybe a special evening out. He is always doing the sweetest things for me. It's time for me to show my appreciation."

Marcy stares at me with furrowed brows. "Since when did this turn into a conversation about making Cam happy?"

I shrug at Marcy's comment. "He plans a lot of fun stuff to do with me, like our upcoming beach trip. I figure it is time for me to reciprocate and do something cool for him."

"Has the word *love* been used by either of you?"

"No, neither of us has used the word because our relationship isn't about that. We are each other's escape from the headaches of our divorces and nothing more."

"Keegan, I like Cam and think he's a fun guy, but please be careful."

"I love the fact that you care so much, but I'm good with him. Promise. Hey, I'm thinking about going ahead and finding a place of my own. Want to go online and see what's out there?"

"Sure."

After checking out rentals and houses for sale, I check my social media pages to find a post from Cameron. Since both of us are dealing with touchy exes, we are careful not to post pictures of the other or mention our names, and we only ever use the Like button when responding to a post. There is no need to give either ex any more ammunition to use against us.

Cameron is away on a business trip today, and he posted a selfie of himself standing by some water with the message, *Thinking of the good times ahead.*

I notice a new name pops up in the Likes on his post. Out of curiosity, I click on the name to view her page. I find myself staring at a profile picture of a beautiful woman in a low-cut dress, showing off her fake assets, lying across a bed in a centerfold pose. Something else catches my eye that is far more unsettling. The cover photo at the top of her page is one taken from an outcropping of rocks looking out over a breathtaking view. There is a farm surrounded by a patchwork of fields and a beautiful stone church off in the distance. It is the same damn place Cameron took me to on our first date.

I hear Marcy in the background. She's saying something about not jumping to conclusions, how it could be a coincidence, and how Cameron wouldn't do something like that to me. But, deep down inside me, I call bullshit.

During the next week, I keep a close eye on Centerfold Chick's and Cameron's pages. I feel like an interloper or stalker. Occasionally, she Likes something on his page, but he never does on hers.

Cameron sounds a little off during our phone conversation tonight.

"Everything okay?" I ask.

"Yeah, sure. Why do you ask?"

"You seem, I don't know, distracted."

"I've got this huge presentation tomorrow. A lot of the guys from the corporate office are here. I just don't want to blow it."

"Hey, I totally get it. I've had presentations like that. You worry yourself to death, and when it's over, there's a huge weight lifted from your shoulders. I just wanted to make sure everything was okay with us."

"What's up with all the questions?"

"I don't know. It seems we've been out of sync for the past few days."

Cameron heaves out a heavy sigh. "Keegan, you are so special to me. I enjoy what we share."

"But?"

"But I'm afraid I can't give you what you need."

"And what is it that you think I need?"

"I don't know. Something more than what I can offer to you right now."

"Do you want to stop seeing each other?"

"No."

"Then, what's the problem?"

"I just don't want to disappoint you."

"You won't as long as you continue to be honest with me. Okay?"

"Okay. Well, I still have a lot to do for tomorrow. I'll give you a call and let you know how it went."

"Okay. Good luck. Try to get some sleep tonight."

"Will do. Night."

"Night."

After ending the call, I'm starting to think that maybe Marcy was right about the picture being a coincidence.

I am wide awake at five thirty in the morning. I got little sleep last night because I was mulling over my phone conversation with Cameron. I power up my laptop to see if I missed anything good on any of the social media sites. You can imagine my surprise when I see a post from Centerfold Chick, announcing she is in a relationship with Cameron.

"What the fuck?" is out of my mouth before I can stop it.

There are no words to express the amount of anger, hurt, and embarrassment I'm feeling right now. It feels as if I've been totally played by Cameron. Before I can stop them, the tears start streaming down my face. *God, I am such a fricking fool.*

Immediately, I pick up my phone and text Cameron.

> *Me: I see congratulations are in order on the announcement of your new relationship. No need to respond back—ever!*

A couple of hours later, my phone starts blowing up with texts.

> *Cam: I'm sorry. I need to explain.*
>
> *Cam: We need to talk.*
>
> *Cam: It's not what it looks like.*
>
> *Cam: I can't let it end like this.*

Similar texts and phone calls go on for the next hour.

Getting tired of hearing my phone going off every few minutes, I finally pick up and snap, "What?"

"Huh?" Cameron answers, caught off guard by my question.

"What is it you so desperately need to tell me that would make me change my opinion of you right now?"

Cameron struggles to find the right words. "Keegan, it's not how it looks. She's someone I dated before I got married. I ran into her at the bar in my hotel. We had a couple of drinks, caught up with each other, and…and…"

"And you took her to your room and had sex with her for old times' sake? Wow, I feel so much better since you explained everything."

"Keegan, please. It wasn't like that. I just thought…"

"How stupid do you think I am? Stop your lying. You two have been seeing each other for a while for her to post something like that. By the way, being monogamous means not sleeping with other women. She has no clue about me, does she? Don't worry. Your secret is safe. She can find out the hard way, like I did. Have a nice life. Peace out. Bye-bye!" With that, I hang up on Cameron, throw myself on my bed, and have a good cry.

I have to get my act together because Kyle is coming home today, and no one is going to ruin my time with him.

Cameron sends another text, asking me to meet him so that we can discuss this like two mature adults. My mature response is telling him to go to hell. There are no more texts from him.

Later in the day, I am beyond happy to see Will pull up because our son always centers my world. Kyle tells Will good-bye and makes a quick exit to come inside to connect with his friends through his video games. Will and I have gotten in the routine of using this time to discuss private matters without an audience. Things have improved between us since the diner parking lot incident, and we're finding some common ground for the sake of our child.

Will senses something is wrong as we take a seat on the front porch swing. "You've got another headache, don't you? You want me to take Kyle for the night?"

"No, I'm fine."

"It seems you're getting more headaches these days. When are you going to the doctor?" he inquires with a tone of concern.

"I've been to the doctor, and they did a CT scan, which was normal. I have migraines caused by stress," I answer him.

"I still worry about you. Promise to take care of yourself?"

I nod in response to Will's question.

He then asks, "Anything else I need to know about?"

I hesitate for a moment and then say, "Can't believe I'm about to do this…"

"Do what?"

"Give you the opportunity to say a big, fat *I told you so* to me."

Will raises his eyebrows and asks, "Why? What happened?"

"Cam turned out to be quite the douche bag after all."

Will cocks his head at me and grins. "Really?"

"It appears the news on the Internet today is, he's in a relationship, and it ain't with me. So, go ahead and have at it. Tell me how I jumped in bed with him too soon, how you knew he was a douche after meeting him the night in the parking lot—yada, yada…"

Will puts his arm around me like a comfy, warm blanket. "Seems like you pretty much covered it all for me. No sense in kicking you when you're down. I'm sorry you got hurt, but I'm not sorry he's out of your life. Please, no second chances for him."

"God, Will, what have we become? Friends? How did we get to this point, but we couldn't do it during our marriage?" I ask, searching his eyes for answers but only seeing pain in them.

"Keegan, I don't know. Some couples are just better apart than together. I guess that's how it is with us. Anything else we need to discuss? Sure you don't want me to take Kyle to spend another night with me, so you can nurse your migraine in peace and quiet?"

"No, I miss him when he's gone. It won't be long before he's out of here for good and going off to college."

"Okay then, I'm out of here." We stand, and Will hugs me, saying, "Keegan, I'm always here for you, okay?"

I nod. "Okay. Thanks for listening, Will."

"Anytime." He gets into his SUV and leaves.

8

Will

Halloween has passed, and we are heading into the Christmas holidays. I hate this time of year. It doesn't help that I'm sitting in a strip bar in the city, waiting for Troy. I look at the paperwork of my second divorce, signifying that the end of my marriage is official. I put the document back in my jacket's inside pocket as I signal the bartender for another beer.

Seven years ago, Troy's mailing provided the golden opportunity for me to go undercover and infiltrate the city's drug ring. There was speculation the local ring had connections with a larger drug cartel operating along the Eastern seaboard, and Operation Skater was born.

The plan was for me to become a dirty cop who'd gone rogue. I would continue my normal duties, maintaining the illusion for Troy that he had a someone on the inside working for him. A system was put into place to distance me from any connection with the arrests made from the intel I collected. It was agreed to go slow and steady, no matter how long it would take for this to be an effective special op.

Before I knew it, days of working undercover had turned into months and months into seven years. We had been successful, and headquarters thought it was important for me to maintain my undercover status—indefinitely. When I'd signed up for this, I'd thought it would maybe take a couple of years to accomplish what we had set out to do. As more information was discovered, our objective would keep changing. Never in my wildest imagination had I thought it would take this long.

After my first divorce, I fooled myself into believing the system set in place would be enough to protect my family and me. I was convinced that it was safe to get back with Keegan, and three years ago, we were married for the second time. I was beyond happy, and then my world came crashing down when I received a call directly from Troy two years ago.

I remember the call as if it were yesterday.

Watching football one Sunday afternoon, I answer my throwaway cell because I'm home alone while Keegan and Kyle are visiting my in-laws, "Yeah?"

"Long time no speak, bro."

I immediately recognize Troy's voice. It's the first time during my assignment when he has personally reached out to me by phone.

"What do you want, Troy?"

"Is that any way to talk to an old buddy? Damn. I thought you would be happier to hear from me, especially since I gave you the chance to line your fucking pockets with some extra cash. It must be expensive, raising that kid of yours and keeping the wife happy."

"I appreciate you thinking of me. Now, what can I do for you? I'm curious as to why I get the pleasure of hearing directly from you."

"I need you to come to the city. You know the place—the strip club we made deliveries to back when we were kids. I was reminiscing with a couple of the girls about the fun we used to have, and they want to party tonight. Tell the wife you've been called into work and won't be home tonight or maybe even for a couple of days. All depends on how much heavy shit we end up doing. It takes about

forty-five minutes to get there from your house—or at least it did when I timed it last week."

He's testing me. Having a pretty good idea of what Troy has in mind, I have no choice but to go. Too much time has been invested in my undercover work not to go. I might also end up doing drugs or, at the very least, smoking some weed. With any luck, I can keep it to a minimum and tell him I need to stay clean for drug-testing at work. There will be no leaving until compromising pictures of me have been taken for blackmail purposes. Troy would not hesitate to send them to Keegan if I stepped out of line.

At headquarters, we knew this was a possibility and discussed what I would have to do.

Passing his test means gaining access to information I can't get from any other source but Troy. The worst part in all of this is, he now knows where my family lives.

This cannot be happening to me again. I know what I have to do to make sure everyone remains safe. It won't be as hard this time because, after tonight, I'll be so damn disgusted with myself that it will be easy to convince Keegan to leave me for the final time.

Arriving at the strip club, I'm escorted to Troy's private office in the back where two girls—a blonde and brunette—are with him.

"Hey, bro, I'm previewing a new routine. Get a drink, and come join me on the couch." Troy points over to a small bar.

I go over for some liquid courage and then take a seat next to him. We watch the two strippers start to do their act as I down my double of whiskey.

They slowly strip and give us lap dances. It isn't long until the blonde is naked on my lap and grinding down on me. She starts kissing me as she pulls off my shirt. Even though I love Keegan, there is something exciting about all of this, and my body starts betraying me as it responds to what is happening in the room.

Being totally distracted by the blonde, the brunette starts tying off my vein, readying it for a needle. Out of the corner of my eye, I see Troy taking pictures of me while I'm half-dressed with two naked strippers appearing to be taking care of my sexual needs.

Troy has staged a scene straight from our younger days and gotten it all on camera. I know what will happen next. We will all shoot up, get high, and have more of the same fun.

All of a sudden, Troy stands. "Thank you, ladies. That's all I need." He then says to me, "If you ever think about fucking me over, remember that I have all of this shit on film, and your sweet little wife will get a copy for the goddamn family album."

After the girls exit, Troy sits down behind his desk.

I ask, "Why in the hell didn't we shoot up like old times? I was just getting into it and having fun."

"Oh, we're going to have more fun, but I can't risk you failing any fucking drug tests. I need to keep you clean and sober. I remember how you get once you start using." Troy continues, "I love it that you're back, man! If you play your cards right, we're going to go places together, and eventually, we'll run the whole fucking show."

I passed his stupid test, and thankfully, I'm still clean. Troy has now made me a confidant and trusts me enough to share information only he knows.

Looking back at the personal cost of my undercover work, I wonder if it's been worth the drugs we've gotten off the street. We have established an elaborate setup where information will be fed to other agencies but never be traceable back to me. It's taken years to build the network, and it's too valuable to dismantle.

I'm proud of what has been accomplished, but I'm not proud of some of the things I've had to do to make it happen. It's a little too late now though to have regrets.

9

Keegan

Marcy: Are you free tonight?

Me: Yeah. Why?

Marcy: Come over.

Me: ???

Marcy: I just miss you.

Me: Time?

Marcy: Whenever.

Me: 7?

Marcy: Sure.

The last thing I want to do is go to Marcy's tonight. It's mid-December with Christmas fast approaching, and my feeling of good cheer is nowhere in sight.

After receiving word in August that I would be laid off effective the first of January, my plans to move out of my parents' came to a screeching halt. Mom and Dad, always being the consummate supportive parents, told me their home was ours for as long as we needed it.

I can't start job-hunting until after January first due to the conditions of my severance package, which offers too much money to pass up. Between my severance and proceeds from the sale of our house, I should be able to afford a nice townhouse in Kyle's school district. The only hang-up is, I need a job before I can sign on the dotted line to purchase or rent any place. My patience continues to be tested in this seemingly unending state of limbo, which is currently called my life.

I'm standing at Marcy's front door when it suddenly opens before I've had the chance to ring the doorbell. I walk in, and Marcy and Roger are standing there with the silliest grins on their faces.

"What's going on?" I ask them.

Marcy is now giggling. "What makes you think anything is going on?"

"Ew, I interrupted you guys having sex on the dining room table or kitchen counter, didn't I?"

Roger starts laughing at me and answers my question by shaking his head.

"Okay, you two are creeping me out now. There's nothing I can think of that could make you act this goofy, except maybe—no, you're not! You aren't finally pregnant, are you?" I screech.

By now, Marcy is bouncing up and down on her tippy-toes with Roger's arm around her.

"Yes, we're pregnant! We didn't want to tell anyone until after we were past the first trimester and into the second. With the way things were going, I was terrified of miscarrying. I went to the doctor today, and everything seems to be okay." Tears of joy are now streaming down Marcy's face.

Roger is standing there with his chest puffed out, wearing an ear-to-ear grin on his face. He hands me a picture of their ultrasound, and says, "Meet the newest member of our family, Baby Bennett—or as we more fondly call him, BB."

"Him? You need to stop that because he could be a *she*, you know," Marcy jokingly scolds Roger.

Now, tears are streaming down my face as I hug Marcy. I am beyond happy for them, but I also feel a little jealous because my personal happiness is nowhere to be found. Guess I now qualify for the Worst Friend of the Year award. I need to snap out of this and celebrate the good news with my BFF.

"OMG! When are you due?"

"Well, if things go well and I carry full-term, the due date is June twentieth."

"Marcy, things will go beautifully. Wait, that's only a few days before my birthday. Who knows? I might have a birthday twin!" Finally, I am getting caught up in their excitement and getting out of my funk.

"We wanted you to be one of the first to know since you'll be BB's godmother," Marcy states in a matter-of-fact manner.

"Godmother?"

"Well, duh! Of course! Who else would I ask? Seth?"

Now, I am bawling like a baby. "Thank you, Marcy. I would be honored to be BB's godmother. Wait, does that mean I need to get up early *every* Sunday morning and start going to church? Maybe I need to rethink this thing through a little bit more. I don't know if I can handle the pressure of keeping BB from going to hell."

The three of us break out into a fit of laughter.

After settling down on the couch with our nonalcoholic drinks, it dawns on me that I haven't seen Marcy drink for weeks.

Why didn't I pick up on this until now?

It's because I've been wallowing in my own self-pity and missing out on what is happening in the world around me.

Marcy snaps me out of my thoughts when she says, "Um…Keegan, I had another reason for asking you over. I've done something you're probably not going to like. I figured being pregnant with your godchild would stop you from killing me."

Roger comes over to sit by his wife's side, as if protecting her, and adds, "Now, Keegan, stay calm. What Marcy is about to explain was done out of her love for you."

"You guys are scaring me. What the hell have you done, Marcy?"

"Keegan, just hear me out. Don't interrupt. Let me get it all out before you start screaming at me and end our friendship."

"What. Have. You. Done?"

She reaches over to the laptop on the coffee table and starts to type. "First, let me start by saying that I hated what Cameron did to you. It was a scumbag thing to do. I've watched my best friend go from being down and out after your split with Will to flying higher than a kite with Cameron, only to crash lower than low after you two broke up. I just couldn't watch it anymore, so I decided to take matters into my own hands by setting up a page for you on a dating site."

"You did *what*?" I scream. "*I'm on a dating site?* Take it down now, Marcy. For the love of God, I will *not* be a piece of meat out there for total strangers to drool over. For Christ's sake, I have a son who is almost a teenager. He does not need his mother on the Internet like some…some…I don't know what! Marcy, I swear…take it down. Now!"

"Okay, okay. But take a look at your page and see some of the guys who have been sending messages. There are some pretty good ones. And although you think of it as a meat market, you can talk to them anonymously for as long as you want. You decide when any personal contact information is exchanged or if you ever meet. You are in total control of where this goes. Isn't this better than being at a bar, randomly meeting guys while drinking? I mean, that went well with Cam, didn't it?"

"That's a low blow, Marcy!"

"I know. I'm sorry. I'll take the page down, but first, please take a look at it. I think there are a few guys you wouldn't mind getting to know."

"Marcy, I just can't put myself out there anymore. I've been left behind by guys who I thought were the loves of my life. It hurts too much."

"You want to know what I think? I think your happily ever after is still out there, waiting for you to show up. What if he's one of these guys?" Marcy asks as she turns the screen around to face me.

I am looking at a string of guys' photos—some with witty pick-up lines and others with simple hellos and introductions.

"Have you been talking to them for me?"

"No, I would never do that to you. I only set it up this morning. These are the guys who have contacted you since it has gone live. By the way, you're IrishEyes-seven-thirty-two."

"I get the IrishEyes, but why the seven-thirty-two?" I ask Marcy.

"There's more than one IrishEyes. It's the perfect tag for you, so I added your parents' house number in reverse, and it worked!"

I am immediately sucked in and start reading all the comments.

> *Congratulations! You have won one free meal, one free movie, and one free trip to the destination of your choice. Please respond quickly. Although*

you're very pretty and smart, this offer will expire. My name is Sam, your host.

"Seriously? This bit works for him?" I ask, pointing to his comment.

Marcy laughs. "Yeah, I know. There are some real gems. If nothing else, you can have a few good laughs while reading them."

For the next fifteen minutes, I scroll down and read the inquiries.

I break the news to a college student.

IrishEyes732: Although flattered, I'm afraid you're a little too young for me.

His response: Being younger just means I stay sexy for you longer. ;) But I understand.

IrishEyes732: Yeah, but my boobs will start to sag! LOL.

I can't believe some of the brazen comments from several guys, like ones asking if the carpet and drapes match.

Do guys really think I will give them the time of day if that's how they ask if I'm a natural redhead?

Some immediately start calling me Ginger, which was Alex's nickname for me, and I have hated it ever since our breakup.

I find the anonymity of it all very freeing. I can be somebody else instead of the responsible mom, breadwinner, and dutiful daughter. I haven't been this carefree person for years, and it's exciting to find her again.

All of a sudden, I stop scrolling when my eyes fall on one particular guy. I click on the pictures of FFCap52. He is hot with a capital H.

Why is this guy even on this website?

He's the whole package in the looks department. After reading his profile, I find out he's a nonsmoker, over six feet, and my age. From the posted pictures, he has a body that rocks, light-brown hair, and hazel eyes. He's also a firefighter, like my dad.

I read his message to me.

> *FFCap52: Hi. I've never done anything like this before, and I'm not sure what the proper protocol is here. I wanted to say hi and see if you have had a good day.*

Before I know it, I am typing.

> *IrishEyes732: Hi. This is my first time on the site, too. My day was awesome! I just found out my BFF is pregnant with her first child. I'm so excited!*

I am blown away when his response is immediate.

> *FFCap52: That's great news. Sounds like your day couldn't get any better after receiving news like that. Congrats.*

For the next few minutes, we go back and forth.

> *IrishEyes732: Nope. I don't see how it could be topped, other than maybe meeting a firefighter on this site. I might be a little biased toward firefighters since my dad is retired from the federal fire service.*

> *FFCap52: Good bias?*

> *IrishEyes732: Most definitely. How was your day?*

FFCap52: Could have been better. We responded to a car accident on the beltway this morning. Saved the mom, but lost the little girl. After fourteen years, I still can't handle losing the kids.

IrishEyes732: I know. My dad felt the same way. If you're still working your shift, I hope things get better.

There's no response back. Maybe he got a call, or I failed my first interview with him, and he started checking out another prospect who was more attractive than me.

Marcy and I spend the evening scoping out all the guys, and I can't believe how late it is. I tell Marcy I will take the site out for a test run and leave my profile up for a few days. It will come down at the first hint of a weirdo stalking me. There's no way I'm going to tell Will about this. He would flip if he knew I was talking to strange men on the Internet.

During my ride home, my thoughts keep going back to FFCap52. It's sad that he lost a little girl today. I know how rough a bad day at the office for a firefighter can be. My dad would often come home from his shifts, carrying the weight of the world on his shoulders. At times, the stories he shared were heartbreaking. Mom found it best to give him time to decompress before starting in with the nonsense of our home.

I climb into my bed and bring up the dating site. I can see this is going to be as addictive as all my other sites. Scrolling down, I find there is still nothing from FFCap52. Other guys have contacted me, but FFCap52 is the only one I want to hear from tonight. I wonder where he works or if he knows my dad or Will. And my thoughts wander on as I doze off with my laptop open to my profile in hopes of hearing from him.

10

Jack—aka FFCap52

Sitting at my desk in my office at Station 52, I scroll down the list of girls the dating site has tagged as possible matches. I'm doing this out of sheer boredom because it is a slow night with few calls and my paperwork is done. Using my mouse, I scroll through pictures with few even registering with me, and then I pass by her. I go back and stop at her picture, taking in the combination of blue eyes, auburn hair, and her smile. It's impossible to resist, and I begin typing a message to her.

> *FFCap52: Hi. I've never done anything like this before, and I'm not sure what the proper protocol is here. I wanted to say hi and see if you have had a good day.*

Her page must be filled with messages, so you can imagine my surprise when she answers me. It's fun, bantering back and forth with her. Just as I reach for the keyboard to start typing another response, we get a call. *Damn firehouse alarm!*

This is the life of a firefighter. The moment the alarm sounds, you immediately stop what you're doing and respond to the emergency.

We have back-to-back calls for the next couple of hours, and we don't get a break until late into the night.

Once back at the station, I go to my office to start processing paperwork. I soon find myself pulling up the site to check if she wrote anything else after her last post. There is nothing.

Damn it!

> *FFCap52: Sorry for being MIA. We had a lot of calls tonight. I'm sure you're in bed now. Wanted to say good night and tell you to have sweet dreams.*

God, if the guys at the station read this post, they would definitely take away my man card, but I don't care.

I was pissed off when I caught my crew, led by Battalion Chief Bob Henley, registering me on an online dating site without my knowledge. Bob was not only my boss, but also a close friend. He had no right meddling in my personal affairs, especially those involving Annie—my former girlfriend and mother of our five-year-old son, Sean.

Thinking back to that night, I don't think I'll ever forget the looks on all of their faces when I caught them in the act.

For a Wednesday evening, things are a little too quiet as I leave my office to walk back to the kitchen. While some stations have a combination of paid employees and volunteers, Station 52 is staffed with only career firefighters. We have three crews who work twenty-four-hour shifts, and twelve people make up each crew—nine firefighters, one master firefighter, one lieutenant, and one captain. Being the captain on duty, I need to find out where my crew is and what kind of trouble these guys are getting into.

No one is in the kitchen or watching TV in the dayroom. I hear voices down the hall, coming from the Battalion Chief's office. It's almost seven p.m., well past the time Bob leaves for the day, so no one should be in there. Ready to bust some asses, I quietly walk up to the door and watch, undetected. I see Bob and the rest of the crew standing at the desk, looking over the shoulder of Nancy—our only woman firefighter—as she types away on the computer.

Listening to them, I hear comments like, "Yeah, that's a good picture," and, "Use the one there, without his shirt on," and, "Nah, not that one. He looks like a dork."

Bob says, "Nancy, you fill in the questionnaire. You know what girls want to hear."

Nancy replies, "It's not about what girls want to hear. These answers are how they match people. He's not going to end up with the right person if it's not the way he would answer them. You guys have to figure out a way for him to do the questionnaire."

"I guess we could make a hard copy and come up with some story of how we're all required to fill out the form for some psych mumbo jumbo from headquarters," Bob says.

"Cap would see through that in a heartbeat. You guys just need to fess up and ask him to do this part. Call me back when it's completed, and I'll get his profile up," Nancy says as she pushes the chair back.

She stands to find me with my arms crossed, blocking the doorway and not looking too happy.

Nervously, Nancy says, "Cap! Um, hey there! Well, I just remembered something I need to be doing."

"Stop right there. I want to know what's going on here."

Bob steps up. "You want to know what's going on? We're tired of Annie calling and stopping by all the time, bugging us about you. For someone you were only living with and never planning to marry, she's become a royal pain in everyone's asses! We have tried to run all sorts of interference, but she's not getting the message. Thought if you started dating, maybe, just maybe, Annie would fade into the woodwork. Christ, it's been a year since you moved out. She still thinks you'll eventually come to your senses and move back in."

I'm left speechless by Bob's disclosure that he and the whole damn crew have been messing around in my personal business. I'm the guy who's supposed to send them into burning buildings, and this is compromising my credibility with them. I am beyond pissed off.

I slowly find my voice and say, "Butt. Out. Of. My. Life."

Bob looks around to the rest of the crew. "Hey, guys, clear out, and give me a minute with him."

Quickly, the room empties, and Bob closes the door behind them, knowing they will be listening from the other side. Bob gestures for me to take a seat in front of the computer as he sits down in a chair on the other side of the desk. I'm staring at an assortment of pictures of me and other personal information, such as height, weight, hair color, and eye color.

I believe in fate and chance meetings. This is not how I do business. I want my profile to come down immediately.

"I know what you're thinking, Cap. Just hear me out on this before giving me your two cents. Annie is not letting go, and she's becoming desperate. It's not only you she still bugs, but all of us on the crew. God, she's even accused Nancy of having the hots for you. This was my idea, and I told Nancy to do it. The plan was for me to show you all the available women out there once it was up and running. It can be taken down at anytime, so no harm, no foul," Bob says in a cavalier manner.

"Did you just say 'no harm, no foul'? Well, let me tell you a few things. You have killed any credibility I had with my crew. I will now be the butt end of their jokes. Forget any respect they had for me as their boss. I can hear the comments now. 'Hey, Cap, seen any good pieces of ass lately?' Or, 'I don't mind your sloppy seconds as long as she's got big tits.' And to have Nancy set up the profile? Seriously, there's got to be a half-dozen sexual harassment suits she could file now. I've busted my ass to make her feel comfortable and safe while working here. God, in one evening, you have blown all my hard work and trust I've tried to achieve with this crew. I don't think I've ever been this pissed off at you! What the hell were you thinking?"

"Watch it, Jack. You need to tread carefully, my friend. That group out there, listening on the other side of the door, would give their lives for you. In fact, they do every time they leave this house on a call!

They have your back—on and off duty. A few of them came to me to speak on the crew's behalf because they care about you and knew it was a delicate situation with your son, Sean. They didn't want to do anything to jeopardize your relationship with him. You know Annie can be a manipulative bitch, and if she saw you out at a bar— talking to another woman, moving on—she would do everything in her power to sabotage it. Now, fill out that damn questionnaire. Give it a week or two. If you're still uncomfortable with it, we'll take it down."

I sit there, staring at Bob, knowing I am not going to win this battle. It would be easier to let it go live, and then after a few days, I can order for it to be shut down.

"Let me make a few things perfectly clear before doing this. One, Annie always has access to me since I am Sean's father. If she's bugging anyone here, let me know, and I'll talk to her. Two, no one makes any comments whatsoever about this website. I don't want to be asked for updates or any details. Three, if anyone here ever butts into my personal life again, there will be hell to pay. Do you understand?"

Bob responds in kind by holding up his hand, counting off on his fingers, as he gives a list back to me, "One, we are a family here. We live, sleep, eat, and put our lives on the line every day we spend together in this house. None of us will ever stop caring for each other. When we stop caring, then someone is going to get hurt or, even worse, killed out there on a call. Two, because we are family, we care about you and what happens in your personal life. We will continue to butt in it from time to time when we see you are hurting or are in trouble. You're always going to get unsolicited advice, just like when you dish it out to them. Get over it. Three, we know Sean is the center of your world, outside of this house, and we would never do anything to risk your relationship with him. Now, stop your whining, and fill out the damn questionnaire." Then, Bob yells at the door, "Nancy, get back in here, and let's get this thing fired up!"

The door flies open with everyone almost falling back into the office. After I complete the questionnaire, Nancy asks me to double-check everything and see if there is anything I want taken off of my *profile. Once it is ready to go, she shows me where to click to make it go live.*

I never knew so many people used Internet dating services.

Nancy explains, although my picture is posted, the anonymity of it makes people feel safe to talk to each other. I have become FFCap52. My tag stands for my profession, rank, and station number. I have to admit, I like it.

By this time next week, I'll have Nancy take it down, and everyone will be happy.

I click over to my social media page and check for any posts from Annie and Sean. Since moving out, I set up this page as another way to share pictures and see what is going on in Sean's life when we are apart. Annie has interpreted my dabbling on social media as having regrets.

The first thing I notice on my page is a post of Annie's new profile photo. She changes this every few weeks. Each one is a little more seductive with less clothing than the last. This picture focuses more on the low top she's wearing, showing off her cleavage, than her face.

Six years ago, I made a huge mistake and had unprotected sex with Annie. I'd thought I was falling in love with her. I had always been honest with her that marriage was never an option because of the hours and commitment it took to be a firefighter. When we found out she was pregnant, for the sake of the baby, I foolishly decided we could live together without the trappings of a marriage.

Thinking back on it, how could I have ever thought an arrangement like that would ever work?

Lessons learned—date, always use protection, and never, ever live together or get married.

$$||$$

Keegan

Slowly rubbing my eyes after waking up, I focus on my laptop that slid off of me last night when I fell asleep. Suddenly, I remember FFCap52, grab my laptop, tap the touchpad to wake it up, and pull up my page.

Scrolling down, I see his post.

> *FFCap52: Sorry for being MIA. We had a lot of calls tonight. I'm sure you're in bed now. Wanted to say good night and tell you to have sweet dreams.*

>> *IrishEyes732: Good morning. And, yes, I did have sweet dreams. ;)*

Immediately, I get a response back.

> *FFCap52: I was afraid I scared you off.*

>> *IrishEyes732: Nah, it takes more than that to scare me off. How was the rest of your shift?*

FFCap52: It was crazy, but, fortunately, no more loss of life. So, is this the time I ask you to tell me about yourself?

IrishEyes732: Heck if I know. I feel like we're having an interview.

FFCap52: I know, but isn't this what it is all about?

IrishEyes732: I guess. Well, here goes. I have my MBA. I'm divorced and a mother of a thirteen-year-old son. I'm getting laid off at the end of this month, so I'm currently living with my parents until I find another job and move out. You?

FFCap52: In the fire service for fourteen years and hold the rank of Captain. Never been married. One child—a five-year-old son. Ended a five-year relationship with his mother a year ago. How long have you been divorced?

Now comes the hard part. *Do I get into the sordid details of how I married the same man twice or act like the first time never happened?* Debating with myself on what to do, I decide it is only fair for him to know the crazy he might be getting into with me.

IrishEyes732: Which time?

FFCap52: How many times have you been married?

IrishEyes732: Twice…to the same guy. First time was for eight years. Then, three years passed until the

*second time that lasted for two years. I
know; nice talking to you, too. Bye.*

*FFCap52: Wait a sec. Why would you think I
wouldn't want to talk to you anymore?*

> *IrishEyes732: You don't think it's
> strange that someone would do that? I
> did it, and I even think it's a little
> weird.*

*FFCap52: No different than me never wanting
to get married and living with a woman for five
years. You know, we're getting into some areas
that are hard to discuss through text. Any way
we can talk to each other? I'm not big on texting
and email. I'm an old-fashioned guy who likes to
talk to people. Would it be okay to ask for your
phone number? You wouldn't have to tell me
your name or any other information until you're
ready. I'm getting tired of typing.*

Oh, crap! Is it too soon to give him my number?

If we had just met in a bar, I wouldn't hesitate after
chatting for a little bit over drinks. I gave it to Cameron.

What's the difference here?

The difference is, I haven't met and sized this guy up
in person.

Am I nuts to even consider this?

I look back at his pictures and wonder if they are
actually of him or of someone else. Maybe everything he's
told me is total bull. At some point, I'm going to have to
throw fate to the wind and see what happens next.

Will would have an absolute conniption if he knew
what I was about to do.

The next thing I know, I'm typing the digits of my cell,
and I hit Send.

Not even five minutes later, my phone is ringing.

"Hi, I'm Keegan," I answer.

"Hi, I'm Jack. No last name?"

"Let's keep it on a first-name basis for right now, okay?"

"Okay."

God, he sounds just as sexy as he looks.

"You sound taller," I say jokingly.

"You sound shorter," he quips back at me.

"I can't believe I'm doing this."

"I can't believe I am either. Why is a beautiful woman like you on this site?"

"I could ask you the same thing."

"My crew set up a page for me."

"And my best friend did mine."

"Thank God for coworkers and best friends."

"You might not think that once you get to know me."

"Talk to me, Keegan. Tell me everything about yourself—the good, the bad, and the ugly."

"Only if you do the same. And when we're finished, we both need to be honest with each other and say if there's any interest to pursue this or not."

"Deal. Ladies first."

When I finish telling all I am willing to share at this time, he does the same.

Jack is a captain at a station in a Maryland suburb just across the District of Columbia line. He loves his job and feels strongly against marriage after seeing too many of them fail because of the job.

He says, "Okay, time for a moment of truth. Could you date a guy who would never want to move in together or get married? If you can't, then we need to end this conversation now."

At first his bluntness shakes me a little, but at the same time, I find it refreshing. "I've been married and divorced twice. Trust me when I say, marriage isn't even on my radar. My primary focus is to find a job and buy a place of my own. Can you handle that? If you can't, I agree, we need to end this phone call now."

I hear the sexy chuckle on the other end of the line, and I can feel his smile when he says, "Yeah, I can handle that."

Before I know it, we have been talking for over an hour. Jack has to go because it is time for him to pick up his son to do some Christmas shopping. I tell him my ex is doing the same. We both feel strongly about keeping our kids out of the mix for now.

When we end our conversation, all he says is, "I'll catch you later."

Whatever that means.

I've never experienced meeting someone like this, and I kind of like it.

Now, let's see if I ever hear from him again.

I decide to take my mind off of Jack by baking Christmas cookies since Kyle is with Will this weekend.

When they left here, something was said about getting a tree for Will's mom. I'm sure Joyce will tag along to personally pick it out herself. Nothing less than perfection will ever do, as her home always looks like a Christmas wonderland every year.

My parents, on the other hand, like having natural decorations all over the house. There are always lots of arrangements and garland made out of pine, fruit, boxwood, magnolia leaves, and nuts. The smell of all the pine is incredible. My favorite decoration is the fruit fan placed outside over the front door. It's filled with magnolia leaves, apples, and a pineapple in the center. The front bushes twinkle with sparkling white lights with each window sporting an individual wreath and single electric candle. The final touch is the pine swag on the front door, adorned with big red sleigh bells and beautiful ribbon. My dad insists his sled with my mom's ice skates—both items from their childhoods—are always propped up by the front door with a huge bow.

Marcy has been bugging me all day about Jack. She can't believe we already made phone contact but only exchanged our first names. Marcy thinks, according to today's dating etiquette, it's perfectly acceptable for me to call him. I know from experience the craziness of a firefighter's life, and having a needy girl bugging him is not cool. I will wait for him to make the next move, and if he never calls back, so be it.

Later in the evening, my phone signals with a text message.

> *Jack: Sorry I didn't get a chance to call back. I had to come in on overtime tonight because the wife of the captain on duty went into labor with their fourth child. Could you imagine having four kids? Anyway, I just wanted to say good night.*

>> *Me: That's wonderful. How exciting. Have a safe night at work. Good night.*

> *Jack: What are you still doing up? Are you out, whooping it up? Should I not bug you tomorrow because of the hangover you might be nursing?*

>> *Me: No, I'm catching up on some things while my son is at his dad's. Mostly wrapping gifts and doing laundry. Now, you know everything about my exciting life.*

> *Jack: Gotta go. Night.*

"Night," I whisper under my breath while crawling under my duvet.

The next day, I hear nothing from Jack. He is probably on his normal shift since he was called into work last night. I knew all about twenty-four-hour-shift work because of my dad. There are several ways the schedule works— twenty-four on and then twenty-four off or forty-eight off. It depends on how many shifts there are to ensure full coverage.

After a couple of evenings of texting and one long telephone conversation, is it okay for me to reach out to Jack?

There was no awkwardness between us, and we seemed to hit it off. If nothing else, he would make an awesome friend.

This is crazy. I've got more important things to worry about than someone I've never even met. He knows how to reach me, so he can make the next move.

Day two goes by, and still nothing from Jack. My insecurities start to kick in as I think he met someone else online and is now talking to them. Even though others have contacted me, I have no interest in them.

Day three, and nothing.

A week later, still nothing but the sound of crickets. Not. One. Single. Word.

Christmas is only days away, and my holiday cheer is circling the drain.

What the hell? Now, I'm mad.

If he doesn't want to pursue anything more with me, then just man up and say so.

Deciding I've been right all along about dating websites not being for me, I consider shutting down the page as soon as Marcy returns from her in-laws after the holidays.

There's no reason for me to be upset. This is how online dating works. Only days ago, I was celebrating the freedom I felt with the anonymity of it, never thinking about the downside. I've had enough rejection in my life. I don't need to set myself up for any more unnecessary heartache.

I hate how things ended with a, *Gotta go. Night*, from him. I pull out my phone and text.

> *Me: I hope all is well. I know you must be busy with the holidays and work, so I won't keep you. I just wanted to wish you a merry Christmas and the happiest New Year. Stay safe. Bye.*

No response.

I guess the silence says it all. I am not waiting for Marcy to return home. I text her and ask her to take down my profile immediately.

12

Jack

I'm escorted to an examination room after arriving at the hospital, following Annie's call, saying she is taking Sean to the emergency room. He's had severe abdominal pains, vomiting, and fever. There, I find her, holding a disposable bag up to Sean's mouth, as he gets sick with tears running down his freckled cheeks.

I walk over to the other side of the bed, taking over holding the bag from Annie. "Hey, buddy. Everything is going to be okay."

In between the heaving, he cries, "It hurts, Daddy. Make it stop hurting."

I helplessly look over at Annie before turning my attention back to him. "Yeah, I know it does, buddy. The doctor is going to make you feel better soon. Just hang in there for a little longer."

Our fears are confirmed by the doctor. Sean is suffering from appendicitis, and he's in need of an appendectomy.

After surgery, the surgeon tells us that Sean's appendix had ruptured, and he will be hospitalized for at least five days, barring any further complications.

Annie and I spend every day together at the hospital as Sean begins to start improving after a minor setback of him having a reaction to one of his medications. By the end of the week, Sean is acting like his old self and laughing at the stories we're sharing of when he was a baby.

As Sean slowly gets better, I begin to think of Keegan and the photos of her with those beautiful blue eyes and auburn hair. This makes absolutely no sense to me because we haven't met and have only talked once by phone. Our conversation was easy and effortless, as if we had known each other for years. There was none of the awkwardness or long periods of silence that strangers often experience when they first meet. I decide to contact her once this whole ordeal with Sean is over and he is safely back home from the hospital.

After a weeklong stay in the hospital, Annie and I load up a happy little boy into the backseat of my vehicle.

Once home, his mom immediately takes him upstairs to bed while I finish unloading all of his get-well gifts from the back of my SUV.

Annie returns a few minutes later and says, "He fell asleep the moment his head hit the pillow."

While Annie is talking, I'm reading the latest message from Keegan.

My disappointment must show on my face because Annie asks, "What's wrong?"

"Nothing."

"Come on, Jack. I know that look. What's going on?" she persists.

"A text from a friend, wishing me a merry Christmas." I shrug.

"How good of a friend?" Annie continues to question.

"Not very. Someone I just met."

"Good. Since you are moving back in with us, there will be no new friends for you." She grins at me.

"Annie, I'm not moving back in."

"Jack, we reconnected this past week. I know you felt it, too. Stay here with us through the holidays and see how things go. Tomorrow is Christmas Eve, and I know church is out of the question, but we can still bake cookies for Santa while Sean rests on the couch. On Christmas Day, we can open gifts and fix dinner. Please, Jack, I need you to come back home," Annie pleads with me.

"Annie, I work on Christmas Day. I can come back over tomorrow morning and spend the day."

Annie wraps her arms around me, seductively rubbing her body up against mine. "I want you to spend the night. I need you, Jack."

"Annie, stop. We can't do this."

"I miss you, baby," she whispers in my ear as she kisses my neck.

"Stop it, Annie." I take ahold of her upper arms, and push her back.

With tears in her eyes, she says, "Please stay. It's going to be hard on Sean with him still recovering from surgery. Please?"

"No, Annie, I'm not staying. Sean has accepted the way things are between us. It will only confuse him if I stay. I'll be over first thing tomorrow." I leave, not giving her a chance to reply.

On the drive home, I think about the text from Keegan. I screwed up by not letting her know what was happening with me.

When I get home, I try to pull up her page on the dating site, and I find it's no longer there. The thought of never seeing those beautiful blue eyes is all the motivation I need to call her.

She picks up on the third ring and answers softly, "Hello?"

"Hi, I'm John Patrick Grady. My friends call me Jack. I wanted to apologize for not calling this past week, and I wanted to wish you a merry Christmas."

Dead air is on the other end.

"Are you still there, Keegan?"

"Yes...I'm Keegan Brigid Fitzgerald Henderson, daughter of Mitch and Sandy Fitzgerald. My friends call me Keegan, but I'm not sure if you're my friend, so Ms. Henderson is fine for now."

I can't help but chuckle under my breath. "I see you're not going to make it easy for me."

She replies, "I'm still here but not sure for how long, so you'd better start talking...fast."

Not to waste a moment of time, I say, "I now get the IrishEyes732 tag. I guess you can't get much more Irish than the two of us. What generation?"

"My great-great-grandfather. How about you?"

"The same."

"So, what's your story for being among the missing this past week?"

"When we were texting the last time, I got a message that my son, Sean, was being taken to the emergency room. He had appendicitis, and after surgery, we found out it had ruptured. I couldn't do or think about anything until I knew he was okay. I don't know what I would do if anything ever happened to him. That little guy is everything to me. I'm sorry for falling off the grid this past week."

"Is he okay?" Keegan asks.

"Yeah, he came home today. It's all good now. Thanks for asking."

"I don't know what I would do if anything like that happened to Kyle. He's my world. I'm glad Sean is better."

"I really would like to meet and talk to you in person instead of the texting and phone calls. We could meet somewhere maybe for a bite to eat. You decide..." I offer, not knowing how she will respond to my suggestion.

More silence follows.

"What's your schedule between Christmas and New Year's Day?" Keegan asks me.

"I'm off on Saturday."

"Does meeting for coffee work for you?"

"Where?"

"Do you know the coffee shop in the strip mall on route ninety-seven, right off of seventy?"

"Yeah, I'm maybe ten minutes away from it, tops."

"Meet you there at nine on Saturday morning?"

"See you then."

"Jack…is there anything I can do?"

"Do?"

"I don't know. Any last-minute Christmas errands or anything to give you more time to hang out with Sean?"

I can't believe she's offering to help after being ignored by me all week and possibly having last-minute things to do for her own son.

"Thanks. I appreciate the offer, but everything is covered. We're all good and getting back to our normal routines."

"That's good. See you on Saturday morning," she says.

"See you on Saturday. Um, Keegan?"

"Yes?"

"Have a great holiday. I want to hear all about it when I meet you, okay?"

"Okay. Bye."

Our phone conversation ends with me smiling and fist-pumping the air.

13

Keegan

Jack calls and texts me throughout the week. It was sad he had to work on Christmas Day and not be able to spend it with his son, Sean. I know how hard it is for firefighters and their families when they are scheduled to go in on a holiday, especially Christmas. When it happened to Dad, we would visit him and bring a tray of goodies that Mom made for the crew. I wish my first meeting with Jack were behind us, so I could have done the same for him.

By the time Saturday arrives, my nervousness over meeting Jack is almost more than I can handle. My day is totally open in case he wants to do something after coffee. I have an excuse to bail if our first meeting turns out to be a bust, but I suspect it won't be needed.

Looking through my closet, trying to figure out what to wear, I wish Marcy were here to help. She is the only one who knows about my date with Jack this morning. I want to look sexy but not slutty. I decide to wear my tight black skinny jeans, black knee-high riding boots, a long white cable-knit sweater over a black camisole, and a purple plaid scarf for a pop of color.

I triple-check myself in the full-length mirror on the back of my bedroom door before leaving. Looking at the time on the way out, I notice I'm running ahead of schedule for once in my life.

Pulling into the parking lot at the strip mall, I notice an open parking space close to the front door of the coffee shop.

Once inside, I get my chai latte, and while looking for the perfect table, I spot Seth in a corner booth.

Damn it!

Of all the people to be here today, it has to be him. He sees me and waves, leaving me no choice but to go over and, at the very least, say hello to him.

"Hey, Seth. What's up?"

He grins up at me. "Not much. How about you? Why don't you have a seat and join me?"

I slide in across from him, trying not to act nervous or divulge the reason for being here. "I can only stay for a couple of minutes—you know, things to do, places to go."

"Yeah, I heard about those things to do…" he answers back with a smirk while bouncing his eyebrows up and down in a Groucho Marx manner.

"What? Wait a sec. You know, don't you?" I ask, squinting my eyes at him.

"Yeah, Marcy asked me to be your wingman today since she couldn't be here."

"You're kidding, right?"

"Hey, she's worried, Keegan. What if this guy is a creep? I'll make an excuse, and we can leave together. If he seems like an okay guy, then I'm out of here."

Shaking my head, I mutter under my breath, "Unbelievable."

Out of the corner of my eye, I get a glimpse of someone walking in the direction of our booth. The person stops, and at the same time, I look up and see an incredibly good-looking guy with a cup of coffee in his hand.

"Keegan?"

"Jack?"

"Hey, it's nice to finally meet you." He then looks over at Seth with a questioning look.

"Hey, man, I'm Seth." He reaches out to shake Jack's hand.

"Jack Grady." He nods, sizing up Seth.

I scoot further into the booth to make room for Jack and start to rattle on, "Jack, please have a seat. Seth's one of my best friends. He invited me to join him until you got here. We go way back to elementary school."

Seth adds, smiling, "Yep, we went all the way through school and graduated from college together."

Laughing nervously, I say, "Yeah, we've been there for each other through it all. He has an appointment and was just getting ready to leave."

"I still have a few minutes. So, Jack, tell me how you know Keegan. I thought I knew all of her friends."

Oh, shit!

Not knowing what Marcy told Seth, I don't want Jack to tell him any more details than necessary.

"Through some guys at work," he says with a straight face, not skipping a beat.

"Oh, so you work with Keegan?"

I decide it is time to take control over the conversation. In an attempt to get rid of Seth, I say, "Jack is a captain at a county fire department down by the DC line. OMG, look at the time, Seth. You're going to be late."

Seth laughs at me as he stands to leave. "Yeah, you're probably right. It was nice meeting you, Jack."

After he leaves, Jack looks at me. "What was that all about?"

"Friends with good intentions, both of whom I would like to strangle right now. My two besties have this need to protect me. I love them both, but there are times when they truly test my patience."

"The guys at the station are like that, too. Sometimes, it's good, but other times, I wish they would back off."

I raise my chai latte. "Here's to good friends with good intentions, no matter how much it drives us crazy."

Jack raises his cup and lightly taps mine. "Hear, hear!"

Our conversation takes off from there. We talk about the holidays, college days, our kids, and our jobs. I find out that Jack knows my dad from a couple of classes he took at the local community college.

I love Jack's laughter, and he gets the cutest wrinkle between his brows when he's being serious. My favorite expression is the one he gets when talking about Sean. We proudly show pictures of our sons to each other. Sean is definitely a cutie, looking very much like his dad.

Talk about our exes is noticeably being avoided.

Before we know it, two hours have passed with a big question looming. *Will our day together continue or end now?*

As we walk out of the coffee shop, he says, "It was nice meeting you for coffee this morning. Wish I didn't have to run off, but Sean is expecting me to come over and spend the afternoon with him."

Shit! He's using my need-to-get-home-to-my-kid excuse.

I put on my fake smile. "It was nice meeting you, too. Have a fun day with Sean."

I'm about to escape before making a further fool of myself when Jack says, "Keegan, this isn't an excuse to bail on you. I really did promise him. I work tomorrow, but are you free for dinner on Monday?"

My fake smile goes to a full one hundred kilowatts. "Sorry, I get my son back tomorrow, and I don't go out on dates when it's my time with him."

"How long do you have him?"

"This week, I have Kyle through Wednesday morning when he goes to school. He's with his dad from Wednesday evening until Sunday."

"So, that takes us up to January fourth, which I work, but I'm off on the fifth. Can you do dinner on the fifth?"

"Yeah, dinner on the fifth works for me. Wait a second. I'm unemployed and available during the school day. Instead of dinner on the fifth, we could do an early lunch on Monday the second, if that works for you."

"Early lunch on the Monday sounds good. I'll be in touch with details, okay?" Jack asks.

"Okay." Smiling back at him, I feel like a silly schoolgirl.

"Great. Now, would you mind if I gave you a kiss?"

"Yeah, a kiss would be nice," I dreamily answer back, getting lost in his eyes.

Jack gently places his hands on each side of my face and tenderly kisses me.

Breaking away, he smiles. "Just as sweet as I thought it would be. Now, which one is your car?"

I point to the black sports convertible a few spaces away.

Jack puts his arm around me as he walks me to my car. "Nice ride for a mother of a thirteen-year-old. I'm sure, Kyle is looking forward to getting his license and cruising for chicks in this baby."

"Please, I'm not ready to hear that! He is still my baby boy," I whine.

Jack turns me around and presses my back to the car while tucking my hair behind my ear to soothe me. "I know. It's okay. He'll always be your baby."

He gives me another sweet kiss on my lips and a warm hug. I inhale his scent to make a memory of this day.

God, he smells good!

Jack steps back and says, "Talk to you soon."

Then, he opens my car door for me to slide in behind the wheel. I watch in my rearview mirror as he gets into a hot-looking charcoal-gray, off-road SUV with a soft top. I immediately find myself picturing us with the top and doors off, doing some serious off-roading in the summer.

Jack follows me out of the parking lot and honks his horn as he turns, heading in the opposite direction.

I turn on the radio and sing at the top of my lungs. All the way home, I have a huge smile on my face, feeling a deep-down-to-the-bones happiness.

14

Jack

During the weekend, I text and talk with Keegan on the phone.

Even though the guys are forbidden to talk about my online dating, they can't help but comment on my new disposition. They keep making comments like, "Cap must have a new hobby. He seems mighty happy these days."

I take it all in stride because I can't wait for my date with Keegan on Monday. I want it to be special, memorable, and unforgettable. I rack my brain on where we can go but come up with nothing particularly special.

Then, it hits me. Keegan mentioned her love for art and going for a business degree in lieu of being an art major.

I discover a clay studio online that allows you to schedule studio time and bring food and wine to enjoy while you work. *Perfect.*

I text her Sunday afternoon.

Me: Can I pick you up as early as 9 a.m.?

Keegan: I know I said an early lunch but 9? Think you have your meals mixed up. Isn't that called breakfast?

Me: Got something special planned. It's over an hour away.

Keegan: Yeah, 9 is good, but you are setting yourself up to meet my parents.

Me: I don't care. Remember, I've already met your dad. Your call.

Keegan: To save some time, what if I drop Kyle off at school, and we meet someplace?

Me: Do you trust me enough to meet at my townhouse, or is it too soon?

Keegan: Yeah, I trust you.

The biggest smile comes over my face as I type in my address. This is going to be the best date ever. I can't wait until tomorrow morning.

After an early run the next morning, I get ready for our date. The doorbell rings a few minutes before I am expecting Keegan. I fly down the stairs to see Annie stepping into the foyer. Talk about bad timing.

"What do you need, Annie?" I stand in front of her, blocking further entry.

"I was in the neighborhood and knew you were off today. Thought it would be a good time to drop off the pictures taken over the holidays. I've picked up a couple of desktop collage frames, one for you and the other for your parents. Maybe this weekend, you and Sean can put them together and surprise your parents. Let me show you how the frames work," she replies.

"Can we do this later?" I ask.

"Don't be silly. You're not doing anything, are you?"

"Well, to tell you the truth, I'm getting ready to leave."

"It will only take a sec," Annie says as she steps around me to head back to the great room. She empties her bag of frames and pictures on the kitchen island, separating the two rooms.

The sooner I deal with this, the sooner she'll be out of here, and an awkward moment with Keegan will be avoided.

"Annie, this looks pretty simple to me. Sean and I will put these together this weekend," I say, hoping this will get her to leave sooner rather than later.

My cell phone rings with the station house number flashing across my screen. I step out onto my patio to take the call.

When I walk back in, Annie is gone from my kitchen, and I hear her ask, "May I help you?"

Then, I catch Keegan's reply, "I must have the wrong townhouse. I'm looking for Jack Grady's house. Do you know which one is his?"

"Shit!" I say under my breath, heading to the foyer.

Before I can get there, Annie answers, "Oh, you're at the right place. Come on in. I'm Annie."

I reach the foyer with both Annie and Keegan anxiously looking at me, waiting for an explanation. And here we have the awkward moment I so badly wanted to avoid.

"Keegan, this is Sean's mom, Annie Burton. Annie, this is my friend Keegan Henderson. Annie was dropping off some pictures for my parents and me. So, Annie, are we squared away?" I ask, hoping she takes the hint and leaves.

Ignoring my question, she turns toward Keegan. "Hi, Keegan. It's nice to meet you." Annie continues to eye Keegan with a smirk. "Yeah, Jack, we're squared away on the pictures. So, what are you kids up to today?"

"Just hanging out," I respond as Keegan stands in silence, taking in our exchange.

Finally, Annie turns toward me. "Well, I'd better get out of here, so the two of you can get on with your day. I'll be back in touch about getting together with Sean." Looking back at Keegan, Annie says, "Have fun today. I look forward to seeing you again."

My breathing returns back to normal. I hadn't realized I was holding it the whole time. To my surprise, especially considering our recent encounter when Sean came home from the hospital, Annie is being cordial toward Keegan. Maybe Annie sees that I'm moving on, and there will be no more unpleasant scenes between us.

After Annie leaves, Keegan remains silent and gives me a small smile. I decide the best thing to do is act as if nothing out of the ordinary happened.

I start to fill the void. "Well, everything is packed and ready to go. I think we'd better head out to make it there in plenty of time. It's a little bit of a drive, but it will hopefully be worth it."

Keegan says nothing in response and gives a slight nod in agreement. We walk out to my garage in silence.

After helping her into the vehicle, I climb in on the driver's side and notice her staring out the front windshield, as if debating on saying something. I hit the button to open the garage door, turn on my favorite playlist to fill the noticeable absence of conversation, and back out.

"I think you're going to like where we're heading," I say, trying to get a conversation going.

Still, there's dead silence from Keegan.

Once we hit the highway, she speaks very quietly, "Jack, I won't be played the fool again by anybody. Do you understand?"

I pull off to the shoulder of the road, put my vehicle in park, and turn to her. "Keegan, look at me. Please look at me."

She slowly looks toward me.

"I didn't know Annie was coming over this morning. If she had called ahead, I would have told her to do the picture thing another time. You have to understand; I have a son with her. She will be at my house from time to time. It doesn't mean I have any feelings toward her. When I'm seeing someone, I'm totally monogamous, and I don't see others at the same time. It's you I want to be with and get to know better...only you. Annie is in my past, and because of Sean, she's going to be a part of my future, too. The same way Will is a part of yours. We both have to accept and understand this for us to move forward with whatever this is between us. We need to trust and be honest with each other when it comes to our exes. Okay?"

"Okay," she replies with a smile.

"Do you still want to do lunch?"

Keegan's smile gets bigger and seems more genuine. "Absolutely."

I smile back. "Good."

We make it to our destination, and Keegan is blown away that I remembered our talk about her love of art. She especially likes that we will have something tangible to remember the day and our time together.

After being warmly greeted by the studio staff, we're instructed to select pieces from the shelves full of pottery that have already been bisque fired and ready for glazing. Keegan and I each pick out a plate and mug. After putting our personal items in a small backroom filled with tables, we are escorted to the glazing room where the process is explained to us. Unbeknownst to me, Keegan is a potter and helps me with my pieces. At a table in the backroom, we enjoy the wine and food that I brought, and we paint our pieces. Our session at the studio passes by too fast.

The drive home is filled with talk, singing along with the radio, and playing a silly game of What Am I? I can't remember having as much fun as I've had today with Keegan.

Once back at my townhouse, I turn into the rear alley to access my detached two-car garage that spans the width of my small backyard.

"Anything I can help carry inside?" Keegan offers as I unload my vehicle.

"No, I got it, but thanks," I respond back.

As we enter the kitchen, I say, "Stay a little bit longer. Don't go home yet."

With the sweetest smile, Keegan says, "Nah, I don't think so. Not today. I have a feeling the best thing to do is head straight to my car, or I might not get home anytime soon."

Smiling back at her, I say, "Yeah, you're probably right. I'm off Thursday and Friday. I don't want to scare you off, but come over and spend those days here…with me."

"What about Sean?"

"He's with Annie during the week because of school. I get him on my days off on the weekends and during my four-day breaks. This week, I'll go over on my evenings off and then get him on Sunday. Please consider coming over. You can stay in my spare bedroom. I just want to spend more time with you."

Keegan doesn't say anything for the longest time as we stare in each other's eyes.

She finally answers after what seems to be an eternity, "Okay, I'll come over. Do you have any special requests for dinner? I feel as though I need to earn my keep." She giggles.

"I'm a steak-and-potato-with-an-ice-cold-beer kind of guy."

"Then, steak and potato with an ice-cold beer, it is. Jack, thank you for today. I had a great time. Talk to you later?"

"Definitely! I'm going over to Annie's tonight to hang with Sean for a little bit before he goes to bed, but I'll call when I get back home. Okay?"

"Okay."

I walk Keegan out to her car. Taking her in my arms before she gets in, I kiss her. Once isn't enough, so I kiss her again.

"I need to get going, or I'm never going to be able to leave if you keep kissing me like this." Keegan smiles sweetly at me.

"I have no problem with that. See you on Thursday," I say, opening the door for her.

"See you Thursday," She slips into her car and then drives off.

Later that evening, Annie lets me into her house.

Sean screams, "Daddy!" as he runs toward me.

I scoop him up in my arms and give him a bear hug. It's good to see him feeling better after being so sick.

"Hey, buddy. How are you feeling?"

"I feel great. You want to play some video games with me?"

Annie interrupts, "Not now, Sean. It's time to get ready for bed. Go upstairs, get your jammies on, and brush your teeth. Daddy and I are going to talk for a couple of minutes, and then he'll be up to play some video games before bedtime."

Uh-oh, here it comes—the grilling. Might as well get it over with now.

"Mommy's right. I'll be up in a little bit after you are all ready for bed."

Sean scampers up the stairs.

I turn to Annie. "Okay, let's get this over with."

"What?" she asks innocently.

"You know what, Annie. Just get it out there, and let's deal with it."

"Okay, how serious is this with Keegan? You introduced her as a friend, which doesn't sound too serious to me."

"If I have my way, we will be seeing a lot of each other," I answer.

"Okay then, we need to discuss how Sean fits into this possible relationship."

"Okay, shoot." I climb up onto a barstool at the kitchen island, bracing myself for Annie's wrath.

Surprisingly, she remains calm and is almost pleasant. "Well, don't get me wrong. I'm happy that you're dating. I just don't want every woman you meet and go out with to be brought into Sean's life."

"I agree, and I have already discussed this with Keegan. She also has a son, and neither one of us wants to add any more confusion to our kids' lives."

"I'm glad to hear that," Annie says, smiling. "So, how did you two meet?"

"That's none of your concern."

"Ah, come on, Jack. You're not the only one out there, dating. I am, too. In fact, I have plans this weekend with a guy named Matt. I have no problem giving you the lowdown on him."

"Nope, none of my business either. The only time we discuss our personal lives is when and if it affects Sean. When you're serious enough with this Matt guy to introduce him to Sean, then I'll be all ears. I'll expect to meet him before Sean does. Other than that, I have no need to know details. You've already met Keegan, so the only thing left is me telling you if and when we reach the point where I want her to meet Sean."

"Wow, I never thought I'd see the day when you shut me out." Annie pouts, crossing her arms across her chest.

"It's not about me shutting you out, but I'm setting boundaries in our personal lives since we're no longer together. I'm thinking it might be a good time to set up some sort of formal child custody and visitation agreement, so there is no chance of us using Sean to manipulate each other," I suggest.

"Manipulate? What do you mean?"

"Well, so neither of us can deny the other to see Sean if we're upset about something. We are no longer together, and with us both moving on, I just don't want to take any chances."

"Have I ever used our son? Don't answer. I don't want to get into an argument with you. Okay, sure. Everything good with how your visitation with Sean is now? You want to add any more times?"

"No, I think the way we have things set up is perfect and working out great. Have your attorney draw up the document, ready for signatures, and then I'll have my attorney review it. Does that work for you?"

Annie nods. "Fine, I'll have it drawn up. Are you happy now?"

"Yep, sure am. Now, if you'll excuse me, I have a son waiting to beat my ass on some video game upstairs."

Annie laughs. "Go on. Don't play later than eight o'clock."

"Yes, ma'am!" I jog up the stairs to Sean's bedroom.

15

Keegan

In twenty-four short hours, I'm going to be with Jack for two days. *What the hell was I thinking?* I'm a nervous wreck.

Kyle suspects something and comes right to the point by asking, "So, Mom, what's going on?"

Since my divorce, Kyle feels the need to be the man of our household and my protector. He's constantly checking in with me to make sure I'm doing okay. If something seems off with me, he worries and asks what he can do to make it better. I'm a lucky mom to have such a caring son. I worry he takes on too many of my burdens and passes up opportunities to have fun, like others his age.

"Going on? I don't know what you're talking about."

"You've seemed distracted lately. Even Dad is starting to notice it," he replies with a look of concern.

"It's nothing but me being anxious to find another job and a place of our own. I know it will all happen, and I just need to be a little bit more patient."

My explanation seems to satisfy Kyle, and he leaves my bedroom to get ready for his dad to pick him up.

Just when I think I'm out of the woods, Mom comes into my room with the laundry I left sitting on top of the dryer. "So, what's going on?"

I knew I couldn't fool her. I come clean by saying, "I met someone."

"Who?"

"A career firefighter. His name is Jack Grady. He's taken a couple of courses from Dad. Mom, he's really a nice guy. He's never been married, but he has a son from a former relationship."

"Oh, I'm not sure if I like the sound of that."

"Jack and the mother of his son lived together for five years, but things didn't work out between them." I thought I'd save the bit about how Jack never wanted to get married. Nope, don't need to go down that road right now with my mother.

Now, it's time to drop the bomb.

"He asked me to come over during his two-day break, starting tomorrow, so I won't be home until Saturday morning." Holding my breath, I wait for her unsolicited opinion of me staying overnight with a guy I've only known for a short time.

"You're a big girl. Make sure all your laundry is done before you leave." Without any further comment, Mom walks out of my bedroom.

Who was that woman who just left? She looked and sounded like my mom, but she definitely wasn't acting like her.

Thursday morning arrives, and I am at the grocery store, picking up ingredients for tonight's dinner, before heading over to Jack's. He is going to have the best steak of his life along with the irresistible sides of twice-baked potatoes and grilled asparagus and cherry cheesecake for dessert.

I hear my name as I'm looking for cherry-pie filling.

"Keegan, I thought that was you leaving the other aisle."

I look up and see Annie pushing a cart half-filled with groceries.

Note to self: No more grocery shopping on Thursday mornings.

"Hi, Annie. How are you?"

"I'm good. I'm picking up a few things on my day off. I can't seem to keep enough food in the house. It seems as if those two boys eat twenty-four/seven. Not that Jack is over every day, but when he does come to spend time with Sean, they eat me out of house and home. I'm sure you know exactly what I'm talking about, feeding a teenage boy yourself. I can only imagine how much your son, Kyle, eats."

Whoa. How does she know I have a teenage son and his name?

She's been successful at sending me the message that Jack still spends enough time at her house to put a hurt on her food supply. What I'm more annoyed at is that, apparently, my son and I have become the topic of their conversations. I'm not sure if I like this. Maybe some ground rules need to be set, concerning how much personal information is shared with our exes.

I find the pie filling and put a can of it in the cart, getting ready to make a quick exit.

Before I can do this, she continues, "Oh, I see you have steaks and cheesecake fixings. That reminds me of the cheesesteak casserole and chocolate cake I took to the firehouse for the crew last night. They love my casserole, and I'm sure your son would, too. I'll give Jack the recipe, so you can make it."

By now, she's smiling so sweetly that I think I might get a toothache from it.

I have absolutely no interest in recipe-swapping with this woman.

"Thanks." I smile just as sweetly back and then add, "Well, I've got to run. Have a great day, Annie."

I push my cart up to a self-checkout line and get the hell out of Dodge.

As I turn onto Jack's street, I spot a space to park. My encounter with Annie is still on my mind, and I don't want to be distracted by it this evening. I get the distinct feeling that she was sending me a message and laying claim to Jack, so to speak. I don't want to come across as being that overly possessive and needy girl by making Annie the topic of conversation tonight.

What did he say to me on our first date?

"We need to trust and be honest with each other."

So, I will trust the right time will present itself for us to talk.

Until then, "Suck it up, buttercup," I say to myself as I pop the trunk before getting out of the car.

As I'm standing at my open trunk, Jack comes jogging out. He wraps his arms around my waist and gives me the most delicious kiss ever.

Annie who?

He breaks away, saying, "God, I've missed you. After we unload your car, go ahead and pull around back. I'll be waiting back there with the garage door up, so you can pull into the second bay. I don't want to take any chances with your car getting dinged or scratched out here."

Once I move my car, Jack shows me the code and buttons to operate the garage doors. He gives me his extra remote and tells me to keep it in my car, so I won't have to park on the street. Feeling a little uncomfortable with this, I question him about taking it, and I am told the code can always be changed along with the remote being replaced if I should ever piss him off.

Once in Jack's kitchen, we start to unpack the groceries.

Knowing my run-in with Annie will bug me all night, I decide to approach the subject sooner than later. "Um...I ran into Annie at the grocery store and found out she made her famous cheesesteak casserole and chocolate cake for the firehouse last night. I can take this home with me if you don't want to have steak two nights in a row." *There.* I put it out there very nicely with no bitchiness or attitude.

"No, let's go ahead and have the steaks. How did you two end up talking about dinner last night?" Jack asks.

It seems to be okay to discuss Annie, and maybe a good time to share my feelings about our conversation at the store.

"Honestly? I have no idea. Annie got into this whole big thing about how much food you and Sean eat. Then, she told me about the casserole she fixed last night and how my teenage son, Kyle, would love it."

"I wouldn't read too much into it. The run-in with you the other morning took her by surprise. We talked about it the night before last, and she's cool with everything. I'm sure Annie was only trying to have some friendly conversation with you. That's all."

"Does she have anything else in her life, other than you and Sean? Like a job or something? It's starting to feel like she's stalking me, especially after her comments about Kyle."

He chuckles a little and answers, "Annie is an interior designer. You can relax. She's not stalking you."

Jack seems a little protective of Annie, and I'm sensing some tiptoeing is needed through this minefield so that nothing blows up in my face.

"Hey, I'm sorry. It threw me a little when she started talking about Kyle. In the future, please try to keep my personal business, like my family, out of your conversations with her, okay?"

Jack leans against the counter, folding his arms across his chest. "I never mentioned Kyle by name or that he's a teenager, only that you had a son. In fact, when Annie started asking questions about you, I shut her down by saying it wasn't up for discussion."

"Thank you, but if you didn't tell her, how did she know Kyle's name and how old he is? Could her impromptu dinner last night at the firehouse been a way to get information about me from your crew?"

"Annie wouldn't do that. The whole dinner thing was so that Sean and I could spend time together, nothing else."

"Have you ever mentioned me in casual conversation at the firehouse?"

"Maybe in passing." Jack shrugs, looking down and kicking some imaginary dirt on the floor.

I'm discovering that Jack shrugs his shoulders when he's been caught with the goods.

"Didn't you tell me that they set up your page on the dating site?"

"Yeah, Nancy did most of it and showed me how to contact someone if I was interested in them."

"Did Annie talk to Nancy last night?"

"Neither Annie or Nancy are like that. Besides, Kyle was never even mentioned on your bio page. You can find out information on anybody these days by doing a search on the Internet. My guess? Because of Sean, Annie went online, searched your name, and found information on Kyle. You never gave me your address, but I know where you live because your dad's personal info is in the county's firefighters' association handbook. Hell, there are all sorts of places these days to find out personal stuff about people." Jack then leaves the kitchen to watch TV in the adjoining room, letting me know our conversation is over.

Well, this certainly is a fun way to start off an overnight date with a guy. Maybe it's too soon for a sleepover, and this is a bad idea.

Do I pack up my stuff and cut my losses before I'm in too deep? Or should I see this through and clear the air with Jack?

I'm a little bothered that he's so protective of Annie. It's pretty clear to me what last night's impromptu dinner was all about, and I find it irritating that she used Sean as a part of her scheme.

"Jack, please don't walk away from me when we're talking like this. Maybe you're right about the Internet, but I still think she made dinner for the firehouse last night to get information about us."

Jack doesn't say anything to me as an uncomfortable silence grows between us.

I continue, "I can't help but wonder why you're so protective of Annie. If there are still feelings between the two of you, then I have no business being here tonight. Tell you what. It's obvious we have rushed this thing between us. I am going to leave and give you time to think about what I said. Call me if you want to talk later."

I pick up my overnight bag, purse, and coat, and then I head to the garage. I expect Jack to jump up and stop me, but he doesn't. He remains seated on the couch, pouting like a baby.

On my drive home, I think he will text or phone at least once, asking me to come back. Nothing. My pride and feelings are now hurt.

Once home, I find my emergency pack of cigarettes and head down to my place of refuge from the world—the dock. I love the lake during the winter. A good portion of it is frozen over, waiting for the ice skaters to come and enjoy. A dusting of snow lies along the shoreline, untouched, except for some small creatures' footprints. It looks as if someone sifted white powdered sugar over the banks. The branches of the bare trees dance in the slight breeze.

I plop down on the dock, light up, and wonder how our conversation got so out of control. The strange thing about it, there was no yelling or screaming, no name-calling, no threats. It was two people rationally discussing honest feelings.

"So, you're a closet smoker, huh?"

I whip around to see Jack standing where the dock connects to the land.

"May I?" He motions with his hand, asking permission to sit with me.

"Yeah, sure," I respond as I flick the fire off my half-smoked cigarette.

For the longest time, neither of us says anything.

Then, Jack begins, "I'm sorry, Keegan. Yeah, I'm protective of Annie but not for the reason you might think. I did a real shitty thing to her. I got Annie pregnant after only dating her for a few months. I really cared about her and tried to fool myself into thinking the feelings I had was love. I did the whole line about never getting married, but I begged her to move in with me, so we could be a family. Of course she agreed, thinking we would eventually get married.

"After five years together, I just couldn't do it anymore. She was talking about marriage and having a little brother for Sean. I was using her for nothing more than sex. I finally got my head out of my ass and did the right thing by moving out.

"Eventually, we found a new comfortable relationship, and things were going great...up to a month ago." He smiles sheepishly at me.

"Until you met me online," I whisper.

"Yep. I saw your picture with that auburn hair and, God, those big blue eyes. I read your profile, and I was a goner. There was no one else I wanted to talk to. I'm sorry if I rushed you, but please don't stop seeing me. I understand if you're not ready to spend the night. I don't give a shit that I had cheesesteak casserole last night. I wanted to eat your steak and cheesecake tonight."

I smile. "You always seem to know the perfect thing to say to me."

"I'm just being honest with you. With honesty comes trust, and that's what good relationships are built on."

"Okay, here's a bit of honesty for you. Annie is a deal-breaker for me. I know she is Sean's mom and will always be a part of your life, as Will is in mine, but that's where it ends. I can handle Annie, but I can't have both of you teaming up against me. I need to feel like you're in my corner."

"Keegan, here's the problem. Annie occasionally uses Sean to manipulate me. Hell, you might even be right about dinner last night. Bob calls her a manipulative bitch. I wouldn't put it that strongly, but she would not hesitate for one minute to keep me from seeing Sean," he explains.

"She can't do that! Don't you have some sort of legal agreement?"

"Up to about a month ago, one wasn't needed. The other day, I asked Annie to have her attorney draw up a custody and visitation agreement. Until everyone signs on the dotted line and the papers are filed with the courts, I'm not willing to rock the boat. Know I am in your corner, but until everything is settled, please work with me on this, okay?"

I nod. "Okay."

"Good! Now, can we go back to my place and enjoy what is left of the day? It's okay if you don't feel ready to spend the night. Just come back with me for dinner, please?"

"Okay. Um, what if I don't have a problem with spending the night? Do I still have to go home?"

"No, but only under one condition. You don't bring those nasty cigarettes with you. Babe, got to tell you. Cigarettes are a deal-breaker for me, no matter how sexy your ass is."

"I'm not a smoker. I have an emergency pack when things get too much for me to handle."

"Throw those things away, and come to me when you're stressed out."

"What if you're the problem?"

"Come to me anyway. Let me hold you until you are calm enough to talk about it. Got it?"

Smiling up to him, I say, "Yeah, got it."

125

Jack kisses me. "Now, go brush your teeth, and then get yourself back over to my house."

When we get up to the house, Mom calls out to Jack from the front porch. "Did you find her?"

"Yes, ma'am. Found her down at the dock, like you said I would."

"Nice meeting you, Jack."

"Nice meeting you, too, Mrs. Fitzgerald."

"Sandy. Please call me Sandy."

"Nice meeting you, Sandy. See you later."

I shake my head at the exchange between my mom and Jack.

Then, I hear her say under her breath, "What a nice young man."

And another one succumbs to Jack's charm and good looks. I see I'm in for a lot of trouble with this one.

16

Jack

On the way back home, all I can think of is Keegan spending the night. I need to take things slow with her and not rush her into anything. Even though I want to explore every inch of her body, I would never want her to feel used.

It does bother me that Keegan felt uncomfortable with Annie's conversation at the store. Probably, the best thing to do is to wait until all the legal documents are filed before having a heart-to-heart with Annie.

Once home, Keegan goes into the kitchen and starts on the cheesecake while I work on my laptop and watch from the kitchen island. Later, we sit down to one of the best dinners I have ever tasted. This woman can seriously cook.

After the kitchen is cleaned up, we watch TV on the couch together. It soon turns into a heavy make-out session.

The next thing I hear is, "Jack, please take me to bed."

"Are you sure?" I ask.

"Yes."

"I'm not expecting you to sleep with me tonight. You can stay in the guest bedroom, if that makes you feel more comfortable." I pray to God she doesn't change her mind.

"Please don't make me beg," she pleads.

"Yes, ma'am," I say, standing and leading the way upstairs to my bedroom.

Keegan's tattoos fascinate me as I slowly undress her. I take in every detail of her toned body and full breasts. As we kiss, she returns the favor by stripping me out of my clothes. Her touch excites me as her hands travel down my body and tenderly wrap around my growing erection.

Fearful of our fun ending too soon, I take Keegan's hands in mine, and I lead her over to my bed. I open the bedside stand, pull out a foil packet, and ask her, "Are you sure?"

"I've never been surer of anything." Keegan starts kissing me again, lowering herself onto the bed and taking me with her.

She softly moans as I begin to explore her body with my mouth. "God, you taste like heaven."

With me craving for more, I position myself over her body and slowly sink inside her. We create a rhythm, as if it is a slow dance, getting lost in the intimacy of the moment. Keegan arches her back off the bed as we come and fall over the edge together.

I find Keegan is a confident woman who feels comfortable in her body. Without giving it a second thought, she walks through my house, naked, with no need to cover up. She wears the few marks left by her pregnancy as a badge of honor, and it is one of the hottest things I've seen.

Later, we lie in bed, sharing a slice of cheesecake. What begins as Keegan playfully tasting some topping from the corner of my mouth, soon turns into deep passionate kisses. The cheesecake is quickly forgotten, and Keegan rides me until our climaxes consume us.

Showering together afterward, we lather each other up, and I watch the bubbles travel past her breast and down the curves of her body.

Damn lucky bubbles!

I can't ever remember a time when I've enjoyed a woman's body like this, and I don't want the night to end.

After our shower, with a towel wrapped around her body, Keegan picks up the plate of cheesecake from the nightstand. As I towel off, I watch her collect some cherry topping on her finger from the plate. She slowly lifts the finger to her mouth and seductively starts licking the topping off. I stand, frozen, taking in every damn movement.

She looks at me innocently, cocks her head to the side, and asks, "Do you want some?"

Walking up to her, I take the plate from her and set it back down on the nightstand. "Yeah, you'd better believe I want some!"

After removing Keegan's towel, I set her on the edge of the bed and push her body back while keeping her legs bent over the side. I part her legs with my knees, fully exposing her to me. Leaning over, I kiss Keegan's lips and slowly continue down to her breasts. Taking her left nipple in my mouth, I caress both breasts and soon give the right one equal attention.

I return to her luscious mouth as my hand travels down between her legs.

Standing, I admire Keegan's beautiful body, and I tell her, "Wrap your legs around me, babe."

I grab her hips with both hands as she lifts her legs up and places them snuggly around me. I tease Keegan by rubbing myself up against her without entering. She silently pleads for more as her legs squeeze even tighter around me.

"Please, Jack, you're driving me crazy!"

"Shh…all in good time. All in good time." I chuckle.

Shifting my hips, I continue to torment by slowly entering her so that she can feel every bit of me. I hold her close and move my hips in a manner that causes her to moan.

Keegan's hips start meeting mine as we move in sync until both of us succumb to the intense pleasure of it all.

As we lie under the covers, exhausted, in each other's arms, I gently kiss her good night.

Keegan lays her head on my chest. "Thank you, Jack, for an incredible night."

"Best night ever! You're an amazing woman, Keegan. I just want to stay like this, with you in my arms, and never leave this bed."

Silence fills the room, making me think Keegan dozed off, when she says, "Jack, maybe we should slow down until your agreement is finalized with Annie. I would hate it if she used me as an excuse to put restrictions on your time with Sean."

"Are you having regrets about tonight?" Holding my breath, I'm unsure if I want to hear her answer.

Without hesitation, she replies, "Even though it seems as if we're going at warp speed, it feels right to be here with you. I just don't want to make things difficult for you, knowing how important Sean is to you."

"Don't worry. It's all good. I want to spend as many nights as possible falling asleep with you in my arms."

"Oh, well, if it's only sleep that you want, then, sure, I'll shack up with you anytime." She laughs out loud.

"Well, you know there is more cheesecake…"

Now, both of us are laughing as we snuggle into each other's arms with sleep soon following.

The next morning, I wake up on my back with Keegan's head on my chest, her arm slung over me and her auburn hair cascading all around. It's the best morning ever—until I hear Annie's ringtone on my phone.

Carefully reaching over to the nightstand for the phone, so as not to wake Keegan, in a scratchy voice I answer, "Yeah?"

"What are you still doing in bed, sleepyhead?" a far too perky voice asks on the other end.

"Um, you woke me up. Why?"

"You usually are up and already back from your run. It's almost eight a.m. Anyway, Sean woke up with a low-grade fever. I need to go into the office this morning to meet with a client. With it being only a few weeks since his release from the hospital, I don't want to leave him with a sitter. Since you're off, I'm dropping him off at your place. I should be there in about ten minutes."

I bolt up in bed, causing Keegan to fall off of my chest and wake up. "I'll come over and keep him at your house."

"Don't be silly. We're already on the way. Be there in a few." Annie hangs up.

I look down at Keegan. "Babe, you have about two minutes to get out of here. Sean woke up with a low-grade fever, and Annie's dropping him off. Throw on some clothes, and you can get the rest of your stuff later. Come on, I'm serious. They're going to be here any minute."

"Seriously?" Keegan says with an incredulous look on her face.

"I don't have time to explain. Just get up and out of here!" I shout at her as I get out of bed to put on my jeans.

Keegan gets up, puts on her sweater, pulls up her jeans, and shoves her feet in her boots, leaving her lace bra and thong on the floor. She grabs her overnight bag and purse on the way out, muttering loud enough for me to hear, "Asshole!"

Keegan no sooner leaves than Annie is letting herself in the front door with Sean.

"Morning! Running late, so I can't stay, but here's all of Sean's stuff he wanted to bring over this morning. This is what I've been giving him for his fever. If he still feels warm, his next dose is at lunchtime. I'll be back to pick him up after work. How about I pick up some pizza on the way home for dinner? How does that sound?"

Still not fully awake and thinking clearly, I say, "Yeah, pizza sounds good."

"Okay, Sean, give me a kiss good-bye. See you around five this evening." And out the door, she leaves.

"Hey, buddy, go set up camp on the couch with your favorite show while I get you some juice and dry cereal to snack on."

I find the spare garage remote lying on the kitchen island. This is not good.

Once Sean is set up on the couch, I run upstairs and call Keegan.

She picks up. "What do you want now, asshole?"

"Have I ever spoken to you like that?" I ask.

"Nope, because I've never disrespected you the way you did me this morning. You literally threw me out of your house, like morning trash."

"What was I supposed to do? Sean's sick, and they were on the way over. The last thing I need to happen is for you to meet Sean under those kinds of circumstances. I thought you of all people would understand, especially after our talk last night about working on an agreement with Annie!"

"Oh, I understand all right. Our dinner date was nothing but a damn booty call."

"You know that's not true. What would you have done?"

"I would have pulled up my big-boy tighty-whities and said something like, 'Annie, you need to know that Keegan is here, and we're not up yet. How about giving us a half hour or so?'"

"You know I don't wear tighty-whities. Annie would have said something about being late for her appointment."

"Then, my comeback would have been, 'Guess Sean and Keegan will meet now instead of at a more appropriate time.' I'll bet my last dollar that she would have said something shitty and then agreed to give us time to get up."

Keegan is right, but she doesn't stop there.

"Jack, I'm not going to be a dirty little secret. We either do this out in the open or not at all. Annie already knows we're seeing each other. Is it too early to involve our kids? Absolutely! But what you did this morning is inexcusable."

"You're right, and I'm sorry. Annie caught me off guard, and I panicked."

"Fine…whatever."

"What's that supposed to mean?"

"Nothing, Jack. I'm tired, and I have crawled back in bed. I don't want to fight. I just want to go back to sleep. I'm a little cranky right now because someone kept me up half the night."

"Yeah, and you enjoyed every damn minute of it! Hey, why did you leave my garage remote on the kitchen island?"

"I don't think I'm ready to go garage steady with someone who sets me out like trash."

"I apologized for that."

"It might take me longer than five minutes to get over it. I assume Sean is going to be there all day."

"Yeah, Annie is picking up pizza on the way home for dinner."

"Well, I guess that answers my question."

"Shit! I was still half-asleep when she offered. I'll call her up and tell her not to bother with it."

"Oh, and make me the bad guy, as to why Sean doesn't get his all-time favorite meal tonight?"

"How did you know it was his favorite?" I ask.

"It's every kid's all-time favorite meal." Keegan lets out a heavy sigh and then says, "Call me when you're able to have a grown-up relationship. Bye, Jack." She hangs up.

Throwing my phone on the bed, I am pissed off at myself for allowing Annie to bulldoze her way into my home. Of course Sean comes first and needs to stay here today, but I could have handled things differently with Annie by taking control over the situation. I need to set some new rules with her, like no more unannounced visits. The last two were disastrous, and I know a repeat of history will mean the end of any chance of being with Keegan.

Time to give serious thought to changing other routines we've become accustomed to. It was my hope to delay this conversation and possibly ease into a new routine with her, but I see this is no longer an option.

At five twenty in the evening, Annie walks through my front door with a pizza in hand.

Sean runs up to her, yelling, "Mommy!"

"Hey, buddy, how are you feeling? Are you up to eating some pizza for dinner?"

"Pizza! Hey, Daddy, Mommy brought home pizza for us!"

"Yeah, I know, buddy. The sooner you let Mommy in, the sooner we can dig into it," I say, picking him up so that he can give his mommy a hug.

Sean giggles as Annie lifts his shirt to give him a raspberry on his belly.

Annie sets the pizza on the kitchen island and asks, "How was Sean today?"

"No sign of a fever all day, and he didn't act like he was feeling bad. Ran around and played all day. He kind of wore me out. Hard to believe it's only been three weeks since he was in the hospital."

"I'm sorry, Jack. When he woke up this morning, he felt a little warm. I didn't want to take any chances. Guess I'm still being a little overprotective with the whole ruptured appendix thing."

"I get it, Annie. I would have probably made the same call. Hey, I want to talk to you. Can we set Sean up in front of the TV with his favorite show, and then we can eat in the dining room?"

"Wow, the dining room. You must have something pretty important to discuss," she says, smiling at me.

"Nah, just want to be out of earshot of Sean, that's all."

As we start enjoying the pizza, I casually comment, "Pretty good pizza."

"Yeah," Annie agrees.

More silence follows until she says, "Okay, Jack, out with it. Tell me what's on your mind."

"You know me well, don't you?" I laugh, wiping my mouth with a napkin.

"I should after all these years. Just spit it out, and let's just deal with it. I'm sure it has something to do with Keegan. What does she want now?"

"Why do you say that?"

"Oh, I don't know. Call it my woman's intuition. There wasn't a need for a legal agreement between us until you started seeing her. She couldn't get away from me fast enough at the grocery store. I shouldn't be surprised though since new girlfriends usually have issues with old ones."

"She's not having any issues."

"Liar, and I noticed you didn't correct me when I referred to her as your new girlfriend."

"Well, your call this morning woke us up. Since you were so close and Sean was with you, I kind of kicked her out of the house this morning," I tell her, feeling a little embarrassed.

"And why does this concern me?" Annie asks.

"We need to set some new ground rules between us, like no more dropping by without calling—"

Annie interrupts, "I called this morning."

I continue, "Yes, you did call. The problem was, you assumed I was here alone and had no plans for the day. It would have been nice to have been asked and gotten a word or two in before you hung up. You also need to stop letting yourself in with your key. Honestly, I think it might be time for you to give it back to me. With Keegan spending more time here, it could become awkward with you having a key, that's all."

"That's all? Boy, this is really happening, isn't it? I never thought the day would come when some piece of ass would become more important than our child!" she says, shaking her head.

"Watch it, Annie. Don't refer to Keegan that way. I made a commitment to both you and Sean to fulfill my responsibilities as his father. That doesn't include me becoming a monk."

"How much notice do you need? Half hour? Hour? Twenty-four hours? Tell me, Jack. What do you feel is a considerate amount of time? Heaven forbid we upset Keegan, so tell me what would she find acceptable?"

"Annie, please don't be this person."

"What kind of person is that, Jack? A bitch?"

"Don't put words in my mouth," I warn her.

"All I know is, things were pretty good between us even though you had moved out. The only real change was you were no longer sleeping in my bed. Then, *bam*, Keegan appears out of nowhere, and everything is changing. It's not fair, Jack. I have never set rules in our relationship, and she's in your life for, what? A few weeks? And life as we've known it is being turned upside down."

"I know it seems unfair, but you knew when we started seeing other people, things were going to change," I say sympathetically.

"I figured when you started dating, it would be out of sight, and I wouldn't even know about it," Annie says with tears running down her face.

I get up from the table, walk over, and pull her into my arms.

"I miss this, Jack. I miss us. Why wasn't I good enough? Why couldn't you love me?"

I have no answer for her.

Annie silently cries in my arms for a few moments. Then, she pulls away and wipes off the tears running down her face with a napkin from the table.

"Okay…new rules. In the future, I'll call in advance and not assume you're alone. I need to use the bathroom. I don't want Sean to see me like this. Um, could you get his things ready to go while I pull myself together?" Annie asks.

"Sure."

It is going on seven p.m. when Annie and Sean leave. I call Keegan as soon as they pull away from the curb.

"Hi," she answers on the second ring.

"Are you busy?"

"Why?"

"I was hoping you would come over, and we could try to salvage what's left of my two-day break."

"I don't know, Jack. How's Sean feeling? Will there be a phone call tomorrow morning with another reason to kick me to the curb?"

I see Keegan doesn't believe in sugarcoating things.

"Sean is fine. He didn't run a fever all day. Annie was just being a little overly cautious because he's still recovering from his surgery. We talked, and I told her no more surprise visits, that she needs to call ahead. I also got my extra key back from her, too."

"So, Sean wasn't sick, huh?"

"I guess not," I answer, unsure of where Keegan is going with this.

"Interesting, and I guess Annie didn't notice there were only two steaks and a small amount of food in my cart. Certainly not enough food...what were her words? To feed a hungry teenager like Kyle."

"What are you trying to say, Keegan?"

"What I'm saying is, Annie played you this morning. Sean was never sick, and she used him to keep us apart today."

"You don't even know, Annie. How can you sit there and judge her like that?"

"How can you not see her for what she is? I've only been around the woman a couple of times, and I see the game she's playing. No wonder you were together for five years. Every time you probably got the nerve to leave, she would do something to make you feel guilty and stay."

"And what's your excuse, Keegan?"

"I beg your pardon?"

"What's your excuse for marrying the same jerk twice?"

"Go to hell, Jack!" And with that parting comment, she hangs up on me.

I call her back several times but no answer.

I decide it is time to go over to Keegan's house and do the appropriate amount of groveling to get her to speak with me again.

I walk up to her parents' front door and ring the doorbell. Her father answers the door and just stares at me, saying nothing.

Feeling like an awkward teenager, I ask, "Is Keegan home?"

He answers, "Yeah, I believe she is. Why?"

"Well, I was wondering if I could please speak to her, sir."

About that time, Sandy comes up behind him and says, "Jack, come on in. Mitch, get out of the way, so Jack can come in."

I step inside the door.

Sandy introduces, "This is Keegan's dad, Mitch. Mitch, this is Jack. I think he's taken some of your classes."

Like a fool, I shake his hand and say, "Mitch, it's good to see you again."

"It's Mr. Fitzgerald."

Sandy tries to save me by batting her husband's arm. "Oh, stop it, Mitch. Go tell Keegan that Jack is here. Jack, why don't you wait for her in the living room? Can I get you anything?"

"No, thanks. I'm good."

A few moments later, Mitch comes back. "Keegan wants you to come downstairs."

Once reaching the lower level, I find Keegan in the rec room, sitting in a wooden rocker, with her arms crossed, rocking like there's no tomorrow.

"What do you want?" she asks.

"To grovel?"

"Is that a question?"

"Nope. I'm definitely here to grovel and beg for your mercy."

"Continue."

"I know Annie manipulates, and I'm dealing with it. I've addressed everything to date with her, and I have set new ground rules. This probably won't be the last time we have issues. As they come up, I'll deal with them. For us to work, you need to trust me, as I do with you."

"Continue."

I notice Keegan's rocking is slowing down. "I want to be with you, but Annie is Sean's mother, and she will continue to be a part of my life. We need to come to terms with our exes, including Will, and how to coexist without stepping on each other's toes."

She stops rocking and brings her finger to her chin, as if pondering something. "Isn't it interesting how Will has yet to be an issue, except for the little backhanded comment you made earlier? But continue."

"My comments about Will, over the phone, were uncalled for and totally out of line. I'm sorry."

"Continue."

By now, I'm running out of things to say and not sure what she wants to hear, but I stumble along with my words. "I will never intentionally make you feel less than the extraordinary woman you are. I've never met anyone like you. Please forgive me and come home with me."

"Is that it?"

"Pretty much."

"Okay. I have some things to say to you."

"Okay, shoot."

Keegan runs her hands along the top of the wooden rocker's arms, feeling the smooth wood. "I've had some bad experiences with ex-girlfriends that I don't care to repeat. I know Annie will be around because of your son, but I won't tolerate being treated like a cheap one-night stand and a dirty little secret. If the two of you have unfinished business, then you need to take care of it, and we end this now."

"I swear, there is no unfinished business with Annie, and you are not a cheap one-night stand. She caught me off guard this morning. Please, give me another chance," I plead with her.

She holds her hand up, indicating me to stop. "There's one other thing you need to know about me. I have a tendency to give my two cents when it's not asked for or welcomed. I'm very outspoken with a small touch of bitchiness that some guys can't handle. I apologize for spouting off about Annie when you had already handled the problem, but it probably won't be the last time it happens. If you can't handle that, then I'm not the girl for you."

I get a shit-eating grin on my face. "Oh, trust me, I can handle all of that and more. You are exactly the girl for me because I don't hold back either. I'm sorry about this morning. Please, come back over tonight."

Keegan sits quietly for a few moments, considering my words. She gets up from the rocker, walks over to me, and puts her arms around my neck. "For some crazy reason, I believe you. I think this is when you're supposed to kiss me."

After a far too short make-out session, we head back to my place, and I show Keegan many times how special she is to me.

17

Keegan

Spring has sprung, and we are into the month of May. Mother's Day is this weekend with Memorial Day only three weeks away, signifying the unofficial start of summer. We've all been taking advantage of the beautiful warm weather by going out on the lake and enjoying the pool whenever possible. It feels good to have my happy back. The only thing that could make me happier is finding a job.

Jack and I have been dating for over four months and are starting to discuss when the appropriate time will be to bring our children into the relationship. Our past experiences are as varied as our opinions on the subject. I see no rush since we both are against moving in together or getting married, and the L word hasn't been uttered by either of us.

I feel it's premature for us to be discussing this, much less acting on it. Jack feels it's not a big deal if our sons met in a casual way, like they do with our other friends, and then we could spend more time together.

We have announced to the world that we are a couple by our social media status of being In a Relationship. The night we lay in bed, changing our status, we joked that it felt like being back in high school, deciding to go steady. Our posts are often filled with pictures of fun times together and sweet messages to each other when we're apart. I don't have to worry about Kyle seeing this since he's banned from having a social media page until he's in high school.

Annie still does little things that irritate me. On Jack's birthday, I noticed on his kitchen island two baseball tickets for one of the area's major league games and a card from Annie and Sean. The tickets were for an evening that fell on one of Jack's two-day breaks, which we typically spend with each other. Sean explained to Jack that the second ticket was his, so they could go to the game together. I knew Annie did this on purpose, but under the circumstances, it was impossible to be upset over it.

Later that same evening, after a quiet dinner at Jack's house, I gave him my present of two custom game jerseys of our favorite football teams. FFCap with the number 52 is on the back of the one for him, and IrishEyes with the number 1 is on the other for me. He didn't quite get the number 1 since my tag was IrishEyes732. I explained custom orders only come in two digit numbers, and I'm his number one gal. He loved them and showed his appreciation numerous times.

Annie is constantly posting pictures of Jack and Sean on her social media page. I'm sure she dislikes the pictures of us as much as I hate seeing Jack plastered all over her page. I try to take it all in stride because what Jack says is true. She can't touch us as long as we remain honest and have trust in each other.

Annie loves amusement parks, and Sean told Jack that he wanted to take her to one for Mother's Day. Since Jack works tomorrow on Mother's Day, they went to one of her favorite parks today. From the pictures Jack has sent with his texts, it sounds as if they are all having a great time.

I wake up on Mother's Day with the sweetest text from Jack waiting for me.

> *Jack: Thinking about the sexiest mom I know today. Happy Mother's Day. Have a great day, babe. Looking forward to tomorrow.*

> *Me: Sending my thanks to the hottest dad on earth. Looking forward to meeting your parents tomorrow.*

I decide it's time to get up when I smell the breakfast Kyle and Dad are cooking for Mom and me. Later today, Will and Kyle are taking me to my favorite restaurant for dinner.

Since Jack is unable to visit his mom until tomorrow, Annie has offered to stop by his parents' today with Sean.

Jack has invited me to go with him tomorrow because this is the first time our schedules have allowed for me to tag along and meet his parents. He thought it would be a perfect time for all of us to spend the day together and get acquainted with each other.

The next morning, Jack and I leave for his parents, who live in an upscale neighborhood along the bay a little over an hour's drive away.

Once we arrive, I follow Jack up the porch steps to the Grady's front door. He opens it and yells, "Mom? Dad? Where are you guys?"

"We're out in the sunroom!" his dad yells back.

I follow Jack to a large room, filled with floor-to-ceiling windows and a spectacular water view of the bay. We find his parents lounging in some oversize upholstered wicker furniture while enjoying some sweet tea.

"Happy belated Mother's Day!" Jack says, walking up to his mom. He hands her a small gift bag containing several ball-shaped beads designed for a special bracelet she owns.

"Thank you, sweetheart," she says, standing up and giving Jack a kiss and hug.

"I love you, Mom," he adds.

"I love you, too," she says back to him.

I stand there, caught up in the tenderness of the moment, not realizing the looks I am getting from his dad.

"Who do we have here, Jack?" his dad asks.

"Oh, I'm sorry." Jack walks over and puts his arm around me. "This is my friend Keegan Henderson. Keegan, these are my parents, Pat and John Grady."

His words *my friend* hurt. I'm not sure what term should be used to define our relationship, but friend wasn't sitting well with me. I so badly want to embarrass him and add, *With benefits*, but I decide to behave myself.

Neither parent says anything, not even extending a polite offer to have a seat.

I speak first, saying, "It's nice to meet you. Jack talks about you so much. I feel as if I already know you."

Without skipping a beat, Pat says, "Strange, we haven't heard much about you, other than what Annie told us when she and Sean were here yesterday for Mother's Day." She continues talking, now directing her comments to Jack, "Annie said you all went to her favorite amusement park for her Mother's Day gift on Saturday. That's all Sean could talk about, spending the day with Mommy and Daddy at the park. They gave me a picture of the three of you. It's up there on the mantel with their card."

"Mom," Jack says in a warning tone.

There, on the fireplace mantel, is a picture of the happy little family sitting on a bench with Sean perched on his daddy's lap. Jack has one arm around Sean, holding him in place and his other one around Annie with her snuggling into him. By looking at the picture, no one would ever guess they were no longer together.

It is an awkward moment, and I add to it by saying, "It's a beautiful picture."

John quickly adds, "Of a beautiful family."

I bite my tongue, forcing a small smile and politely nodding my head. After all, I'm only Jack's friend.

Jack decides to ignore the tension in the room by asking, "Keegan, would you like some sweet tea?"

"No, thank you. I'm good."

He leaves me standing in the sunroom to get a glass of it for himself. I try desperately to think of some small talk to fill the dead air, but nothing comes to mind. I continue to stand there self-consciously, looking out the windows at the water view.

A short time later, Jack returns with his drink. "Are you working on any new projects, Dad?"

"I sure am! I'm making some improvements on Sean's tree house. Come out back, and tell me what you think," John says, getting up from his chair, and then heads outside with Jack.

I'm left alone with his mom and decide to sit down because, obviously, it would be a cold day in hell before she was going to offer me a seat. Minutes pass with nothing being said.

"According to Annie, you have a teenage son from a man you married and divorced twice," Pat blurts out of the blue.

I cringe at how my past sounds when thrown back in my face in such a blunt manner, and I'm irritated to find out I was the topic of their conversation yesterday. Yet again Annie knew details about me that I had never shared with her.

I answer the only way I can, "Yes."

"I also understand you and my son met online?"

"Yes, we did."

"You need to know that we're upset Jack hasn't done the right thing by marrying Annie. Sean needs his father, and we thought they'd be married by now." She continues,

"Instead, he finds you online and leaves them. I'll never understand how he could do such a thing to Annie."

I'm now wishing for Pat to start ignoring me again.

She continues droning on, "Nothing personal against you, Keegan, but Jack needs to get back with Annie and marry her, so they can provide a happy home for Sean."

I can't take another second of this rude, deplorable woman's behavior. "With all due respect, Pat, what you don't seem to understand is that Jack isn't in love with Annie, and that is the reason he left her. It was a year after they broke up that we met online. I'm not the reason for their breakup. As for my past, it's my story and only fair I get to tell it. Now, if you'll excuse me, I'll wait for Jack outside since you've made it clear I'm not welcome here. I apologize for ruining your Mother's Day visit with him. Please, let Jack know where I am and for him to take his time." I get up to leave, only to find Jack and John standing at the doorway with a look of shock.

I squeeze by them, saying, "Excuse me," and leave the house.

Minutes later, Jack comes jogging out to find me sitting on the top step of his parents' front porch, hugging my knees to my chest. "I'm sorry, Keegan. Do you want to go home?"

I look up at Jack, amazed at his stupidity. "What do you think?"

As I stand, he offers a hand to help me up. I ignore it and walk past him to his SUV.

Once we are settled in his vehicle and before he starts to back out of the drive, Jack turns to me. "Again, I'm sorry. I don't know why they behaved that way."

I can no longer maintain my cool. "You don't know why they behaved that way? I'll tell you why! A day with Annie spewing all the sordid details of my life is why. Your mom said, and I quote, 'Nothing personal against you, Keegan, but Jack needs to get back with Annie and marry her, so they can provide a happy home for Sean.' End quote. Once again, dear sweet Annie strikes. And I want to know something. If you aren't telling her stuff about me, then who is? Annie told your mother I'd been married and divorced twice. Where is she getting her information? Did you tell her?"

"No, I do not discuss you with her."

"I'm getting sick of Annie's manipulative ways."

"Keegan, now, don't start jumping to conclusions about Annie. Mom could have easily taken Annie's comments out of context."

I hold my hand up. "Stop coming to Annie's defense right now. I don't think I can take any more. Just take me home."

Later, I find out, after dropping me off, Jack went back to his parents' and had a long talk with them. The next day, I get the sweetest bouquet of flowers with a written apology from Pat attached to it.

I'm looking forward to Jack's next two-day break, which starts tomorrow. We create our own bubble during these times together and enjoy both great food and sex.

Kyle is with Will until Sunday, and my parents are visiting friends in New Mexico. I've turned on the evening news for background noise to fill the eerily quiet house.

While arranging freshly baked brownies on the plate I made on our first date, something on TV catches my attention.

"Earlier today, two firefighters from Engine Company Fifty-Two were taken to a local hospital. One was pronounced dead on arrival while the other is being treated for minor injuries."

I stand, motionless, listening to the broadcast and watching the accompanying video of a house engulfed in flames.

I pick my phone up from the kitchen counter to text Jack and see how he's doing. Being the captain on duty, I know the devastation he must be feeling. I wait for over a half hour for a reply, and nothing. The need to see him is slowly becoming more than I can handle.

Another ten minutes pass, and the urge to find him surpasses all common sense. I tear out the front door to my car. I'm confident he's safe because officers of his rank don't fight the fires but manage the attack from a command post located outside of them.

The first place I look for Jack is at the hospital where they took the one firefighter for treatment. After parking my car, I run toward the entrance and see Annie coming out of the doors, crying.

I quickly approach her and ask, "Annie, what's wrong? Tell me what's happened!"

She looks at me and cries, "Jack fell down a flight of stairs."

Trying my best to remain calm, I ask, "What? Jack fell down some stairs? How? He's not even supposed to be inside, working the fire. But Jack's okay, right?"

She slowly shakes her head, looking me straight in the eyes. In the most mournful cry, she says, "No, he's not okay! He's…he's…oh God, don't make me say it!"

"I don't believe you." I start to walk past her.

She grabs my arm and says, "They won't let you in. I had an awful time getting in. Bob Henley had to wave security off and take me aside to break the news about Jack to me."

I stand there and start shaking from the shock, which is starting to consume me.

Annie continues, "I don't know what to do. God, how did this happen?" She hurries off, leaving me standing alone in disbelief.

Annie's right. I'm nobody. I'm not family or even his significant other. As he told his parents, I'm a friend. They would never let me in. Feeling lost, I return to my car and leave.

After arriving home, I walk into the kitchen and see the brownies on the plate. Picking it up, I throw everything at the wall and scream, "No!"

The brownies splatter all over the place, and the plate breaks in pieces. I fall to my knees, curling up into a ball, crying my heart out.

I have to get out of here. All I see are things reminding me of our times together. I see Jack sitting on the couch, watching games with my dad, out in the boat on the lake, and us down at the dock, talking.

I grab the overnight bag packed for my two-day stay with him and head out to my car to find someplace where there are no memories of us. I head east until I end up in a hotel along the water, somewhere near Annapolis. Exhausted, I enter my room and collapse on the bed. I allow myself to fully feel the pain of losing Jack, and I cry myself asleep.

The next morning, after searching both purse and car for my phone, I remember leaving it behind on the counter at home.

I spend the morning on my room's balcony that overlooks the water mourning my loss. I have no communication with the outside world. It's only me, alone, lost in my grief, discovering I had fallen deeply in love with Jack.

Watching a pair of geese flying low over the water, I begin to think about Jack's parents and Sean. Pat and John have lost their only child, and it's a burden no parent should bear. Then, there's Sean, who is now living with the heartache of losing his father. Feeling embarrassed for allowing my grief to consume me to the point of running away, I check out of the hotel.

Once back home, I find my phone and call Will. "Hey, it's me. Um, can you keep Kyle for a few more days? I'm coming down with something, and I don't want him to catch it."

"Yeah. Just let me know when you're feeling better and ready for him to come home. The only thing I have on the books is the funeral, on Monday, for the firefighter who died yesterday."

I lie to Will, "He was my former secretary's cousin. I was thinking about going to the funeral. Can I go with you?"

"Sure."

After ending the call, I clean up the brownie mess and carefully wash the pieces of the broken plate. I make sure all pieces are accounted for, so I can glue them back together. After everything is cleaned up, I head to the dock with cigarettes in hand and light up.

Pulling my phone out from my pocket, I dial Pat Grady's number and she answers, "Hello?"

"Hi, it's Keegan."

"Keegan, where are you? Jack's been going crazy, trying to get in touch with you! Why haven't you been answering your phone? Are you all right?"

What? Did she say Jack's been trying to call me? But he's dead.

"I'm sorry. What do you mean Jack is trying to get in touch with me? He's gone."

"What do you mean, gone?"

"Annie said he fell down some stairs and…"

Pat then understands and says, "Oh, sweetheart, he's not gone. Whatever made you think that? Jack was hurt from falling down some steps, and he has a broken arm. Other than that and an injured shoulder, he's fine."

I replay my conversation outside the ER with Annie and realize she never actually used the words *died* or *dead*.

Lost in my own thoughts, Pat's words are no longer registering with me.

I cut her off, "Thanks, Pat. Sorry to cut you off, but I've got to call Jack."

I hang up and immediately dial his number, only for it to go over to voice mail. After disconnecting the call, I notice some voice messages I previously ignored because they were from an unknown phone number. I pull each one up and hear Jack's voice speaking to me.

"It's me, baby. I'm okay. Where are you? Call me back at this number."

"Keegan, where are you? I'm starting to get worried. I've lost my phone. This is Annie's phone. Call me back at this number."

"Since I haven't heard from you, Annie is taking me home. Call me back at this number."

I am so pissed off at Annie for what she said to me in the hospital's parking lot yesterday. She's the last person I want to talk to now. Instead, I decide to head over to Jack's townhouse, only to find him not home. I have no other choice but to call Annie.

"Hello?" she answers a little louder than a whisper.

"Annie, it's Keegan. Where's Jack?"

I hear Annie walking and closing a door before she answers in her normal voice, "So, you finally decided to call him?"

"Annie, I'm not getting into this with you now. Where's Jack?"

"He's here with me. Where else would he be since you abandoned him at the hospital?"

"You know I didn't abandon him."

"Funny, I don't remember seeing you there with him or getting any calls from you after all of his messages. So, if you didn't abandon him, what exactly would you call it?"

It then hits me. Jack doesn't know I thought he was dead and why I was gone for the past twenty-four hours. *How will I ever explain it all to him?*

"Put him on the damn phone now," I demand.

"No, he's finally fallen asleep, and I'm not waking him up. In fact, I was getting ready to crawl into bed myself. I'll let him know you called when we wake up tomorrow morning. Have a good night, Keegan." She hangs up.

There are no words for the rage I'm feeling toward Annie and this whole messed-up situation. My ability to think rationally is lost, and I'm clueless as to what to do next.

I wake up the following morning, disconnect my phone from the charger, and check for a text, a missed call, or a voice mail—anything from Jack. All day, I call and text Annie, trying to contact him. She doesn't answer. There are no return calls or texts. Nothing.

I decide to call his mother, hoping to get a message to Jack through her. She doesn't answer, and I leave a voice mail.

"Uh, hi, Pat. This is Keegan. I've been trying to get in touch with Jack with no luck. If you should talk to him, could you please ask him to call me? Thanks."

It's soon late afternoon, and I still have heard no word from Jack. Not knowing what else to do, I ask Marcy and Seth to come over for moral support. Once they arrive, I tell them about the whole mess.

Marcy immediately says, "What's the problem? Just go over to Annie's and confront the bitch. Where's my girl who takes control of the situation instead of allowing it to take control of her?"

"You don't understand. If Jack rejects me in front of Annie, I will never be able to handle the humiliation of it all."

"Seriously? Since when have you ever backed down from a fight?" Marcy asks out of exasperation with me.

Seth chimes in, "Marcy, back off. I hear what Keegan is saying, and I know exactly how she's feeling."

"Then, what do you suggest, Seth?" Marcy asks him.

Seth looks over at me. "Let's think about this for a second. Either Annie is not telling Jack about your calls, or he's mad and doesn't want to talk to you. No matter which one it is, it'll do no good to keep calling or going over there, pounding on the door. Don't forget. It's the weekend, and Sean will be there. Do you really want to meet Sean for the first time like this?" He pauses for a moment and then asks, "Do you think Jack has feelings for Annie?"

"No, he doesn't have feelings for her—or at least, not in the way you're implying," I answer with confidence.

Seth asks, "Do you trust him, staying at Annie's?"

"For God's sake, Seth, he has a broken arm and messed up shoulder. I'm pretty sure sleeping with Annie is the last thing on his mind. It pisses me off more than anything that she's the one taking care of him, but, yes, I totally trust him staying there," I tell him.

"Good. Then, I think there's only one thing you can do, and that's to wait until Monday to see him at the funeral."

Marcy and I both shout at the same time, "What?"

Seth explains, "Calm down for a second, and listen. The funeral is the only place I can think of where Annie can't stop you from seeing him. In the meantime, maybe he will eventually call to talk things out. I mean, you've done everything you can by calling, texting, leaving messages, and even calling his mom. I'm not sure if you have any other choice but to wait until Monday."

I think it over, and although it's going to kill me to wait three more days to see him, Seth is right. I have no other choice.

After I hear nothing back from Jack, Monday morning finally arrives. The doorbell rings, and I find Will waiting on the front porch all decked out in his dress uniform. "Are you sure you're up to going to this funeral?"

"Good morning to you, too. Yes, I'm feeling much better. I forgot how handsome you look in your uniform."

Will ignores my compliment. "Are you ready?"

"As much as I'll ever be." I close the door behind me, hoping my plan works to get things sorted out with Jack.

We pull up in front of the church in Will's unmarked state car. I can't believe the number of apparatuses there, representing other fire departments. Many are from bordering states, coming to show their solidarity and support.

Once Will parks where the funeral home staff directs him, we walk toward the massive crowd, entering the church. The street in front of the church has been blocked off to accommodate Station 52's various pieces of equipment draped in black. The first fire engine in line has been designated to transport the casket to the cemetery. Before entering the church, mourners pause at the fire engine as the casket covered with the American flag lies in repose in the empty hose bed.

Relief sets in as I know all of this pomp is in honor of someone other than Jack.

As we get closer, I see the back of Annie's head as she talks to a group of firefighters all standing in their dress uniforms worn on ceremonious occasions such as this. With their backs to me, I stop in my tracks, seeing Annie's arm around Jack. His left arm is in a cast and sling while his good arm is around her.

Will asks, "Are you okay?" He stops and puts his arm around me, thinking I am about to get sick.

As though Jack senses my presence, he turns and looks straight at me. Annie looks up at him and turns to see what he is looking at. Her face goes ashen. I can tell by

Jack's expression that he has totally misinterpreted Will's gesture.

"Just give me a second. I'll be okay," I plead with Will, trying to decide if I should go to Jack now or wait for a more private moment. "I'll be fine in a minute. I need to catch my breath."

The decision is made for me when funeral staff informs us it's time to go inside and take our seats. Annie is gone when I look back over at the fire engine, and Jack along with the other members of his company are getting last-minute instructions from Bob.

Once inside, I notice Annie is sitting with a group of women, who I assume are the firefighters' wives and significant others. Before the service begins, the station's crew files into their designated pews. Jack is not among them.

The service starts as the fire department's chaplain and the pastor of the church lead the procession of the casket and family with Bob and Jack escorting the widow and the mother. I glance at the program and see I'm attending the funeral of Ronald Clyde Green.

Jack looks over his shoulder at me during the service. I see a combination of hurt and anger on his face, and my biggest fear of him not wanting to talk to me is slowly becoming a reality.

When the ritual of loading the casket back onto the hose bed is completed, the firefighters board the different pieces of the apparatus. Many have already gone to predetermined locations along the funeral procession route to stand at attention as the funeral motorcade passes.

As luck would have it, Will's car is right in front of Bob's SUV, and Jack is his passenger. I feel his eyes boring into me as Will escorts me to his car and holds the door open as I get in.

At the cemetery are two aerial ladder trucks on each side of the entrance. Their ladders are extended up high to create an arch for the procession to pass under. An

American flag hangs proudly from the middle of the arch where the two ladders meet. A pipe and drums corps formed by local firefighters leads the procession to the gravesite, playing a funeral dirge. Along each side of the road inside the cemetery are firefighters standing at attention. One by one, they salute the fire engine that carries the casket as it passes by them.

I decide to stay close to the car during the graveside service. As they lower the casket from the hose bed of the fire engine, listening to the pipe and drum corps play "Amazing Grace" gives me goose bumps.

Mourners are slow to leave at the end of the service, and off in the distance, Will gets caught up in a conversation with a few other police officers.

I begin to search for Jack in the crowd when I hear him say from behind me, "So, you finally show up out of the blue after going missing for, how long? Five days? Is that the infamous Will Henderson?" He nods in the direction where Will is standing.

I look up into Jack's eyes. "Please don't, Jack. I can explain. We need to talk."

"I think your actions have pretty much said it all."

"Jack, you said as long as we are honest and trust each other, nothing can touch us. Please, trust me and know there is a good reason I haven't been here for you."

As if on cue, Annie walks up and wraps her arm around Jack's good one. "Hi, Keegan." She looks up at Jack. "Excuse me, babe, but are you ready to leave? We should get back home, so I can massage your shoulder and do physical therapy."

Game, set, match.

Annie has finally won Jack back. She is letting me know, in no uncertain terms, she is the victor.

Pleading one last time, "Jack, please remember trust and honesty…you promised."

Looking at Annie, he says, "Yeah, I'm done here."

And I watch him walk out of my life with Annie.

As Will turns into my parents' driveway, I tell him, "Thanks for letting me come with you today. What time will you be dropping off Kyle?"

"I think you need a couple of more days to rest before Kyle comes back home."

"I'm fine. Kyle can come home today," I insist.

"Keegan, you almost got sick in front of the church today. I'll just have him stay with me until Wednesday."

Being too exhausted to argue, I simply say, "Okay."

After Will pulls away, I go inside to my bedroom to take some headache meds and try to figure out what to do next since today was a total disaster. Not bothering to change out of my clothes, I crawl under my duvet feeling defeated. I no sooner get comfortable than the doorbell rings.

Now, what does Will want?

I open the front door to find Jack standing there.

"What? How did you get here?" I ask, peering out the door and spotting his vehicle.

"I drove. It hurt like hell, but I need to hear what could have made you disappear and end up at the funeral with your ex. You're right. I did promise honesty and trust would protect us, so this story had better be a good one."

"Where's Annie?"

"At her place and not very happy with me at the moment. Can I come in, or are we going to talk out here on the front porch?"

"Come on in. Go to the TV room, and get comfy in Dad's chair. I'll get some ice for your shoulder. Are you even supposed to be driving?"

"Nope," he says, walking past me into the house.

I see him pause at the kitchen counter, looking at the plate that I glued back together.

Jack gets settled with an ice pack resting on his shoulder and reclines in Dad's leather chair. "What happened?"

I tell Jack everything from the moment I was cutting the brownies until I saw him today at the funeral. At times, I break down in sobs, choking on my words, while describing the heartache and how lost I felt without him.

Then, I tell him, "But, Jack, the worst part of it all was sitting outside on the balcony of my hotel room, discovering too late that I had fallen in love with you. I'm not letting another second pass without saying I love you."

Jack stares at me, speechless, as I sit across from him, baring my soul.

After a couple of minutes, Jack brings the recliner back to its upright position. He speaks in a low voice, "I heard over the radio that Ron had collapsed on the second floor. I slipped and fell on the yard's front steps while helping with the stretcher.

"Annie took me to her house when I got discharged from the hospital because you never came after I'd left all those messages for you. We even stopped here, but no one was home. The only place I've been able to get any sleep has been in Annie's recliner, and that's why I stayed with her.

"Damn it!" Jack slams the fist of his uninjured arm down on the recliner, making me jump.

"I kept asking Annie if you had called, and she said no. She told me the only person who had called were my parents. Since I couldn't find my phone, I asked Annie to keep calling and texting you. Didn't you get any of her messages or texts?"

I shake my head.

"For five days, I heard nothing from you, and then you showed up with Will today. You're right. We need to be honest with each other, so here goes nothing."

I feel the bottom of my stomach fall out because I know whatever is coming next isn't going to be good.

The tone in Jack's voice changes, and he looks over my shoulder at a painting on the wall to avoid making eye contact as he continues, "I went home with her today, thinking you and I were through, especially after seeing you with Will. God, I was so pissed off, tired of the damn pain, and I missed you. I wanted to turn the clock back to five days ago and forget about everything that had happened. I just wanted it all to stop, so I could feel good for a few minutes.

"When we got back to Annie's, she took me up to her bedroom. After she helped me out of my shirt, I sat on the bed, waiting for her to massage my shoulder. Annie stood in front of me and stripped down to her bra and thong. She climbed up onto the bed behind me and started to massage my shoulder. God, it felt good. I closed my eyes and imagined it was your hands as hers slowly came around to my chest and held me."

I gasp in my sobs, knowing what he is about to tell me.

"I was snapped back to reality when Annie climbed off the bed and onto my lap and started kissing me."

"No, please don't tell me any more!" I whisper through my tears.

"I can't lie to you, Keegan. It would have been so easy to have sex with her, but I couldn't because it was you who I needed, not her. I pushed Annie off and told her I was in love with you."

I stare at him, not knowing how to respond or what to say.

"That's right. I told her you were the only woman I ever wanted to make love to. I got up, put my shirt back on, and came here to fight for us. Do you hate me? Have I ruined us to the point that you'll never be able to forgive me?" he asks with tears welling up in his eyes.

I walk over and pull my dress up high enough to crawl onto his lap with my knees on each side of his thighs. Facing him, I remove the ice pack and gently place my hands on his shoulders. "Am I upset that happened between the two of you today? Yes, I am."

I see his expression fall. His tears release and slide down the cheeks of his face. Taking my hand, I lovingly wipe them away.

"Do I understand how it happened? Maybe a little. Does it make me happy that you stopped it and set her straight? Yes, it does. Do I still believe in us? Yeah, I do. After all that's happened this week, the bottom line is, I love you, Jack Grady, with all my heart. Does that answer your question?"

He gives me a soft kiss. "I'm sorry for everything. Annie's not who or what I want. It's you and only you."

"I know…I know…" I tell him.

Our kiss deepens.

He tugs at my dress. "Take it off. Take it all off. I've missed you, all of you."

I stand up in front of him and unzip the black dress I wore to the funeral. I let it drop to the floor, standing in a plunging push-up bra and thong. I slip one of my bra straps down, followed by the other. Unfastening the single hook closure located in the front, I expose my breasts to him. My bra falls to the floor. I slide my thumbs under each side of my thong, shimmy it down to my ankles, stepping out of it.

The whole time I am stripping in front of him, I never take my eyes off of his. I watch him take in every move I make as each part of my body is revealed.

After all my clothes are off, I carefully climb back onto his lap, making sure not to disturb his shoulder and arm.

In a hoarse voice, Jack says, "Help me with my pants, babe."

Once unbuttoned, I tease him by taking my sweet old time unzipping his fly and exposing him.

"God, you're killing me, Keegan. Please don't make me come all over your father's recliner. I would never be able to look the man in the eyes again." He laughs.

"Do you have a condom with you?"

"Front left pocket. I brought it just in case." He shrugs.

"In case you got lucky?" I ask, reaching into his pocket and pulling the foil packet out.

We make love until both of us cry out as we come.

Afterward, I cover us with a quilt from the couch as Jack holds me on his lap with my head resting on his good shoulder. Reclined in Dad's chair, we sit like this for the longest time, saying nothing to each other while lost in our thoughts.

Jack breaks the silence, "So, you want to tell me what happened to the plate?"

"I kind of went crazy and threw it up against the wall. Let's just say, it wasn't one of my finer moments."

"I need to find out why in the hell Annie would do such a sick thing to us," Jack says angrily.

"I think it was a simple case of me being in the wrong place at the wrong time."

"There's no excuse for what she did," Jack replies back to me.

"Leave it," I say, not believing what just came out of my own mouth.

"Why in the hell would I do that?"

"What would be accomplished by confronting her? I mean, you spelled it out to her today. What else is there left to say?"

"To tell her that what she did was fucked up and to never do anything like that again or else," Jack says in his authoritative voice.

I interject, "Or else what? You'll never see or speak to her again? We both know that's never going to happen because of Sean. Anything you say will be an empty threat. Why even go there? Anyway, it will drive her batshit crazy if you say absolutely nothing about it." I smile evilly up at him. "Jack, one thing is still bugging me about all of this."

"What's that?"

"I talked to your mom. Why didn't she tell you I'd called?"

"I haven't talked to Mom since Thursday morning. It seems like we've been playing phone tag all week. Ever since I lost my phone, Annie's been taking care of my calls for me. The first couple of days I was doped up on pain meds. Once the pain eased up, I had trouble using the cell phone with one hand. That's why I asked Annie to keep trying to get in touch with you."

"Well then, that's the first order of business once we get up and moving."

"What's that?"

"Getting you a new phone. I'm now the nurse on duty. Maybe we can pick up one of those sexy little nurse outfits while we're out, too."

"God, I love you, babe," he says, kissing my head.

"I love you, too."

18

Will

Keegan calls me the Wednesday after the funeral, as promised. She can't wait for Kyle to come home. I can hear in her voice how much better she is feeling.

"Will, I need to discuss something else with you," Keegan says to me.

I notice Keegan's tone has taken on a nervous edge. I'm not sure if the next part of this conversation is something I'll want to hear.

"Yeah? What's going on?" I brace myself for her answer.

"I have been seeing a firefighter named Jack Grady since the first of the year. We're ready to take our relationship to the next level."

"What do you mean by the next level?"

"I want Kyle to meet him."

Fuck! I knew this day was going to come, but I prayed it would never happen. After the whole Alex Parker debacle, I never wanted to share my son with another man again.

I say nothing in response.

"Jack wants to meet you."

"Why?"

"It's Jack's idea. He has a son, too, and if the roles were reversed, he would want the same consideration."

"What? Is this joker going for sainthood or something?"

Ignoring my sarcasm, Keegan continues by saying, "You need to know Jack is a permanent part of my life. It's not like before with Alex. You can either meet Jack now or later, but you will eventually meet."

"How can you be so sure it's permanent?"

"You'll just have to trust me on this one. I know," she answers back with confidence.

After heaving out a heavy sigh, I ask, "When and where?"

We decide to meet on Friday morning at Keegan's favorite coffee shop.

Being the first to arrive, I get my coffee, take a seat in an empty booth in the back of the shop, and wait for their arrival.

A couple of minutes later, the bells over the front door jingle, and I see Keegan enter with a guy who has his left arm in a cast and sling. I observe them as they walk over to the counter. It looks as if he orders for the both of them as she looks around and spots me. Keegan tells him I'm here and points me out. He nods back at her, and she then walks over to where I'm sitting. When she reaches the table, I stand and hug her, knowing he's taking it all in and not particularly liking it.

Good!

"Good morning, Will. Thanks for meeting with us," Keegan says to me once we break our embrace.

"It remains to be seen if it's a good morning. Is that your guy walking over here now?"

"Yes, it is," she answers with a starry-eyed look on her face.

I remember the days when I was the one responsible for putting that look on her face.

A moment later, this guy comes up to the booth. He places their drinks on the table and extends his good hand out to me. "Hi, I'm Jack Grady."

I fucking hate him.

"Hi, Will Henderson. Have a seat." I motion to the other side of the booth.

I watch him with Keegan, and I notice he steps back, allowing her to slide into the booth first. He sits down beside her but not too close. I've got to give the guy props for respecting her personal space in front of me. He places her chai latte in front of her. I like how he takes care of my girl.

"Will, Jack and I have been dating for almost five months, and I'm ready for him to meet Kyle. We've been discussing it for a while, not always agreeing when would be the appropriate time for us to introduce each other to our sons. I'm saying all of this because we did seriously take into consideration how it would affect everyone involved, including you. Jack wanted to give you an opportunity to meet him and address your concerns."

I look at Jack. "Why?"

"I'm a dad of a five-year-old. If his mom wanted to bring another man into his life, I would want the same common courtesy to have the chance to meet him before Sean. I guess so that I could see if he measured up."

"And what if you don't measure up? Are you going to step out of my family's life?"

"Listen, I get how hard this is for you. I'm not here to take your place or get in a pissing contest of who's the coolest guy. I'm here to get to know you. I want to be able to have your and Keegan's backs with Kyle."

"What if Keegan and I don't share the same viewpoint? Whose back will you have then?"

"Neither. That's when I'd butt out. I won't be your kid's go-to guy when he doesn't get his way with you two." He points between me and Keegan.

"What happens if the day comes when you walk away from them? That happened once before, and Kyle was a mess. I don't like cleaning up other guys' messes."

"I would like to be able to promise that it'd never happen, but I don't have a crystal ball."

"What if something on the fire scene takes you away from them?"

Keegan and Jack exchange a look, as if they have already experienced the feeling. I suddenly remember Jack from the funeral.

I look down at his cast. "Guess you two had a taste of that last week. How's the arm doing?"

Jack looks me dead in the eyes. "It's getting better."

Damn it, I'm starting to like this guy.

I know he's going to do everything in his power to keep my family safe and happy. I can leave today, knowing he'll take good care of them if my greatest fear becomes a reality.

Isn't this why I ended my marriage with Keegan—to make sure they would be safe from harm? She can go off with Jack, be totally off Troy's radar, and have her happily ever after. It still hurts though, knowing it can never be with me.

"So, what's your plan? Are you two planning on moving in together?" I ask Keegan.

"I'll first start mentioning Jack in casual conversations with Kyle. Hopefully, Kyle will ask if or when he can meet Jack. He might not want to meet him at all. If that turns out to be the case, I'll respect his wishes and not force it. Jack's work schedule has a four-day break in it every seven weeks with the next one starting a week from today. We thought it would be a good time to get everyone together at the lake next Saturday. Kyle will probably ask if you know about Jack, and I'll tell him about our meeting today. And, no, we're not moving in together or getting married. Jack knows how important it is for me to be independent and have my own place. There will be no sleepovers when our kids are around. We want to spend time together with them, like we would with any of our other friends. Does that work for you?"

I nod. "Yeah, that works."

"Do we have your blessing, Dad?" Keegan asks, giggling.

"I wouldn't so much call it my blessing, but, yeah, I'm okay with all of it." Looking over to Jack, I ask, "How does your ex feel about all of this?"

"I have no idea. Guess we'll find out later tonight when we meet to discuss it with her." Jack reaches across the table, shakes my hand, and says, "I'll take good care of Keegan. I know what she means to you."

We exchange a look, each knowing I am still in love with her.

"You'd better, or I'll track down your sorry ass and become your worst fucking nightmare. And I'm not joking!"

He responds, "I know."

After they leave, I sit in the booth, feeling alone and empty. I've finally accomplished what I set out to do. I've pushed her into another man's arms, so she and Kyle can have a new life, far away from me. Troy should never consider them as a form of retaliation if he ever finds out I've been working undercover.

I still remember his look in court twenty years ago.

Troy and I were caught delivering drugs, and we are being charged with possession with the intent to distribute. The cops knew we were just punks and wanted our dealer, but neither of us would give them any information because we enjoyed breathing too much.

Yeah, I had become hooked on drugs in two short years. It'd started with weed and escalated to cocaine. Troy had introduced me to some local strippers during our deliveries to a club. The strippers had not only taken my virginity, but they'd also taught me how to shoot up and snort lines. Thought I was a real badass and untouchable back then until I got arrested and spent the night in jail. I was scared shitless and cried like a baby.

Dad forced me to make a deal with the district attorney's office to testify against Troy. If I go to rehab, I'll get probation, serving no time, and my records will be expunged.

I would have been a fool not to agree to the deal and testify against Troy. My other two choices were serving time in a juvenile detention center or ratting out our dealer. I barely got through one night of being incarcerated, and I valued my life way too much to be a snitch.

At almost sixteen years old, I'm sitting in court, getting ready to testify against my best friend. Dad is with me, but Mom was too embarrassed to come.

Troy is a couple of years older than me and is being tried as an adult.

Nervously, I sit on the stand and answer every question. In the process, I throw Troy under the bus, causing him to serve time. I feel horrible, but I have no choice. As I step down from the stand, one of our dealer's flunkies gets up and leaves the courtroom. Troy stares me down as I walk past him and out of the courtroom with my dad.

I've been scared straight, and I want to get as far away from Baltimore as humanly possible. We already moved to the suburbs, and I will be in a rehab facility close to our new home. After today, I can walk away and forget this nightmare ever happened.

Brittany is the only one who knows all the ugly details of my life. I trust her and can always count on her to be there for me.

What have I done in return to show my appreciation to her? Absolutely nothing, except treat her like some common hooker by meeting her at that damn seedy hotel. It's time for all of that to change.

I dial her number.

"Hey, sweetie," she says after answering on the first ring.

"Hey, baby. I'd like to take you on a date. Would you like to go out to dinner with me tonight?"

"What? Who is this? What have you done with Will?"

I laugh at her. "Hey, I want to take you someplace nice for dinner."

"Are you serious? What about Troy?"

"I'm tired of hiding. We still have to be careful. We'll stay out of the city and keep our outings to remote places. I never want to go back to that damn hotel though."

"God, I must be dreaming. I've been waiting for this moment for forever. Yes, I would love to go out to dinner with you. What time do you want to pick me up?"

"See you at seven?"

"See you then. I look forward to it."

"Me, too. Bye, Britt."

"Bye, Will."

God, I hope I didn't just make the biggest mistake of my life.

19

Annie

On Wednesday evening, Jack is waiting in front of my house when I come home from work. My first thought is that he misses me and wants to apologize for how he left after the funeral. But I know this isn't the case because he's leaning up against Keegan's black sports convertible.

"Mommy! Look at Daddy's cool car!" Sean shouts from the backseat.

"Yeah, I see it."

It takes Sean no time to jump out of my van and hurry over to Jack. "Daddy, can you take me for ride?"

"Sorry, not tonight, pal," Jack tells Sean.

"New car?" I ask, knowing all along that it belongs to Keegan.

"It belongs to a friend. I borrowed it because it's an automatic and easier to drive with my injured arm."

"You're not supposed to be driving at all," I remind him.

Jack chooses to ignore my comment as we enter the house.

I'm waiting for Jack to confront me about the sob story Keegan has probably told him to justify her absence during the past week. No doubt it involves me and what I said to her outside the ER the day of the fire. I only told her the truth—that he had fallen down some stairs. It's not my fault if Keegan is a silly girl who doesn't know the first thing about firefighting, so she jumped to the wrong conclusion. Surprisingly, he doesn't even bring the topic up, and he heads upstairs to spend the evening with Sean.

At eight o'clock, Jack comes back down. "School must be hard work. I was in the middle of reading his favorite book to him, and I looked down to see he was out like a light."

I smile at Jack and watch him gather up a few things he left behind last week. He then asks, "Hey, Annie, do you have a few minutes to talk? There's something I need to discuss with you."

Here it comes. I knew we would eventually talk about what had happened. "Sure, have a seat."

He sits down. "Keegan and I have something to discuss with you, and we were wondering if you were free for dinner on Friday night. We can go to a restaurant, or you could come over to my place."

"You and Keegan? So, you went running back to her after you left here?"

"Yep, that's exactly what I did."

Shaking my head, I mutter under my breath, loud enough for him to hear, "Missing for five days, doesn't give a shit about you, shows up with another man at the funeral, and you run after her like a dog in heat."

Jack responds back, "I'm not discussing it with you."

"What about Sean on Friday night?"

"You'll need to get a sitter. Maybe he can spend the night at your parents'."

"Jack, what's going on? What do you and Keegan need to discuss with me?" I know in my heart that it's something I don't want to hear. *Are the two of them going to tag-team me about recent events?*

"Don't worry. It's all good. So, do you want to go to a restaurant or have dinner at my place?"

"Your place works."

"Okay. Does seven o'clock sound good?"

Feeling uneasy about the whole dinner thing, I tell him, "Yeah, that works. Anything else?"

Jack stares at me for a second, as if he's debating on saying something else. "Nope. Guess I'll head out. See you Friday, my place at seven."

"Do you want me to help you with your physical therapy before you leave? I promise to behave," I say with a small smile.

"Nah, I've got it covered. Keegan went with me to physical therapy yesterday and learned how to do everything. I'm good. See you Friday."

Before I know it, the dreaded night is here, and I'm now standing at Jack's front door, debating on ringing the bell or surprising them by using my key. It was a good thing I already had a duplicate made months before giving mine back because you never know what emergency might come up. Last week is a perfect example. I was able to stop by and check on his townhouse the whole time he was staying with me.

After I ring his doorbell, Jack opens the door. "Hey, Annie. Glad you could come over tonight. Keegan is in the kitchen, putting the finishing touches on dinner," he says, as if I give a shit about what she's doing.

"Great." I smile back.

When we walk back to the TV room, Keegan walks in from the kitchen, saying, "Well, the casserole is in the oven. All that is left is throwing the salad together. I hope

175

you like stuffed shells, Annie. Jack said you did, so it's his fault if dinner is a bust."

Jack invites me to have a seat and offers to get me a glass of wine.

While he is gone, I turn to Keegan and say, "Please let me apologize for my meltdown at the hospital when I saw you in the parking lot. I guess Ron's death and Jack's injury were too much for me to handle. I can only imagine how scary it must have been for you, being new to all of this and unfamiliar with fire departments."

Keegan takes a few seconds before responding, "As it turns out, I'm very familiar with fire departments because my dad is a retired fire chief. It's all in the past, and we've moved on from that horrible week. I'm just thankful that Jack is okay."

Jack must have overheard our conversation from the kitchen because he returns and says, "I appreciate you apologizing, but we want to discuss something else with you tonight."

"Okay, I just wanted to get that off my chest. By the way, who was the handsome state trooper you were with at the funeral? Did he have anything to do with you not being around that week?"

Jack chastises me, "Annie!"

Keegan holds up her hand, signaling for Jack to stop. "The handsome state trooper you're referring to is my ex-husband, Will Henderson. In a roundabout way, he's part of the reason we invited you over."

Jack picks up the conversation from there. "Yeah, we met him for coffee this morning for the same reason we've invited you for dinner."

"Now, you really have me curious."

Jack continues, "We're at a point in our relationship where I'm ready for Sean to meet Keegan."

Keegan adds, "Annie, I want to assure you that I do not intend on taking your place as Sean's mother. You set the rules, and I follow them. I will support both you and

Jack in all of your parental decisions. Being a mom myself, I know how I would want to be treated if Will brought another woman into Kyle's life. I promise to treat you with the same respect."

Seething inside but making sure not to show it on my face, I say, "Thank you, Keegan. I know you will keep my son's—I mean, *our* son's"—I point between Jack and myself—"best interests at heart. When were you thinking about doing this?"

Jack is the one who answers, "My four-day break is next weekend. Keegan's parents' house is on a lake, and they also have a pool. We thought a day of fishing, boating, and swimming would be a great way for everyone to meet."

"Sounds like you two have put a great deal of thought into all of this. I know Sean will enjoy the day. All I ask is, there should be no sleepovers between you and Keegan when Sean is around. I think that would be a little too soon and inappropriate."

Jack looks a little surprised. "Absolutely. So, you're okay with all of this?"

"Well, it is what it is. I knew this day would come when you had someone else in your life. Thanks for telling me ahead of time and for being considerate of my feelings."

Keegan and Jack seem to let out a collective sigh of relief.

Keegan says, "If you'll excuse me, it's time to pop the bread in the oven and put the salad together."

"Anything I can help with?" I ask.

"No, thanks. I've got it. I'll let you know when everything is ready."

A few minutes later, I hear Keegan say from the kitchen, "Damn it! I forgot to bring garlic."

Jack pops up and says, "I'll run to the store to get some. It will only take a few minutes since it's just down the road. Do you need anything else?"

"Thanks, babe. That's all I need."

Once Jack leaves, I walk out to the kitchen, lean against the counter, and watch Keegan for a few minutes before asking, "Are you sure there's nothing I can help with?"

"Nope. Everything is done, other than the bread. Can I get you more wine?"

"Yes, please." I hold my glass out for a refill. I let a few more minutes pass as I sip my wine. "Keegan, again, I'm sorry for my behavior at the hospital and when Jack was staying with me."

Keegan looks at me, unsure of where this conversation is going. She attempts to nip it in the bud by saying, "Like I said, over and done with. Time to move on."

This is just going to be too easy. I continue, "That's very gracious of you, especially with what happened between Jack and me after the funeral."

Keegan snaps back at me, "Annie, I know what happened after the funeral. Jack told me."

"Seriously? I've got to admit to being a little surprised that he told you how I undressed him and then stripped naked in front of him. If Jack told you all that, then I'm sure he didn't leave out the part of how I straddled him as we made out. But don't worry. Even though he begged me to have sex with him, I said no, not until he moved back for good."

I can see Keegan's anger building on her face with each word.

She maintains her composure though as she confronts me. "Annie, I don't know what game you're playing, but I do know you're lying."

"Game? Lying? I'm only stating the facts. Think about it. Do you really think a guy would own up to what I just told you?"

I see something flash across Keegan's face for a fleeting moment, and then it was gone. I don't know what it is, but I know I have hit a nerve. "God, don't be so naive, Keegan." I add for good measure.

"If what you said were true, he would never have invited you over for dinner tonight with me here."

She has a point, and I have to think fast to come up with a convincing argument.

"Doesn't mean what I said isn't true. You abandoned him for five days. I was there for him. Not you. It was my hands massaging him night after night, taking care of his needs. After seeing you with Will at the funeral, he was pissed off, feeling abandoned and betrayed. Hell, you should be thanking me for stopping it. We probably wouldn't even be here tonight if I had gone ahead and fucked him."

Jack walks into the kitchen, returning from the store, as Keegan loses it and screams, "You bitch!"

Jack stands between Keegan and me while yelling, "What the hell is going on?"

Keegan directs her anger at Jack. "So you begged her to have sex?"

"What?"

"That's what Annie just told me. So, who do I believe, Jack—her or you?" Keegan asks, enraged.

"Annie, get the hell out of here! Now!"

"Jack, you know where to find me if you want to talk later," are my parting words before I leave.

With any luck, I've put enough doubt in Keegan's head, so she won't believe anything Jack tells her. I know he's furious with me, but he'll get over it.

20

Keegan

It's Alex and Cameron all over again. It's like a reoccurring nightmare with each one being a little worse than the previous one.

"Well, Jack, who do I believe? You or Annie?"

"Since I wasn't here, why don't you enlighten me as to what Annie said?" Jack says as he sits down on the couch. He motions me over with his good arm, indicating he wants to hold me.

Is he crazy?

"You're nuts if you think I'm going to curl up next to you right now!"

"Remember, after our first fight on the dock, when you told me why you smoked? What did I tell you—even if I was the problem?" he asks.

I let out a sigh. "Come to you anyway. To let you hold me until I'm calm enough to talk."

"So, get your ass over here, so we can talk this out," Jack orders me.

"No!"

"Then, I'll wait."

Maintaining my stance as Jack remains seated, we stare at each other in silence. My heart rate slows as my anger dissipates enough for me to think rationally. I walk over to the couch, and he pulls me down beside him.

Jack puts his arm around my shoulders and holds me tight as he nuzzles his nose in my hair. "When you're ready, tell me what Annie said to you."

His arm around me is soothing, and it's hard to stay mad, but I have to get to the real truth.

After sharing the details of my conversation with Annie, Jack says, "Christ, she's delusional! It happened exactly the way I told you. Keegan, think about what she said. With everything we've talked about this week, do you honestly believe anything Annie said tonight? Trust your gut, baby. What is it telling you?"

"It's total bullshit. What you said is the truth," I answer.

"Continue."

"You love me, not her."

"Is there anything else?" Jack asks.

I climb up on Jack's lap and look him straight in the face. "What are we going to do? Annie's not going to be happy until she tears us apart."

Jack gazes into my eyes and says, "Annie can try all she wants to break us up, but if we keep communicating and working through our issues, like we did tonight, we're golden. Now, be honest. Isn't this a much better stress reliever than lighting up one of those nasty cancer sticks?"

I softly kiss him and answer, "I'm not sure. This talking it out and holding me just isn't as satisfying as I thought it would be. I'm still feeling really stressed out."

Jack kisses me back. "I've got just the thing for you upstairs to relieve your stress. Shower, bed, or tub?"

I smell something burning, and a few moments later, the smoke detector goes off.

"Shit! Dinner! I totally forgot to turn off the stove." I jump up from his lap and run to open the sliding glass doors in the kitchen to air out the house.

Jack leans back on the couch, laughing his head off.

I come back in. "Are you hungry?"

Jack gets up, walks overs to me, and starts to nibble away at my neck. "Only for you, babe. Again, shower, tub, or bed?"

"Bed."

21

Jack

In the past, I've trusted Annie, but now, I wonder how well I know the mother of my son and the woman I lived with for five years. I can no longer ignore the things she's been doing, and I need to have a serious heart-to-heart with her before taking Sean to the arcade center today.

Giving Sean a hug as he lets me in the house, I say, "Hey, buddy. How are you?"

"Good since you're here, Daddy!"

Annie walks up behind Sean, smiling, as if all is right between us. "Hi! So, what are you guys up to today?"

I lean down to Sean. "How about you head upstairs and set up the race car video game? If you beat me, I'll take you out for ice cream, and if I beat you, I'll take you out for ice cream."

Sean giggles at my wager and heads upstairs to his bedroom.

Giving Annie a stern look, I say, "We need to talk."

We head to the kitchen, and making sure Sean can't hear us, I turn to her and say, "What the hell were you thinking, telling Keegan those lies the other night and pulling the shit you did after the fire? I was hoping we could remain friends, for Sean's sake, but you're making it awfully damn hard for that to happen. Get it through your head. I'm with Keegan, and there is nothing you can do about it!"

Annie answers in a contrite voice with tears filling her eyes, "I'm sorry, Jack. The week before the funeral, everything seemed to be the way it was before you'd moved out. Everything was perfect until after the funeral when it was all snatched away from me for the second time. Before I could readjust to things, you invited me over to dinner, refusing to tell me why. I tried to accept things the way they were, but watching you play house with Keegan was more than I could handle. I felt ambushed by the two of you when I found out the reason for being there. It was as if you were giving me notice that I was being replaced as Sean's mom. I was scared and hurt. I'm not very proud of myself for lashing out at Keegan. Please forgive me. Sean and I need you in our lives." No longer being able to hold the tears back, she asks, "Are things okay with Keegan, or do you want me to explain things to her, too?"

I stare at her for a moment, and then say, "Yeah, everything is good with Keegan. Are you still okay with our plans for Saturday?"

"Yeah." Annie nods.

Leaving out a sigh of resignation, I give Annie a reassuring hug with my good arm. "Annie, I'm sorry. It was never our intent to make you feel that way. I would never let anyone take your place as Sean's mom. Next time, can we just talk to each other instead of you pulling that kind of shit?"

"Okay."

Feeling sorry for Annie as she wipes her tears away, I ask, "Are you up to going to the arcade and getting some ice cream later?"

"Yeah, that would be nice. Thanks, Jack."

After playing games with Sean, we get ice cream from the snack bar at the arcade center.

Sean watches a group of teenagers laughing and taking selfies of themselves. "Daddy, what are those kids doing over there?"

Looking over at the group, I answer, "They're taking selfies."

"What's a selfie?" he asks innocently.

Annie and I explain what they are and why people take them. We end up taking a few of ourselves, making silly faces, with Annie's phone to show him how it's done.

The day flies by, and soon, I am dropping Annie and Sean off at their house. On my way home, I call Keegan to see if it is too late to stop by.

"I'm on the way home and thought I would stop in to say hello to my girl. Is that okay?"

"Yeah. Sure. Come on over."

Sensing something is off with her, I ask, "Everything okay?"

"We'll talk when you get here."

As I park my SUV, I find Keegan is waiting for me outside.

She walks up to me. "Let's go down to the dock. I need a cigarette break."

"I'm not going to the dock if you're going to smoke!"

"Did I say I was going to smoke? I said I needed a cigarette break."

"Is that code for we need to talk?" I ask.

She nods.

"Then, let's go down to the dock for a cigarette break." I motion for her to lead the way.

When we get there, Keegan sits down and pats the spot next to her on the dock. Once I'm sitting, she lifts my arm and puts it around her.

"Okay, tell me what's on your mind," I tell her.

"This is." She holds her phone up, showing a social media post that I was tagged on.

It includes the selfies, taken at the arcade this afternoon. I was unaware Annie had posted the pictures.

"Why?" I ask.

"You seriously don't see why I have a problem with this post?"

"I confronted Annie today about the other night. She said having dinner with us at the townhouse was harder than she'd thought it would be. She felt ambushed and being replaced as Sean's mom. I guess I was feeling a little sorry for Annie, and invited her to go with Sean and me to the arcade. We saw some teenagers taking a bunch of selfies at the snack bar. Sean asked what they were doing and we ended up taking some of the three of us. They're innocent pictures of us joking around. No, I don't see a problem with them." I find myself getting a little irritated with Keegan.

"You felt sorry for her?" Keegan asks in an accusatory tone.

"Yeah, maybe a little. I mean, think about it for a moment. One of these days, Will is going to bring another woman into Kyle's life. How are you going to react?"

"I sure in hell won't act like Annie!"

"You're not going to feel just a little bit threatened?"

"No."

"Then, I guess this is where we respectfully agree to disagree. Personally, I'm not so sure what my reaction would be under the same circumstances. Maybe I was identifying with her a little bit, knowing that day is coming when the tables will be turned. With that being said, I'm still not understanding why you're upset. This isn't the first time pictures like this have been posted of when Annie and I do stuff with Sean. Why are these so different from the others in the past?"

"After everything that has happened, it hurts to see these pictures and their comments. Let me read a few to you, *What a beautiful family*, *It's good to see you guys back together*, *I'm so happy for you guys.*"

I listen as Keegan reads from her phone.

"How would you feel if you saw comments like that about me and Will?"

"Keegan, I have no control over what people post about our pictures."

Nodding her head in confirmation, she says, "So, you don't see a problem with any of this? Okay."

I sit there, not knowing what else to say. "So, we're okay?"

Keegan nods. "Golden. Peachy-keen. Well, tomorrow is a workday, so you'd better head out."

She gets up and walks back toward the house, leaving me at the dock as I wonder what the hell just happened. I catch up with her as she enters the house through the downstairs entryway, and the door closes behind her. I go to open it to follow her in and find the door is locked. I knock on it for her to come let me in, but I get no response.

"What the hell?" I mutter under my breath.

I stomp around the front of the house to my SUV. I see Mitch standing on the front porch.

"Evening, sir. How was your trip?" I smile and wave at him.

He nods and says, "Good. Chilly night, isn't it?"

"Excuse me?"

"I said, it's a little chilly out here tonight."

I walk up to the front porch. "For some reason, I think you're trying to tell me something, sir."

Mitch sits on the top step and says, "I normally stay out of Keegan's business, but I like you, so I'll clue you in on something. Those tattoos of hers? They all represent moments of disappointment in her life by the people she's loved and trusted. Keegan doesn't think I've noticed when she gets them. They might look like innocent Celtic symbols to you, but they are her reminders of past mistakes. Don't fuck it up with her, so she has another damn excuse to mark up her body any more than it already is. You understand what I'm saying?"

"I'm in love with your daughter. The last thing I want to do is hurt her, sir."

"Then, don't. Have a good night, son." He gets up, walks inside, and turns off the porch light, signaling to me that it's time to leave.

The following day at work, I'm sitting at my desk, playing back the events of the previous day. I pull up my social media page to look at the picture to try to figure out why Keegan was having such a big issue with it. As I scroll down through the News Feed, another picture catches my attention. It's a selfie of Keegan and Will laughing, as though they were having the time of their lives.

What the hell?

I know what she is doing, and it's working. I start reading the comments.

Sexy.

You two are the hottest couple ever.

Does this mean you guys are back together?

She's made her point, and I have to figure out how to fix things.

I text her.

Me: Sorry for being such an idiot.

    Keegan: Hello? Did you say something?

Me: I'm sorry for the pictures.

    Keegan: You still don't get it, do you?

Me: You're upset about the pictures taken at the arcade center.

    Keegan: Continue.

Me: And you posted the pic of you and Will to show me how it feels.

    Keegan: Continue.

Me: I understand why you're upset.

    Keegan: Continue.

Me: I can't believe you took that selfie of you and Will to post.

    Keegan: It's an old one of us. Continue.

Me: Continue what? I don't know what else to say.

    Keegan: You're a smart guy. Let me know when you've figured it out.

Days have passed, and our contact has been a few short telephone conversations and even shorter texts. I haven't seen or, even worse, held Keegan since our talk Sunday evening down at the dock. I'm beginning to miss her. In a few days, everyone will meet each other, which is already going to be stressful enough without this tension between us.

Friday afternoon, I pick Sean up from school.

During the drive home, he says, "My two friends got in a fight at recess today. When I sat with one of them at lunch, my other friend got mad, and now he's not talking to me."

"That's a tough one, pal. I guess his feelings were hurt because he thought you had chosen your other friend over him. I'm sure it will all work out."

After we get home, Sean settles in the TV room, watching his favorite programs, and I order pizza for us. While waiting for the pizza to be delivered, a ton of bricks of realization hits me.

Shit!

Keegan told me the first time down at the dock how important it was for me to be in her corner when it came to Annie. After everything that has happened since the fire, my comments came across as though I was siding with Annie.

Now, what do I do?

Since Sean is here, I reach for my phone to text Keegan.

> *Me: I'm sorry.*

> *Keegan: Hey, smart guy, did you figure it out? If you have, please continue.*

> *Me: Annie has done some real mean shit to you and us. The picture made you feel like I wasn't in your corner.*

> *Keegan: Continue.*

Me: It was thoughtless of me. I need to be more sensitive about how it makes you feel.

Keegan: Continue.

Me: I need to stop doing stuff Annie could misunderstand.

Keegan: Stuff? Explain.

Me: You know, stuff like being nice to her.

Keegan: How nice? Please, by all means, continue.

Me: Like the way Will was with you at the funeral.

Keegan: Apples and oranges. He thought I was about to hurl all over him.

Me: It gave him an excuse to have his hands all over you. If you haven't noticed, he still loves you. It was written all over his face when we met at the coffee shop.

Keegan: No, he doesn't. You never saw how he used to be. It's been a long process to get to where we are today.

Me: Christ, you're blind. You have no problem seeing it in Annie but not Will. I'm telling you, he's still in love with you. He threatened to hunt me down and do bodily harm if I ever hurt you.

Keegan: Consider yourself lucky. He cuffed the last guy I dated when he met him. Anyway, this isn't about me and

Will. Stay on topic. It's about stuff with Annie. I want details.

Me: *When she's upset, I might hug her or put an arm around her.*

Keegan: *What? Are you serious?*

Me: *Calm down. It sounds worse than it is. I don't rock her world like I do yours.*

Keegan: *Rock my world? You don't think much about yourself, do you?*

Me: *Seriously, no more stuff, so she doesn't get the wrong message. No more selfies or group pictures unless we're at least 10 feet apart.*

Keegan: *If you make it 20, I might let you rock my world again.*

Me: *Okay, 20. I love you and only you. Please never forget that.*

Keegan: *I'll try not to. I love you, too.*

Me: *See you tomorrow?*

Keegan: *See you tomorrow.*

22

Keegan

On Saturday, the weather is perfect for a day of fun out on the lake. Dad is pulling the kids on their tubes with the boat while Jack and I act as spotters, laughing as they go airborne and crash back down. Jack is upset he can't go tubing because of his injured shoulder and arm being in a cast. Dad has promised to take him once everything is fully healed.

Later, Kyle shows Sean how to fish off the dock with the new fishing rod we gave him as Dad grills hamburgers on the grill. We end the day with making s'mores around the campfire as plans are made for next weekend when Jack and I will have our sons. At the end of the day, everyone is exhausted, and Jack loads a sleepy Sean into his vehicle to head home.

Surprised as to how worn out I am from the previous day's fun out on the water, Sunday is a day to recover and run a few errands. I need to start going to church if I am going to take my responsibilities of being BB's godmother seriously. Marcy and Roger have found out they are having a boy, and they decide on the name Aaron, but BB has stuck for some reason. With any luck, the nickname will fade away once Aaron enters the world.

After I return home from dropping off Kyle at Will's mother's, I stop by Jack's. Sean shows me a picture he drew of him and his dad fishing at the lake, and he thanks me for letting him come over. Before I leave and say good night, Sean reads a book to me before his bedtime.

Feeling true contentment, it has occurred to me that I have been headache-free for the past two days, only proving they are caused by stress. Now, if only I could find the elusive job, my life would be perfect.

Monday morning, I pick up some freshly baked doughnuts and wait on Jack's front step for him to return from taking Sean to school. He is having a new recliner, exactly like Annie's, delivered this morning for the upstairs TV room.

After the recliner arrives, Jack informs me that it needs to be taken for a test drive. He tells me to stand in front of him as he reclines back in it. I know exactly where this is going and feel myself getting excited in anticipation of our fun.

"Strip for me, baby," Jack says with the sexiest grin on his face.

When the last piece of my clothing falls to the floor, Jack then says in a pathetic voice, "My shoulder is killing me. Could you help me with my shirt?"

I know it doesn't because he has stopped wearing his sling, but I do as I am told. With me on his lap, we begin with gentle kisses and caresses, only for it to quickly escalate to us both wanting and needing more.

"What about a condom?" I ask him.

"I got one right here, babe." He reaches over to the end table next to the chair, and takes a foil packet out of its drawer.

Our lovemaking is passionately wild, and I collapse on him afterward.

He mutters under his breath, "And another world is rocked!"

Tuesday morning, while enjoying a scone and chai latte at the coffee shop, I pull out my phone and check my social media sites.

I notice a selfie of Annie and Sean on my page.

She tagged Jack with the message, *Thanks for taking care of us Sunday night. You're the best!*

I look at the selfie, trying to figure out what it means or what it's referring to. Trying hard not to be that insecure girlfriend, I keep telling myself that there is a logical explanation for the post. Yeah, exactly like there was with Cameron and Centerfold Chick.

The only way to find out what the post is referring to is to call Jack at work and ask him.

"Morning, babe. What's up?" Jack answers his phone.

"Nothing much. I got a craving for a chai latte and stopped by the coffee shop before heading down to pottery class. Hey, I was checking out my page and saw the cutest selfie of Annie and Sean."

"On your page? Why would you see a post from Annie? Have you guys become friends?"

"No, when she tags you, it shows up on my page because you and I are friends. Remember, that's how I saw the selfies at the arcade?"

"Yeah, I keep forgetting that. I haven't seen it yet. What are they doing?"

"Nothing. She's thanking you for taking care of them on Sunday night—whatever that means."

There's silence on the other end.

"Jack, from your silence, I'm guessing this isn't as innocent as it appears. Want to explain what it's about?"

"It's nothing. Can we talk about it tomorrow when I'm not at work?"

"No, I think we should probably talk about it now. Stop stalling, and start talking."

Jack heaves out a heavy sigh. "After you left Sunday night, Sean woke up sick around nine o'clock. I called Annie to let her know he wouldn't be going to school the next morning. She freaked out because of the whole appendix thing and came over to check on him. By the time she got there, he had fallen back asleep. She wanted to take him home, and I convinced her not to wake him up. Annie was ready to leave when that huge string of storms hit the area along with the tornado advisory. I thought it was best for her to stay until the storms passed and the advisory lifted. While working on my laptop at the kitchen island, Annie fell asleep on the couch, reading a book on her phone. I covered her up with a blanket and went to bed. End of story."

"So, let me get this straight. Annie spent the night at your house, and you didn't think it was important to mention it to me. I have a question. If she hadn't posted this picture, would you have ever told me?"

"Please, don't do this, Keegan."

"Do what, Jack?"

"Make a mountain out of a molehill."

"Seriously? I just want to understand. Why didn't you think it was important to mention this to me?"

"First, Annie didn't spend the night. Supposedly, she left a little bit after eleven. Christ, it wasn't a big deal. Do you want me to file a report with you every time we talk or she comes over?"

"Is this really the story you're going with?"

"I guess so since it's the truth."

"I cannot believe you are so gullible when it comes to Annie. I'm so tired of having the same conversation over and over with you about her."

"What conversation is that? Your insecurities or how shit like this is going to happen since she's Sean's mother?"

By now, I'm so mad that all I can say is, "Fine. Think I'll give Will a call and see if he wants to have a sleepover tonight. Talk to you later."

For the rest of the morning, I stew over the picture and my conversation with Jack. After giving it more thought, under the circumstances, there really wasn't anything else he could have done, other than have her stay. The real issue with me is being blindsided by a post from Annie instead of Jack telling me about it yesterday morning. If I had known up-front, my reaction might have been different instead of me acting so childishly with Jack.

Lunch comes and goes, much like my initial anger. Trying to decide what to do next, I pull up Annie's selfie once more and notice the background this time. Chuckling to myself, I find it funny to see that Annie took a selfie next to the crumpled condom wrapper Jack and I had forgotten to throw away. I'm glad that it wasn't noticed, especially by Sean, because—

Wait a minute! The wrapper is lying on Jack's end table. They're sitting on Jack's recliner, not Annie's chair that is the same as his. The only time this picture could have been taken is this morning after Jack left for work and before Sean went to school. How did Annie get in Jack's house? She gave her key back to him. Did she have another one made before giving hers back?

Annie purposely tagged Jack for me to see it, so I would know they were together on Sunday night.

That little conniving bitch!

I think back to all the times during the past five months when she has skewed the truth just enough to make it appear to be something totally different, causing issues between Jack and me. After Jack confronts Annie, he eventually forgives her because of his guilt over leaving her and Sean.

I need to talk to Jack, and I decide to do it face-to-face instead of over the phone.

Mom confirms that she will be home for Kyle while I go to see Jack at the station.

I pull into the parking lot of the firehouse and see Annie's car. I shouldn't go in because I'm not sure if I can contain my anger, but she counts on me to keep my mouth shut and let Jack handle things. I have to go in there and show her I will no longer be manipulated.

Walking through the side door, I head to the bays of the station where the apparatuses are housed. I know from past personal experience that all kids want to play on fire trucks. Stopping at the door, I see Jack lifting Sean into the squad truck. Noticing Nancy down the hall, I motion her over to me and ask her to take Sean to visit the candy machine in the dayroom. I stand out of sight as she brings Sean back through the station.

I quietly walk down the opposite side of the engine where Jack and Annie are standing, and I eavesdrop on their conversation.

"Keegan is upset over your post this morning," Jack says to Annie.

"I'm sorry. I didn't even think about her seeing it when I tagged you. I don't know what the big deal is."

Here is my signal to enter stage right. Walking around to them and making my presence known, I say, "The big deal is you are constantly trying to cause issues between Jack and me."

"Excuse me?" Annie turns around in surprise.

"Excuse you? Nope, don't think so. First, hand over the key to Jack's house," I order with my hand extended out.

"What? I don't have a key to his house. I gave it back to him. Didn't I, Jack?" she asks, turning back to Jack.

"Keegan, she gave it back to me."

"Sure she did—after having another key made. The picture posted on your page? Take a good look at the background. She and Sean are sitting in your new recliner. Notice anything else in the picture?"

Dumbfounded, Jack drops down to sit on the side step of the engine, looking at his phone. "You've got to be kidding me. Is that the condom wrapper from Monday?" he says, shaking his head.

Panic comes across Annie's face.

I continue, "Sure is, and you want to know why she posted it on your page instead of texting you directly? So that I would see it. She played me, just like all the other times when we fought over her."

I walk up to Annie and get into her personal space. In a deliberate low voice, I tell her, "This shit stops here and now, Annie. Keep your damn key because Jack's locks are getting changed tomorrow."

Annie tearfully looks at Jack. "Are you going to let her talk to me like that?"

Jack nods. "Yeah, I am."

"Do you even care if you ever see your son again?"

"Yes, I do, and I will because we have a binding legal agreement. Try me, Annie, and I'll haul your ass into court in a heartbeat."

I look at Jack and ask, "Are we good?"

"Golden." He gets up, kisses me, and whispers, "God, I love you, babe."

"I love you beyond the stars and back," I repeat the words that Sean read to me the other night.

While Annie goes to gather up Sean, Jack walks me out to my car.

"Jack, I'm sorry for making a scene with her, but someone had to spell it out to her. Don't think you're totally off the hook even though I understand her staying because of the storms. In the future, please give me a heads-up, so Annie can't blindside me, okay?"

"I know. I screwed up by not telling you that she came over. I didn't think it through until your parting words about a sleepover with Will. I did the whole shoe-on-the-other-foot bit, and I understand why you were upset. In fact, I was getting ready to call when Annie and Sean showed up."

"Continue," I say with a wink.

"I'll always tell you the good, bad, and the ugly," he adds.

"Me, too."

"Love you beyond the stars and back, too." Jack kisses me.

I climb in my car and put the top down since it has turned out to be a beautiful day. I pull out of the station's parking lot, feeling oddly pleased with myself.

23

Jack

By the time I walk back into the station, Annie has Sean ready to leave. I'm so annoyed with Annie and her behavior that I can't even put a game face on for Sean's sake.

After getting him in his car seat, I take Annie aside, and with a clenched jaw, I say in a controlled low voice, "Don't you *ever* interfere in my life again! Do you understand what I'm saying to you?"

Annie's eyes get bigger with each word I emphasize, saying nothing and only nodding. She quickly gets in her car and leaves. Once more, all is right in my world—until the alarm sounds, signaling we have a call.

There is an accident involving three vehicles with one person trapped. The location is a few minutes away from the firehouse on a three-lane stretch of the interstate going northbound. County and state police have already closed down all three lanes of the road and are redirecting traffic.

We take a route that brings us north of the accident, so we can drive south on the vacant interstate in the wrong direction down to the scene. I follow the rescue squad, fire engine, and ambulance, being the last to pull up behind the other pieces of the apparatus.

Off in the distance, I see a full-size pickup truck rammed into a car, forcing it into an SUV. The car is sandwiched between the two vehicles. I see gas flowing out of one, if not all, of the vehicles and order the crew to throw absorbent material down on the spills. I can't see the top of the car and assume it was crushed in during impact.

Within a few seconds, I surmise from the damage of the vehicles that there are serious injuries. Fortunately, there is a trauma center only a couple of miles down the road from the accident scene. There will probably be no need for the medevac helicopter.

Once reaching the vehicles, I am able to take in more details of the scene. I freeze when reality hits that the top of the car in the middle is not crushed in, but it is a black sports convertible with its top down. I see auburn hair and a body hunched over a deflated airbag…and blood, lots of blood. My worst nightmare is happening. It's Keegan, and my feet are not moving fast enough to get me to her.

I jump on the hood of her car, scrambling over the debris of the accident lying on top of it. A paramedic is already in the car, assessing her injuries and tending to the bleeding, while other people of the crew are figuring out the best way to free her from the wreckage.

I feel someone pulling me off the hood and away from the car.

I try to fight the person off, and then I hear Bob say, "Jack, listen to me."

I turn and yell at him, "That's Keegan! I've got to get back to her. I've got to get her out of the car and to the hospital. Let go of me! I've got to get back to her and help."

Bob grabs me by both shoulders. He shakes me and says in his no-nonsense voice, "Jack, look at me. Look at me now, Jack. Let them do their job. She's in good hands.

I'm taking you off duty and putting Joe in charge of the shift. You and I are going to follow the ambulance to the hospital in my vehicle. Do you understand?"

"Yeah, I got it. I've got to be with her. Let me go and be with her," I plead.

"No, Jack, stay here with me. They're getting ready to use the Hurst Rescue Tool to get her out of the car. Once she's freed and on the stretcher, you can see her. I promise."

A Hurst Rescue Tool—or what we commonly refer to as the Jaws of Life—is a hydraulic rescue tool for extracting trapped crash victims. It takes minutes to either push or cut metal away, so the occupant can safely be removed.

Although it seems everything is happening in slow motion, I see them starting to lift Keegan out of the car. She is strapped down to a backboard. Her eyes are still closed, and I see no movement in her arms or legs. Once out of the car, they carry her on the board over to the stretcher and rush her to the ambulance.

Bob and I meet them at the back step of the ambulance. I look down at Keegan and yell her name.

Nothing.

I yell her name again, and I see her eyes flutter open, looking up at me, confused.

"Baby, you've been in an accident. Everything is going to be okay. We're getting you to the hospital. Stay awake. Try to stay awake," I instruct her.

Her eyes start to close.

"Keegan, stay with me. Stay awake. You've got to stay awake."

She is disoriented and scared.

I appeal to the paramedics. "Please let me ride with her."

"Sorry, Cap, no can do. Got to get her loaded up and out of here. It looks like a possible closed head injury and fractured back. We've got to roll."

I look back down at Keegan. "I love you, babe. Stay awake. I'll see you at the hospital."

They load her into the ambulance while Bob and I sprint to his SUV.

We pull up at the trauma center a few minutes behind the ambulance. The doors of the unit are still closed.

Why aren't they unloading her?

The next thing I know, the ambulance doors burst open, and I see them doing chest compressions on Keegan. I see the defibrillator monitor lying on the stretcher, meaning they shocked her but with no response. Once on the ground, one of the paramedics climbs on top of the stretcher and continues chest compressions as they wheel her into the trauma center.

Standard procedure is shock with the defibrillator, and if there is no response, chest compressions are done before the defibrillator shocks again.

It's vital they get her inside as fast as possible. One of the paramedics tells me she started seizing during transport and then went into cardiac arrest.

This is not happening!

Once inside, Bob asks about contacting family members. I tell him we need to get in touch with her ex, Will Henderson, through the state police. He would have the contact information for her parents and brother.

Now, all we can do is sit and wait.

About forty-five minutes later, Sandy and Mitch arrive with Kyle. I tell them everything I know. The Fitzgeralds become terrified when they hear about the seizure and CPR being administered. I reassure them that she is in good hands and getting the best care available.

Less than ten minutes later, Will arrives with another couple, who introduce themselves as Keegan's brother and sister-in-law, Ryan and Liz.

A little over an hour passes before two doctors finally come out to speak to us. Bob sees the doctors approaching and takes Kyle to grab a bite to eat.

Both men introduce themselves.

Dr. Metcalf, the trauma doctor, says to the Fitzgeralds, "Keegan is a lucky young lady. She has a moderate concussion, a fractured spine at L5, and a nasty cut on her head, requiring ten sutures. The spine seems to be in line, and no surgery will be required. We will reevaluate tomorrow to see if a back brace will be needed. It should heal fine on its own. As I said, her concussion is moderate, but I ordered an MRI due to the seizure. It shows no swelling of the brain or bleeds. However, we did find a large tumor, called a meningioma, located on the left side of the brain."

All of us are shocked by this news.

The doctor continues, "I'm going to let Dr. Osborne, the neurologist assigned to her case, take it from here."

Dr. Osborne explains, "A meningioma is a slow-growing, usually nonmalignant tumor on the covering of the brain, called the meninges. If she is going to have a tumor, this is the best kind to have. Does Keegan have a history of chronic headaches, numbness, or any slurring of speech?"

"She has a lot of headaches, but it was diagnosed as migraines. They ran tests and did a CT scan, but nothing showed up," Sandy tells the doctor.

"I'm not surprised. Unless you know it's there, they are hard to detect on a CT scan. What about seizures?"

"Not that I'm aware of," Sandy answers.

"Then, she's a very lucky lady since she hasn't been symptomatic, other than her headaches. From the size of the tumor, it looks like it has gone undetected for ten to fifteen years. The tumor is located in the communication area of the brain. Depending on the size and slow growth of these tumors, it's not unusual for surgeons to put off removing them until they get bigger. In Keegan's case, surgery is needed sooner, not later.

"She's on a high dosage of pain meds for both her back and head along with seizure meds. She is resting comfortably.

"We are getting ready to move her up to the neurology floor in a few minutes. Once she gets situated in her room, a nurse will come and take you up to her. I know all of you want to see her, but please keep in mind the meds she's on and what her body has been through today. Any questions?"

"How long will she be hospitalized?" I ask.

Dr. Osborne answers, "She'll be here for a few days. I'll explain the different options she has available to her. When released, Keegan will have a referral to a neurosurgeon of her choosing. It could take a couple of months before her surgery is actually scheduled. Keegan has a long road ahead of her, but I see nothing from today's examination and MRI that would prevent a full recovery. With that being said, the surgery itself is serious with its own set of risks and complications."

24

Will

It is good news that Keegan's injuries are not serious, but it's a shock to hear about the tumor. As I listen to the doctors, it kills me to watch Jack's interaction with them and the family. He is taking my place, playing the role I used to have. I feel insignificant. It is spelled out loud and clear to me. I am Keegan's past, and Jack is her future.

As the doctors walk away after giving us an update on Keegan's condition, I promise myself that, if I get wind that Troy is involved, it will be the sorriest day of his life.

The next day, I enter Keegan's hospital room and see it's already decked out in flowers. "Wow, someone is popular around here."

"Will! I was wondering what happened to you."

"Work has me busy. Sorry I couldn't stick around to see you yesterday. I was called back into work while they were getting you settled in your room."

The real truth is, this is the first time I could visit with her without Jack being around.

"So, a tumor, huh?" I say.

"Yeah. I'm so scared. The thought of someone opening my head and messing around with my brain is creeping me out."

I stand beside her bed, lean over, and press my lips to her hair in comfort. "Shh, don't think about it now. Focus on recovering from your injuries. How are you feeling?"

"I'm having a lot of pain with my back and concussion. I'm not complaining. It could have been a lot worse."

"Can you remember anything about the crash?"

"I remember driving and a white truck coming over in my lane. After that, nothing. I get an occasional flashback, like one of a black motorcycle and the color red."

I almost lose it because Troy rides a black bike trimmed out in chrome and red flames on the gas tank. I immediately shift into investigative mode and press Keegan for more information. "Can you remember anything more about the bike? Did it have artwork on it?"

"Nope. I've got nothing but a black bike and the color red."

Pressing harder, I ask, "Is there a design on the gas tank? Maybe a flame?"

"Will, I can't remember any more. Why is it so important?"

"The police are still investigating the accident. Any little bit of information might help them piece together the cause of it. Do you know why the truck came into your lane? Did another vehicle cut him off, forcing him over?"

"No, I don't remember anything, other than the truck coming over."

"Could it have been the motorcycle?"

"I'm sorry. I really don't remember anything."

Jack walks in at that moment, ending all talk about the accident. I say my good-byes and make a quick exit.

After hearing about the motorcycle, I decide to plant a bug in Troy's office to see if he talks about the accident to anyone. Nothing is mentioned, but I hit the mother lode of information about the drug cartel and its organization.

From Troy's conversations, I now have names, phone numbers, and detailed information about some of the deals. It's much bigger than I originally thought, and it involves one of New York City's biggest crime families.

Realizing I obtained this information with an illegal surveillance device, I have to find a way to make it admissible in court. I call Federal Agent Aiden Collins, who is also assigned to this case. I've known Aiden since college. We were dorm roommates until he moved out in our senior year.

"You have any information for me?"

"I've got a ton of stuff, but it was obtained by an illegal surveillance device."

"Why in the hell did you do that?"

"Long story. I'll explain later. Can we meet?"

By the end of our phone conversation, plans are made to meet, so we can figure out how to use the newly acquired information.

Around the time I discover this information, I start to notice Troy acting differently toward me. He hasn't found the bug in his office because I am still getting feed from it. I need to remain vigilant.

25

Keegan

It's been four weeks since my accident, and my body is still screaming out in pain. Now, instead of only my head hurting, the pain permeates throughout my whole body. My family physician says I will start feeling some relief soon, and after six weeks, the pain will be minimum. I can do this.

I miss my life prior to the accident. Being out of work for the past six months, I was filling my days with things that brought me joy. I was a PTA volunteer at school and being the ultimate soccer mom who made sure to make it to all of Kyle's games. The best was finding a pottery studio not quite an hour's drive away, enabling me to throw clay on the wheel again.

My life now consists of pain, constantly popping pills, and restrictions.

My family along with Jack and Sean have been phenomenal. I would never have made it to this point of my recovery without them. Between not being allowed to drive and still needing assistance with the smallest of tasks,

I've become cranky. At times, I'm a total bitch. I don't like myself much these days.

I know what is at the heart of my misery. It's not the pain and meds but the loss of control of my life. I'm frustrated the job search has been put on hold indefinitely, and my nest egg is slowly dwindling. My dream of buying a house is slipping away a little more each day.

I'm going to lose it if one more person tells me to hang in there or be patient or—my all-time favorite—that it's going to get better soon. I'm sick of the well-meaning platitudes being shared with me.

It surprises me that Will hasn't been around more. I was told he was there immediately following the accident. He has only been back once, and he acted as if he was the investigative officer, grilling me on what I remembered about the accident.

The accident report said the driver of the pickup truck was making a video of himself lip-syncing to some stupid song. According to eyewitness accounts, he drifted over into center lane, colliding into both my car and the SUV in the lane next to me. The accident was over within a matter of seconds.

Fortunately, there are traffic lights along this part of the interstate, and our speeds were greatly reduced. The only reason I'm alive is because the SUV was there to keep my car from flipping. Instead, I was violently jerked around, and that caused my fractured back. It was like bumper cars on steroids.

The man in the SUV died from his injuries. He was an elderly gentleman who lived at a huge retirement center close to the accident site.

I know the accident was not my fault, but a small part of me feels responsible for his death because it was my car colliding into his vehicle.

The only thing keeping my sanity is thinking about the what-ifs and realizing how blessed I am for surviving the crash. The alternative is bone-chilling.

My days are filled with worries about my upcoming surgery. After researching all things meningioma with the help of my parents and Jack, I decide to have the procedure done in Baltimore.

Walking into my bedroom, Jack finds me on a website where others post their personal stories about their tumors and recovery. "Will you please stop reading those websites? Everyone is different."

My response back is, "Yeah, my outcome could be worse than anything I've read. Jack, I've made Ryan my power of attorney and executor of my will."

"What exactly does that mean?" Jack asks as he gently lowers himself beside me on my bed.

I take a deep breath, not wanting to have this conversation with him. I close my laptop. "It means, if I become incapacitated, Ryan has my living will to follow to refuse or take me off life support. I do not want extreme measures used that could cause me to live a life where I would be unable to think or care for myself."

I can tell by Jack's body language he's becoming upset with me.

"Why? Why are you getting your affairs in order? The neurosurgeon is very optimistic for a full recovery."

"Jack, you know I'm the type of person who needs to have all the I's dotted and T's crossed, especially in a situation like this one. It's one small way for me to take back control of my life."

"If the decision needs to be made to pull the plug, I want to have a say in it, too," Jack demands.

"Your heart would never be able to do it."

"This is bullshit!" Jack stands and storms out of my bedroom to sulk.

I slowly stand up to head outside to the comfort of my feel-good place. Dad set up a comfy chair down at the dock, so I could visit there during my recovery. I see it is also where Jack has disappeared to. He's looking out over the lake, lost in thought.

"I see you needed a cigarette break, too." I walk up to him, wrap my arms around his waist, and hug him ever so gently from behind.

He holds my hands at his waist. "Yeah, I'm just thinking."

"Continue."

"About us…the kids…where we're heading…just things."

"Continue."

He heaves out a sigh and then chokes on his next words. "What will happen if you are taken away from me? I'm not ready for that…not ready for us to end. The day of the accident…when I realized it was you in the car, I felt a loss so great that there are no words to describe it."

"Yeah, much like how I felt when Annie implied you were the one who had died at the fire. Jack, I'm not expecting to die during surgery. I just want my affairs to be in order if the unexpected happens. This, right here, is why it can't be you to make the decision of when and if to pull the plug. Ryan knows the parameters to base the decision on if, God forbid, the time comes. Please try to understand. I'm not going into this surgery, thinking I'm going to die. I want to see where our story takes us."

He turns around and looks into my eyes. "Continue."

"I want to have my happily ever after with you and no one else. We've been through some things that I'm not sure other couples could have survived."

"Continue."

"You've taught me how to remain calm enough to talk things out and what it is to trust someone. I cherish those gifts."

"Anything else?" Jack asks.

"I hate to bring it up, but because marriage is not in the cards for us, we have to accept the limits of our legal rights as a couple and come to terms with it."

He nods. "Yeah, I know. That's what I was coming to terms with before you came down here."

"Continue."

Jack walks me over to my chair. "My viewpoint on what I thought I wanted is changing."

While getting comfortable and motioning for him to sit next to me, I tell him, "Jack, we'll get through this, and I truly believe it will make us stronger. When we get to the end of this little detour, we can pick up where we left off. I promise."

"I'm going to hold you to your promise, Keegan."

It's the last day of June. Marcy is now ten days overdue. She's getting bigger by the day, but her OB/GYN is old school and decides to let nature take its course.

Barely the next day, my phone rings, waking me at two a.m. "Hello."

"It's me, Roger."

I am now wide awake, knowing what he's about to tell me. "Is Marcy in labor?"

"Yeah, we're at the hospital. Marcy wanted me to call you."

In the background, I hear Marcy groaning, and then it stops.

The next thing I hear is her telling Roger, "Give me the phone." Then, Marcy says to me, "Keegan, it's me. I can't talk for long. I know you can't come, but you would have killed me if I hadn't called. Contractions are about four minutes apart. And—oh, shit, here comes another one. Talk to you later."

And then there's dead air.

The rest of the day consists of me waiting by the phone and calling for updates.

I am having a good day and insist on going to the hospital when Marcy's mom text, saying they are prepping her for the C-section. Fortunately, Jack is off and is able to take me to the hospital. We get there in time to witness Roger coming out to the waiting room. He informs us that my godchild, Aaron Francis Bennett, has arrived. He weighs nine pounds, six ounces, and he has ten toes and ten fingers.

A little while later, we are allowed to see Aaron through the nursery windows. I look at Jack and watch him being fascinated by the nursing staff completing the tasks they do to all newborns.

I then remember that he missed all of this with Sean. When Annie went into labor, he was a firefighter and inside a burning building. By the time they got word to him and he was able to get to the hospital, Sean had arrived. Jack was heartbroken that he'd missed the birth, and it has only added to his guilt throughout the years.

During the ride home, Jack and I can't stop talking about Aaron.

Jack then asks me the ten-million-dollar question, "Do you want any more kids?"

I don't say anything for a few moments. "I don't know. If you had asked me that question four months ago, my answer would have been an unequivocal no. I probably would have pulled out the age card as my excuse. I would still have to take that into consideration today. Now, I'm not sure."

"Why aren't you sure?" Jack asks.

"Oh, I don't know. Maybe it's because of what I'm facing. I'm finding myself getting restless and reevaluating what I thought I wanted in life. I had the marriage, a son, a great job, a beautiful house in the suburbs, and a cool car. I was living the dream. I even got to do it twice. Maybe Will and I didn't make it because what I thought was the dream, in reality, wasn't my dream. Looking back, I felt more like a hamster on one of those wheels. I think maybe that's why I am so against getting married. Now, I feel as if I'm at some sort of crossroads. Things are changing, and it's the first time I can remember having choices. That's the only way I can explain it."

"Yeah, I hear what you're saying. I've been feeling very much the same way. Like there's been a paradigm shift," says Jack.

"Yeah, something like that," I agree.

Then, we both grow silent, getting lost in our own thoughts, for the rest of the drive home.

26

Jack

The week prior to her surgery, Keegan had me drive her to the hairdresser. She had the left side of her head, where the incision would be located, shaved. The rest of her beautiful long hair was cut severely short with long bangs.

Each day, Keegan's need to be in control of her life became clearer to me. This was just another way of taking charge of when and how her hair would be cut, not leaving it up to the neurosurgeon. When finished, she had a punk-rocker vibe going on. I found her new look hot and sexy.

On the day of the surgery, I drive Keegan and Kyle to the hospital with Sandy and Mitch following in their car.

Once Keegan finishes the process of checking in and getting prepped, her assigned pre-op nurse comes out and says two of us can go back at a time. It is then we find out the hospital has some stupid rule about being at least sixteen to see someone in pre-op. I promise Kyle to do my best to find a way for him to see his mom before surgery, if only for a couple of minutes.

Sandy and Mitch go back first. When they return, I tell Ryan and Liz, who are now here, to go on back. I don't need to hear any last-minute instructions Keegan might want to tell Ryan. It is my turn after they come back to the waiting room.

I step through the curtain to find an anxious Keegan trying to keep it all together.

I look at her and ask, "Do you need a cigarette break?"

Keegan nods with her eyes glistening with unshed tears. I sit next to the bed, holding the hand free of medical monitoring devices and IV needles.

I lean over and whisper in her ear, "Talk to me, babe."

"I'm scared," she says in a quivering voice.

"Continue."

"They won't let Kyle come back."

I look up at the pre-op nurse. "Anything we can do about getting her son back here? In the waiting room is a young man who desperately needs to tell his mom he loves her and good luck. Mom is falling apart here because she wants to reassure that young man that everything is going to be okay."

The nurse nods. "When we're ready to take her down to surgery, I'll come get you to stand in the hall outside of pre-op with her son, so he can see his mom."

"Thank you." I look at Keegan. "Anything else?"

"Thank you. I love you," she answers back with a little smile.

"I love you, too."

I am told it is time to leave. I lean over, kiss Keegan, and whisper in her ear, "I'll see her later, okay?"

She nods as she tells me, "Okay."

It takes everything I have to walk away and leave her to face the unknown by herself.

The nurse keeps her promise and shows us where to stand to see Keegan one last time before she enters the surgical suite.

When the double doors of the pre-op area open, Kyle holds it together and says, "Hi, Mom."

"You know everything is going to be okay, right?" Keegan asks as tears start to seep from her eyes.

"Pinkie promise?" Kyle asks, chuckling at a personal joke between them.

"Yeah, pinkie promise." She winks at him and giggles.

"I love you, Mom." Kyle's voice cracks with a small sniffle following.

"I love you, too," Keegan answers back.

Kyle holds on to his mom's hand, walking beside the gurney all the way down to the surgical suite doors, with the rest of us following behind.

It seems like an eternity until Keegan's neurosurgeon comes out to speak to us after her surgery.

Thank God we aren't being directed to the room.

Throughout the day, I noticed they would take some families to the room for their post-op conferences. When they came out, you could tell by the look on their faces the news was not good.

I start to breathe a little easier, knowing he is going to talk to us in the waiting room.

The neurosurgeon said the surgery went well, and he sees no reason not to expect a full recovery. We all breathe a little bit easier hearing this news.

We are then shown to the Neuroscience Critical Care Unit—or more fondly referred to around here as the NCCU waiting room—until we are permitted to go back to see her.

When we are finally allowed to see Keegan, only a few of us are granted entrance into the unit at one time. I tell the family to go ahead while I wait here because I'm spending the night. I am surprised Will hasn't been around today—if not for Keegan, then at least for Kyle.

Watching an ambulance tear down the city's street to the hospital, I think about how my life could have changed today. For the past couple of months, I have been putting on a brave face for Keegan's sake. The truth is, I've been terrified as to the outcome of today's surgery. This past hour has been the first time I've been able to relax since her accident.

Mitch jolts me out of my thoughts when he places his hand on my shoulder. "She's awake and asking for you. You go on back. It's the fourth room on the left. Since Keegan is doing so well, we're heading out and taking Kyle home with us."

"Okay, I'll call you with an update in the morning."

Mitch smiles. "Thanks. That would be great."

Sandy decides to walk back with me to see Keegan one last time before leaving. On the way to her room, Sandy says, "Make sure she listens to her nurses tonight."

"I will," I try to reassure her.

"Here's her room." Sandy points to a door next to a nurse's station.

From the doorway, Sandy watches Keegan sleep for a few moments before leaving.

Walking into her room, the first thing I notice is the size of the dressing wrapped around her head. Then, I see the pale color of her skin. I sit quietly in the chair next to her bed as she sleeps.

Slowly, her eyes flutter open, and she looks at me.

Smiling down at her, I say, "Welcome back."

She gives me a small smile and says in slurred speech, like a drunk, "Missed you."

"I've been right here, all day, waiting for you, babe."

"You must be tired. Go home."

"I'm spending the night with you. I'm not letting you out of my sight."

"Love you." She cringes. "Head hurts."

"I'll get the nurse for more meds. I think they are going to keep you pretty doped up tonight."

The nurse comes in with Keegan's meds, and she is out like a light. I open the chair provided for overnight guests into a bed and get settled in for the night.

Around seven a.m. the next morning, Keegan is moved out of NCCU and into a private room. I stay outside in the hallway while the nurses and the hospital orderlies get her situated in the room.

When I walk into Keegan's room after the hospital staff has left, she tells me, "They said my bandages are coming off today. I wasn't sure if you wanted to be here when they did it."

"I wouldn't miss it."

The morning passes by uneventfully. My parents along with Mitch, Sandy, and Kyle come down at the start of visiting hours at ten a.m., and they leave after having lunch with us.

Shortly after everyone has left, the nurse returns. "Are you ready for the big reveal?"

Keegan nods as I get up and hold her hand.

The nurse prepares Keegan by describing in detail how her head was shaved and the incision. After all the bandages are removed, I see a line of staples marking her incision. It starts at the front of her left ear and goes above it, making a wide sweep up to the top of her head, before it continues along the left side, from back to front, ending above the left eye behind the scalp line. It looks very much like a zipper.

Keegan gasps when she sees her incision and stares at it in the mirror with fascination. "This completes my new punk-rocker look."

She looks over at me, and we both crack up laughing.

The following days are rough for Keegan. The nurses are constantly fussing and reminding her that she just had brain surgery and needs to rest. Her neurosurgeon is impressed at the progress she has been making and talks about possibly releasing her a day early. Keegan is ecstatic over this news and starts not owning up to how she is really feeling.

The third day after surgery, she wakes up with the left side of her face so badly swollen that I cannot see the left eye. Keegan's speech is slurred to the point that it is hard to understand her. Before she loses her speech entirely, she tells me to call Ryan and tell him to get to the hospital.

I leave her room and contact Ryan, Mitch, and my mom.

When Mom answers, I say in a panic, "Mom, something is happening to Keegan. I'm scared."

"Oh, Jack. Your dad and I are on our way."

"No, sit tight until we talk to the neurosurgeon."

"Jack, she's going to be okay. She's a fighter, and she loves you and Kyle too much to give up. You've got to stay strong and keep the faith. I'll be praying for all of you."

"Thanks, Mom. I've got to get back to her room. I'll talk to you later."

I return and find Keegan in tears. During my absence, an intern stopped in to put the tiny pads she had worn during surgery back on.

Since she's having trouble talking, she texts me.

Keegan: Taking me for MRI. Pads are back on in case surgery is needed today. Call Mom and Dad.

I hold her hand. "After I talked to Ryan, I called your dad, and they're on their way here. Let's see what the MRI shows before going into a full-blown panic. You're going to be okay."

She nods.

Minutes later, an orderly comes to take her for the MRI.

Ryan and Mitch arrive before she returns to the room, and they plan on staying with us until we know what's happening. Sandy stayed home with Kyle in an attempt not to alarm him and to maintain a normal routine.

Her neurosurgeon stops by to let us know the results of her MRI and that no further surgery is needed. He is adjusting Keegan's meds and she should start seeing improvement within the next twenty-four hours. He is keeping Keegan for a few extra days to monitor the situation and avoid any reoccurrences of what happened today. He removes the pads from her head and leaves.

Ryan and Mitch leave shortly after the neurosurgeon, and the nurse brings in Keegan's meds for the night.

After we are alone, I turn the lights down low, shut the door to her room, and crawl into bed with Keegan. I hold her as she gently sobs onto my chest and falls asleep.

Within three days, Keegan's face and speech are almost back to normal. Half of her tongue is numb, and she has trouble finding the right words at times. There are some words she can't say correctly even if her life depended on it.

The neurosurgeon says this should eventually clear up in time. He agrees to release her from the hospital if Keegan promises to follow his instructions and restrictions for the next six weeks. At the end of six weeks, she will have her post-op appointment. If all is good at the appointment, she will be released from the neurosurgeon's care, only to return for a baseline MRI and routine checkups.

On the ride home, Keegan is quiet.

"What's going on in that head of yours?" I ask.

"I haven't heard from Will. I wonder what's going on with him."

"Don't know. I do know he's been spending a lot of time with Kyle during your hospital stay. Maybe he figures that's how he can pitch in—by keeping Kyle occupied."

"It's not like him."

"Keegan, I know you don't want to see it, but the guy still loves you. Maybe he just couldn't handle you having brain surgery. Only he knows why. When Will's ready, he'll come see you and possibly explain his absence."

"Maybe, but I doubt it."

"Don't worry. He's okay."

"I'm glad he's been there for Kyle."

Keegan dozes on and off during the rest of the ride home.

27

Will

Keegan is home from the hospital, recovering from her surgery. I feel bad for not stopping by, but I have my reasons, even though they might be selfish ones.

My cell phone rings with Jack's number showing on the screen. It's strange, having his number among my contacts. While waiting in the ER for news on Keegan's status after her accident, we both agreed to exchange numbers.

I answer the call, "Yeah? Everything okay with Keegan?"

"Everything is fine. I was wondering if you were available to meet at the coffee shop tomorrow morning."

"Why?"

"I have something important to discuss with you."

"Let's discuss it now," I tell him, trying to avoid seeing him any more than I have to. The more I stay away from Jack Grady, the happier I am.

"No, this is something I want to discuss face-to-face. Can we meet at ten tomorrow morning?"

"Guess you're leaving me with no choice. Yeah, see you at ten," I tell him before disconnecting the call.

Entering the coffee shop, I see Jack sitting in a booth. After getting my coffee, I join him.

No sooner do I slide into the booth than he starts in on me. "Keegan is worried about you. Why haven't you been around?"

"I've been busy at work."

The real truth is, Jack is always there, and quite frankly, it's starting to piss me off. Even though Keegan and I are divorced, I miss my friend and the private moments we used to share when dropping off Kyle.

"So, why the big meeting?" I ask to change the subject.

"I'm proposing to Keegan as soon as she's feeling better."

Son of a bitch!

Jack continues, "I wanted you to hear it from me. I also want to assure you that I will never try to take your place as Kyle's father."

I cannot believe the audacity of this fucking asshole thinking this could ever be a possibility.

I politely shake his hand. "Congratulations. Keegan has had enough heartache and disappointment to last a lifetime. You'd better do good by her, or you will have me to deal with."

I then get up and leave, putting an end to our little coffee chat.

Since Keegan's release from the hospital, it's become my routine to drive by the Fitzgeralds' to see if Jack's SUV is gone, so I can stop in for a visit. Since I met with him yesterday, I make the educated guess he is working today and drive over to see Keegan. Noting that Jack's SUV is nowhere in sight, I decide to seize the moment and stop for a visit.

28

Keegan

It's the end of my first week home from the hospital. Mom and Dad are still hovering over me and overseeing my distribution of meds. I'm having a difficult time focusing on routine tasks and conversations. My sensitivity to loud noises and bright lights is off the charts. Sunglasses and earplugs are now my new best friends. I become easily overstimulated and can't follow conversation if more than one person is talking at once. It all results in my head hurting worse than it already did. I knew there would be pain but never to this degree.

With Jack back at work and Kyle away at soccer camp, it seems everyone is getting back to their lives and routines, except for me. My frustrations are getting the best of me, and I feel as if I will be an invalid for the rest of my life. When I am fully recovered, I don't even know what the new normal will be, never mind being able to get back to doing the things I used to enjoy. Depression is starting to set in, and I need to get a handle on it before it consumes me.

I think spending some time out of bed and getting some fresh air might do the trick. I ask Dad to help me down to the dock. He has replaced my comfy chair with a lounger with upholstered cushions and brought down a few chairs for people to sit with me. Dad putters around the dock for a while and does a little fishing. I tell him there is no need to babysit me.

Before he can respond, I hear a familiar voice say, "I thought this is where I would find you. Hey, Mitch, I'll stay with her if you have other things to do."

"Thanks, Will. Don't let her walk back to the house alone," Dad instructs him before heading up to the house.

"Still daddy's little girl. Nice look, by the way," he says, sitting down in the chair next to me and motioning to the ball cap I am wearing.

"Hey, stranger. Where have you been?"

"Work has kept me away," he answers.

"Working on a big case, are you?" I ask, not quite believing him.

"Yeah, it's been keeping me really busy. So, how are you doing?"

"Hanging in there. I'm trying not to get too discouraged, but I'm tired of being in pain and popping pills twenty-four/seven to manage it. I miss my life. I miss pottery. I can't focus when there are more than two people talking at one time. And please don't ask me to say the word *banquet*!"

"Banquet?" Will repeats.

"No, *banquet*!"

"That's what I said—banquet," Will says once more.

"No! *Banquet*—the thing you cover yourself up with when you're cold."

"Do you mean, *blanket*?" Will asks as he crinkles his eyebrows.

"Yes! That's it. Don't ask me to say *banquet*."

Will breaks out in laughter.

"It's not funny." I try hard to keep a straight face and then start laughing, too.

We spend the next couple of hours talking and reminiscing about our happier times together. There is no more talk about my surgery or accident, and neither of us mentions Jack.

"God, I miss you, Keegan," Will blurts out. "I owe you an apology for being such a dick when we were married. I'm sorry that things turned out the way they did. You deserve so much better. I wish it were me who could have made you happy."

"Will, what's going on? Is everything okay?"

"Yeah, everything is fine. I guess with what's happened to you this summer, I'm learning not to take things for granted. Your accident and then the whole tumor thing really shook me up. I'm finding myself reevaluating my life. I don't know what I would do if anything happened to you or Kyle."

Sensing something is terribly wrong, I plead, "Will, please talk to me. Tell me what's going on. You can trust me."

"That's the problem, Keegan. I can't trust anyone. Listen, I've got to get going. I'll send Mitch back down."

Now standing, Will leans over and kisses me softly on my lips. Before I know it, the kiss turns deeper with an unexpected desire.

He pulls away. "I never stopped loving you, Keegan." He walks away, leaving me stunned by both his actions and words.

Dad comes down and sees I'm visibly shaken. "Everything okay?"

"I honestly don't know. Will is acting strange. It was almost as if he was saying good-bye…forever."

29

Will

A month has passed since the last time I saw Keegan. Before leaving her that day on the dock, I apologized and gave her a kiss. It was a shitty thing to do, but when Jack pops the question, I want her to be thinking of me.

I have decided to cut off all contact with Keegan and keep updated on her progress through Kyle. This is a new chapter in my life, and Keegan is no longer a part of it, except when it deals with something involving our son.

Brittany and I are now officially a couple, much like we were back in college, and we spend all our free time together.

After our candlelit dinner this evening, Brittany and I walk, hand in hand, along the waterfront across from the restaurant. I sense something is bothering her, but I know Brittany will eventually tell me once she gets it sorted out in her head.

She stops to say, "I need to tell you something. You probably already know this, but I have loved you since the day we met in college. I thought for sure we would end up married with children and the white picket fence. You were all I ever wanted. God, I was shattered when you left me for Keegan."

I interrupt her and start to say, "Britt, you don't—"

She holds her finger up to my lips. "Shh…let me finish. It's taken me a long time to build up the courage to say this. You know the girl I was in college and the one standing here today but not the person I was while we were apart.

"When you married Keegan, all my hopes and dreams of being with you ended that day. I met someone who helped ease the pain through sex and drugs, but he wasn't you. Eventually, we got back together, only for you to turn around and leave me for Keegan a second time.

"When you remarried Keegan, it was probably the lowest point in my life. I ended up going back to the same guy, who was more than happy to feed my growing addiction to prescription painkillers. I hit rock bottom the night of my overdose, and I ended up in rehab. God, I did some stupid shit during that period of my life."

Taking Brittany in my arms, I kiss the top of her head. "I'm sorry for causing you so much pain. God, I've hurt so many of the people I care the most about in my life."

"It would be easy to blame you, Will, but it's all on me. I was the one making the bad choices, no one else. I'm trying very hard to make things right in my life to become a better person. No matter what you might hear, I have only ever loved you, and I would never have done…I never thought we…" Brittany pauses and takes a deep breath, as if collecting her thoughts. "I just wanted you to know in case any of it would come up in court."

"How would your past come up in court?" I ask.

"Come on, Will. I was passing on information from my clients! Prosecutors have ways of finding out stuff to discredit witnesses."

"Relax. I'm the only one who knows, Britt," I try to reassure her.

Looking up, she gives me a small smile. "I will always love you, Will Henderson."

When we get back to my condo, I make sweet, gentle love to Brittany and worship her beautiful body. With every kiss and caress, I make sure she feels how strong my feelings are for her. She is no longer the woman I use as my filler to try to forget Keegan. She is someone who has become very special and dear to me.

I hold her in my arms as we fall asleep.

I wake up the next morning and smack Brittany's ass. "Rise and shine, sunshine! Hey, listen, I've got to get out of here. Got a lot on my plate today."

After getting dressed, I kiss Brittany good-bye and leave for the office. My day is filled with conference calls, discussing the legalities of using the information from the bug in Troy's office and coordinating a plan of action with the Feds. It won't be long until key arrests are made.

At the end of the day, I return to my condo, surprised to find visitors inside, waiting for me. Brittany is sitting on the couch with Troy standing not far from her while pointing a gun at me.

"Look who's home, sweetheart. Does he know about us, babe?"

I shout, "What the fuck is going on here?"

Brittany looks over at me. "I'm sorry, Will."

Troy chuckles. "Hell, by your reaction, Will, I would think you didn't know. You see, Brittany and I go way back. We met one night at a party, both higher than fucking kites, and she told me all about a college boyfriend who broke her heart. You can imagine my surprise when I found out it was my old buddy, Will, the fucking snitch. It sure is a goddamn small world!"

I say nothing and start taking inventory of where my guns are located around the apartment.

"By the way," Troy says to me, "drop your gun on the floor, and kick it over here."

I do as he instructed.

Troy nudges the gun closer to him with his foot. "Anyway, Brittany and I've been fucking on and off ever since that night. I was the one who had her reach out to you about that kid she was working with. She was keeping an eye on things for me to make sure you weren't screwing me over."

I look over at Brittany for some indication that Troy is lying, but deep down, I know it's all true. She tried to come clean with me last night, but she couldn't bring herself to tell me the guy she was referring to was Troy.

His ramblings interrupt my thoughts. "The whole time in jail, all I could think of was you walking out of that goddamn courtroom and going back to your fucking life. I decided back then, one way or another, you were going to serve your time.

"Finding out you were a fucking cop was perfect! It was just too damn easy, sucking you in by sending that picture of your family. I knew you would be the good guy and do anything in the world to protect them. The plan was to collect a bunch of shit on you, and for it all to mysteriously show up on the DA's desk one day.

"After you ran some interference for me on some of my drug deals, Brittany pointed out your usefulness and talked me into keeping you around."

It's then I realize that, for all these years, Brittany has been manipulating Troy to protect my cover and keep me safe. The information she gave me was never connected directly to his operations but random things her clients would share about their neighborhoods. A lot of it was gang-related, and I would pass it on to others on the force to use. When I did use her information, it was to arrest some small-time punk dealer who was cutting into Troy's business. It was her way of giving him more reasons for keeping me around. Brittany hasn't been an informant but my protector.

He continues, "I got rid of all the shit I had on you because you had me fooled, bro." Shaking his head slowly, he says, "You really had me fucking fooled." Troy reaches in his pocket with his free hand and throws my surveillance device at me. "Man, I never once thought you would try to get shit on me to take over my fucking business. Don't even try to say this isn't yours. I had big plans for us, and now, you've fucked everything up by doing this!"

Could there possibly be a chance to talk my way out of this face-off since he thinks I'm trying to take over the business instead of being undercover?

"Okay if I sit down, so we can fucking talk about this before you end up doing something stupid?" I motion to an upholstered chair where a gun is hidden between the cushions.

Troy slightly nods, indicating it is okay for me to sit.

"I think maybe you've got the wrong fucking idea about what's going on here. I'll make a deal with you—"

Troy interrupts, shouting, "There are no fucking deals when it comes to my business!" He picks up my service revolver and tucks it in the waistband of his pants.

In return, I shout back, "Just give me a fucking chance to explain!"

Troy yells, "Shut the fuck up! I don't want to hear shit from you!"

Then, Brittany tries to reason with Troy, "Hey, baby, maybe you should hear what he has to say. It could be important."

He yells even louder, making Brittany jump, "Listen, bitch, I said, shut the fuck up. I'm the only person talking here!"

I look down at the coffee table and see what appears to be residue from a line of coke that has been snorted with a few more lines ready to enjoy. I can tell by looking at Troy that he is the one who did the line, not Brittany. I also see a couple of glasses of whiskey sitting on the table. It looks like a private party was interrupted, but I know that is not the case. No, this is a setup because he no longer has anything on me.

What doesn't make sense is why Brittany is even here.

Several lines...two drinks...

Jesus Christ, he's setting us both up.

All of a sudden, her safety becomes more important to me than mine. This is no longer about me just saving my family, but I also need to save Brittany. I think back to us making love last night. It's a hell of a time to discover that I've fallen in love with her.

Troy carries on, "Now, hand over what you've recorded, especially the little conversation from last week. Either give me what I want, or watch me kill Brittany."

Jumping to my feet in reaction to his words, I yell, "What the fuck, Troy? This is between you and me, not Britt. Why in the hell don't you just let her leave?"

Troy starts shouting again, "You can stop with the fucking games! I know the two of you are fucking each other and are in this together! I trusted Brittany. I told her everything. She was the only one who knew about the deal that went down last week. You think I'm stupid enough to believe it was a fucking coincidence that you planted a bug in my office the same time that deal went down? Now, decide. Do I get the recordings, or do I kill Brittany?"

It's ironic that Brittany is getting blamed for information I got from a bug she never knew existed.

I try one more time to talk some sense into Troy. "I swear, Britt had nothing to do with any of this. She's never told me jack shit about anything, and she didn't know about the bug. It was all me. I swear to God!"

Troy's only response as he pulls my revolver out of his waistband and points it at Brittany is, "Fuck you! You got five seconds. Recordings or Brittany?"

Troy's drug-induced paranoia is setting in, making him even more dangerous with one gun pointing at Brittany and the other one at me. The backup of the recordings is on a thumb drive here in the condo, and the original is with the Feds. I decide that keeping Troy calm so that I can try to stall for more time is the best plan of action.

"It's over there in the wooden box on the bookshelf. There's a false bottom to it, and underneath is a thumb drive," I tell him.

Troy tells Brittany to go over to the bookshelf and get the box as he tucks my revolver back in his waistband. Still standing from jumping up from the chair moments ago, I'm desperate to find a way to get to the gun. I flop back down into the chair, acting defeated, as I let out a heavy sigh of resignation. Troy chuckles to himself, thinking he's beaten me. Once Brittany has the box in her hands, he tells her to open it. Standing a couple of feet away from him, she pretends to act as if the false bottom is jammed to divert Troy's attention from me.

It works as Troy starts telling Brittany different things to try until he yells out in frustration, "Just smash the fucking thing!"

To retrieve the gun out of Troy's sight, I position my body at a better angle, enabling me to ease it out between the two cushions of the chair. Troy is too distracted by Brittany smashing the box open to notice what I'm doing.

As I quickly take my stance to shoot, he sees my movement out of the corner of his eye. We simultaneously fire our guns, and both of us fall to the ground as Brittany screams.

Feeling a sharp pain but still conscious, I look over and see no movement from Troy's body. I try to get up, but the pain immobilizes me, making it more difficult for me to focus on what is happening around me. I see Brittany taking both guns from Troy before tossing them away from his body. She sobs as she calls 911.

Moments later, she's sitting on the floor with me, lifting my head to her lap and putting pressure against my wound. I look up at Brittany as she strokes my hair with her free hand, and our eyes meet.

"Hold on, Will. Troy's dead." She tries hard to get her crying under control. "I'm sorry. I should have told you. When Troy found the bug in his office, he thought you were undercover. I had to come up with something, and I told him you couldn't be undercover because you were quitting to work for him full time. He asked how I knew that and somehow figured out we were together. Then he jumped to the conclusion that we were taking over his business. I tried to tell him he had it all wrong."

I feel her tears hitting my face as I fight to stay conscious, trying to comprehend all she's saying to me.

"We're going to get you to the hospital. I love you. God, please don't leave me again. Hold on."

I'm beginning to feel weaker by the minute. There are things I need to say to Brittany while I still have the strength. "Shh…it's okay, Britt. Everything is going to be okay. Please stop crying, sweetheart. Listen to me…"

Brittany begins to calm down. "I'm listening."

"I know what you were doing. It's not your fault," I tell her as her tears begin once more. "I love you."

Brittany cries even harder. "I love you, too. Shh…don't talk. The ambulance is coming. Everything is going to be all right. Hold on. Don't leave me."

Feeling exhausted, I close my eyes and want to go to sleep.

"Will…wake up. Open your eyes for me, baby. Stay with me. Please stay with me."

I hear Brittany sobbing. I try hard to do as she asked, but I'm just too tired.

I hear a lot of commotion in the room, but I don't have the strength to open my eyes to see what's causing it. I just want to sleep.

30

Keegan

Six weeks have passed since my surgery. At my post-op appointment with my neurosurgeon, I am given the green light to start returning to my normal routine. I'm still experiencing some issues with speech, but I'm slowly improving as each day passes.

On the way home from my appointment, Jack asks, "Do you feel up to going out to dinner tomorrow night?"

"I won't know until we try it."

"Since we're celebrating, I think we should dress up for the occasion."

"What are we celebrating?"

He simply replies, "You."

It has been a month since Will's last visit. I haven't told Jack yet that Will kissed me. There never seems to be a good time to talk to Jack about it. Either I'm doped up from all of my meds and too tired to get into it, or someone else is around.

Kyle is going out to dinner and catching a movie with his cousins this evening. Before leaving, he comes downstairs to my bedroom and gives me a hug. "I love you, Mom. Have fun tonight."

At five thirty, I come upstairs to find Jack talking to my parents. He's wearing a navy blazer, a pale blue button-down shirt opened at the collar, and khakis with deck shoes and no socks. God, he looks good enough to eat. Jack faces me and takes in my outfit of a low-cut floral sundress with white sandals and a scarf tied around my head to hide my incision even though my hair has started to grow back.

"You are beautiful." Taking me in his arms, he gives me the gentlest of kisses on my cheek.

"You're looking mighty fine yourself." I giggle back.

Mom insists on getting some pictures of us before we leave. It feels like senior prom night. The only thing missing is the pinning of the corsage and boutonniere. In fact, I notice Mom and Dad are full of smiles tonight. Mom is always pleasant when Jack comes over, but Dad gets his kicks out of making Jack feel uncomfortable. It gets downright weird when they walk out with us and wave as we drive off down the driveway.

Looking out the window and waving back to them as we pull out, I say, "I wonder what that was all about."

"What?" Jack asks.

"Dad being all smiles tonight. We both know Mitch Fitzgerald is never all smiles, especially around you. He gets his jollies by intimidating you, if you haven't noticed."

Jack shrugs. "I didn't see anything strange about them tonight."

I point my finger at him. "You're shrugging. You always shrug when you're caught with the goods. Spill it. What's going on?"

"Nothing is going on."

I look at him suspiciously.

"Nothing! Did you ever think they are just happy to see their beautiful daughter feeling well enough to go out to dinner with her boyfriend? This is kind of a milestone for you, Keegan."

I smile. "Yeah, it is. I'm starting to get my happy back."

"I know, and it makes me happy to see it."

Jack turns into a county recreational area that is on the other side of the large lake where my parents live. He pulls into an isolated area and parks.

"Here we are." Jack hops out and reaches in the backseat, grabbing a picnic basket and a couple of beach chairs.

I watch Jack unload the picnic paraphernalia that I overlooked while getting into his SUV. "We aren't going to a restaurant?"

"I thought maybe a picnic close to your happy place at home—without the prying eyes of parents—might be better. Do you want to go to a restaurant?"

"Absolutely not," I answer, smiling at him.

Jack gets busy with setting up our picnic. He places beach chairs beside the lake's water edge. From the picnic basket, he pulls two prepared plates, each having fried chicken, potato salad, and some fruit. He informs me that my mom is responsible for dinner. He puts the wooden lid back on top of the basket and sets it between us to serve as a table.

Jack has thought of everything, even down to the citronella candle he lights to keep the mosquitoes away along with the music playing from his portable media player. Everything is perfect.

During dinner, we talk about our kids, the guys at the firehouse, Aaron's birth. You name it, and we talked about it. The one thing we didn't talk about was Will's kiss. We are having too much fun for me to ruin it.

"Keegan, lately, I've been thinking a lot about us and all that we've been through," Jack starts to say as both of our phones begin to ring.

We look at the screens. Mom is calling me, and Dad is calling Jack. Something horrible has happened for them both to be calling at the same time. The coward in me decides to hit End on my phone and let Jack get the bad news from Dad. I know in my gut that the call is about Kyle. I simply can't deal with any more heartache.

Jack says, "Hello? Yes, sir. Not yet." Then, he looks my way with his brows furrowed and continues, "When? Where? I don't know. What do you think? Okay. Okay, we'll be there shortly. Bye."

"Just tell me. What's happened to Kyle? God, just tell me what's happened!" I scream-cry at him.

Jack takes my hands in his. "Shh...calm down, babe. Kyle is fine. It's Will. They've taken him to shock trauma. I'm taking you back to your parents' house. If you want to go down to the hospital, your dad and I will take you."

Jack quickly gathers everything up from our picnic as I stand, helpless, trying to process that Will is at shock trauma. I feel lost in a thick fog, and I can't find my way out of it.

When we get back to my parents', Dad is waiting on the front porch for us.

Without saying anything, his grave expression tells me Will is dead, and I cry out, "No...he can't be gone."

Jack holds me in his arms. "What's happened, Mitch?"

With a heavy sigh, Dad answers, "From what I understand, he and another guy were shot. The other guy was dead at the scene. Will was still alive and rushed to shock trauma. He lived for a couple of more hours before dying."

By now, I'm a blubbering mess.

"Let's get you inside," Jack says as he comforts me in my grief.

The rest of the evening is a blur. A state trooper is dispatched to Will's mother's home. Dad calls over to check on Joyce and asks the trooper to bring her to our house. When Ryan brings Kyle home from the movies, Jack meets them on the front porch. He tells Ryan to see his dad in the study and then brings Kyle down to my bedroom. When they walk into my room, I'm sitting in bed with my arms out to Kyle, signaling for him to crawl into bed with me.

"Do you want me to give you a few minutes of privacy?" Jack asks.

"No, please stay." I need all the support I can get to break this heartbreaking news to my son.

Jack sits down in a winged chair across from us.

How do you tell your child his father is dead?

I soon find out I don't have to when Kyle asks, "Dad's dead, isn't he?"

I nod and hold Kyle as we both cry over our loss.

I look across the room to where Jack is sitting, but I see he's gone, leaving us to grieve in private.

The week following Will's death is surreal. It is full of memorials, viewings, the funeral, and all the ritual that happens when state troopers die in the line of duty.

Jack is by my side through the whole ordeal. He is also there for Kyle, who is having a particularly hard time. Both Dad and Jack help Kyle carry the burden of his grief. They make sure he has full access to them whenever his sorrow becomes too heavy for him to bear.

The details as to what transpired the night of the shooting are sketchy at best. At this time, the state police is giving out very little information on the incident. According to the media coverage, I find out Will was working undercover. The other man killed was a suspected drug dealer in the city and the person who shot Will.

The day after Will's funeral, I am contacted by his attorney, Daniel Shrewbridge, asking me to come to his office for the reading of the will. He says Kyle is mentioned in it, but since he is a minor, I can represent him, so there is no need for him to be present.

My parents take me to the attorney's office since I'm still not cleared to drive, and Jack is at work. I feel as if I've reached the end of my rope, and I'm hanging on by only a single thread. My parents wait in the reception area as the receptionist takes me back to the conference room.

Entering the room, I find Mr. Shrewbridge and Joyce sitting at a massive wooden table having a casual conversation.

Mr. Shrewbridge stands and gestures to the chair across from Joyce. "Good morning, Keegan. Please have a seat."

During our first marriage, Will received a sizeable inheritance from his paternal grandparents. I refused to include that money or his retirement in either of our divorce settlements. I assume Joyce is here because Will is leaving these funds to her and our son. I am shocked to discover he has left the bulk of his estate to me. Between his inheritance, retirement, and savings, our family will have few financial worries. I'm stunned by his actions.

After Joyce leaves, Mr. Shrewbridge says, "Keegan, I need to speak to you privately in my office."

He shuts the door of his large office filled with leather upholstered chairs and dark wooden furniture. My head begins to throb as I smell the mixture of leather and furniture polish with a hint of pipe tobacco in the air. I take a seat in one of the chairs in front of his desk and pray this doesn't take too long. I watch Mr. Shrewbridge remove something from a file cabinet. He then walks over and sits in the chair beside me.

He's holding a slim accordion type folder with a tied string closure. Looking at it, I am clueless as to how something so innocuous is going to turn my life upside down.

Mr. Shrewbridge studies me for a moment before he speaks, "Will left specific instructions regarding this folder. It contains three sealed envelopes. The two addressed to you are to be opened in the order of the dates on them. Once you have read what's in them, the contents are to be destroyed. You are to deliver the third envelope to the person at the address written on the front of it. Do not leave it with anyone else other than that person. I've contacted him, and he is expecting your call at the phone number found on the back of the envelope. You are not to show or mention these envelopes to anyone, not even your son or parents. They contain information that could put your family at risk if the wrong people knew about them. Do you understand what I've said to you?"

"Yes," I answer quietly.

"Good. Once you have taken possession of this folder, I will deny ever seeing or giving it to you. Understand?"

"Yes."

Mr. Shrewbridge stands, hands me the folder, and watches me put it in my bag. He then holds my hand. "Again, my condolences to you and your family, Keegan. Please leave here knowing that Will was a good and honorable man."

I walk out of his office, almost in a dazed state.

When I reach my parents, my dad asks, "Is everything okay, princess?"

I nod. "I'm not feeling well. Can we go home?"

Once I get back home, Jack calls me to check in and see how things went. I have yet to tell him about Will's visit and kiss. The guilt is slowly becoming a weight too heavy for me to carry. I'm starting to feel a disconnect with my life, and I can't seem to grasp everything that is happening to me.

One moment, I was spending one of the best evenings of my life with Jack by the lake, and then it all fell apart. I feel myself losing grip of that one last piece of thread I've been desperately holding on to.

I go to my bedroom and lock the door behind me. I carefully untie the string closure and dump the three envelopes out on my bed. Two have my name and dates written in Will's handwriting. I gently run my fingers across his writing as if it will magically bring him back. The other one has a name of a man that I don't recognize, and I can feel something hard and flat in it.

I open the envelope addressed to me dated the furthest back. It contains a letter where Will confesses all his past indiscretions, lies and secrets to me. The only thing missing are the words, *Forgive me, Father, for I have sinned…*

It starts with Will declaring his love for me. He writes about his teenage years, being addicted to drugs, and his arrest along with testifying at Troy Martin's trial. He describes how Troy blackmailed him, followed by his undercover work. Will talks about the day he spent with two strippers and his involvement with Brittany. Will claims he did it out of his love for our family and the need to protect us.

The letter ends with the same instructions given by his attorney.

I lie in my bed, stunned, finding it difficult to concentrate, because there is too much information for me to process. Picking up the second envelope, I notice the date is the last day we saw each other, the day he kissed me. I rip it open.

Enduring you

My dearest Keegan,

I'm sorry.

I love you with all my heart.

Be happy.

Will

It is then I lose grip of that one tiny last thread.

31

Jack

The shock of Will's sudden death has left us all struggling this past week. It is especially difficult for Keegan with it happening in the midst of her recovery from surgery. The last official order of business related to Will's death was completed yesterday with the reading of the will. Hopefully, now, our lives can gradually get back to some type of normalcy.

I decide to put off proposing to Keegan until she's feeling better and back on her feet. I'm anxious to see her today because we haven't spoken to each other since yesterday.

Shortly after lunch, I pull up to her parents' home to find Mitch coming out the front door to meet me.

"Something's wrong with our girl, Jack," are the first words out of his mouth. "I can't seem to reach her."

"What are you talking about?" I ask, confused by his statement.

Mitch goes on to explain, "Keegan came home yesterday and locked herself in her bedroom. Late last night, she built a bonfire and burned something. Seth picked her up early this morning. They came back a couple of hours later, and she went straight to her room. Seth said they went to Baltimore. Keegan made him wait in the car while she ran an errand that took about twenty minutes. I went down to her bedroom after he left and knocked on the door. When she didn't answer, I went to open the door, and it was locked. I threatened to bust it down if she didn't open up. She eventually opened it, looking like she hadn't slept all night. I asked her what was wrong and was told she was fine and to leave her alone. She shut the door in my face and locked it again. I called Joyce to see what had happened during the reading, and she said everything was fine. Keegan stayed behind talking to the attorney for about ten to fifteen minutes after Joyce left. I think something happened during that time, and I don't know what to do."

"Where's Kyle?" I ask.

"He's over at Joyce's house. She missed him and asked if he could come over to spend time with her."

I immediately go down to Keegan's bedroom and find the door is still locked. I knock.

No answer.

I start pounding on it. "Open the damn door, Keegan!" I shout.

I hear her unlock the door, but she doesn't open it. When I enter her room, I find Keegan sitting on top of her bed with her knees to her chest, rocking back and forth, almost in a catatonic-like state.

Sitting behind her, I wrap my arms and legs around her while pulling her up against my chest. "Talk to me, baby."

"I can't. I can't talk to anyone."

"You can always talk to me. What happened?"

"I can't. I can't tell anyone. Will told me I couldn't, or something might happen to Kyle, my parents, or even you."

"Will's gone, baby. He can't talk to you anymore."

"Oh, yeah, he can. He has the power to reach right up from his grave and snatch me down in it with him. He told me secrets I could never repeat. I've already told you too much."

"Keegan…stop it. You're starting to scare me. Tell me what's going on."

"I can't. We can't be together anymore. There are too many secrets. Secrets are just silent lies. We're supposed to be honest with each other. Will took that away from us the day he died. I can't be honest with you anymore. There is one thing I have to tell you before you leave."

"I'm not going anyplace, baby. What do you need to tell me?" I ask her.

"Will stopped by one afternoon right after my surgery, and we kissed each other. I'm sorry, Jack. I'm so sorry."

My world stops. I can't believe what I am hearing.

"What happened after the kiss? Did you have sleep with him, too?" I ask sarcastically.

"Oh God, no. I love you, Jack. I would never betray you like that. I don't know why I let it happen. It was the first week I was home from my surgery, and I was doped up on drugs. I love you and only you. Don't ever forget that. Please leave before I won't be able to let you go."

"Keegan, I'm not leaving you. We'll get through this. I promise you."

She stands up and starts flailing her arms, screaming, "Get out! I don't want you here anymore! We're done! Don't you get it? Will has made it so that we can never be happy. Get out of here now!"

Mitch and Sandy come running into the bedroom, pulling Keegan off of me while she's kicking and screaming. She collapses on the floor, sobbing hysterically.

Keegan is broken, and there's nothing I can do to help her.

I get up and walk out of the room. Sandy stays with Keegan, trying to get her to calm down.

Mitch comes out of the room and finds me frantically pacing in the hallway. "I think she's having a nervous breakdown. I'm going to call the hospital."

I know he's calling the psychiatric facility located a few miles away.

Mitch returns. "They told me to bring her in."

"Let me go with you."

"No. For some reason, your presence seems to be setting her off. I'm worried she's going to hurt herself. It's only been eight weeks since her surgery. Go home, and I'll call you with an update."

Mitch calls me later to say Keegan has been admitted and isn't allowed any visitors until further notice. He promises to contact me immediately if there is a change in her status.

It is a week later when I finally get a call from Keegan.

"Hey, baby. How are you?" I ask her.

"I'm better. It's been a rough week, but I'm getting there. Um, I want to see you."

"Tell me when, and I'll be there."

"Thursday at nine, okay?"

"Okay. See you Thursday at nine. I love you."

Keegan sniffles. "I love you, too, Jack."

It's killing me not to be able to take her in my arms and comfort her. "Baby, please don't cry. You're getting better, and before you know it, we'll be back together."

I can tell she's crying harder and barely able to talk.

"I've got to go. Bye, Jack."

The call ends before I can say good-bye and tell her once more how much I love her.

I enter the hospital, thinking I'm on my way to getting my girl back. I enter a room with a table and two chairs with what looks to be a two-way mirror spanning one of the walls. Keegan is standing on the other side of the room, looking out the window. She turns to me as I walk up and hug her. She stiffens in my arms, and I release her.

"Please, sit down, Jack," she says to me, as if we're in a business meeting.

I sit down, and she takes the seat across from me.

Keegan continues, "Jack, I've got a lot of things to get sorted out in my head. This is something I've got to do on my own. You can't make this all better and make it go away for me. I don't know how long it's going to take for me to get healthy. I want you to go on with your life and not wait for me."

Shocked by her words, I say, "Keegan, this is bullshit. I'm not going anywhere. I don't care how long it takes."

She stands. "Jack, please don't argue with me about this. I worked hard this week, so I could say this to you. I don't know if I'll ever be whole again."

I stand and go to her on the other side of the table. She stops me with a kiss before I can get any words out.

She breaks away and says, "Good-bye, Jack."

I hold on to her and tell her, "I'm not going anywhere. I have no life without you in it. You're going to get better. We will be together again."

She pulls out of my arms in tears and leaves the room.

A doctor comes in to see if I'm all right and if I would like to talk.

I shake my head and leave.

32

Jack

I've kept the faith that, one day, Keegan will reach out or give me some indication to contact her, but there has been nothing.

For the longest time, Mitch would contact me with updates on Keegan's progress. Gradually, his calls became more sporadic over time until they eventually stopped.

The timing of Will's death on top of everything else Keegan had been through was more than she could manage. Instead of leaning on me to help her through the pain, she chose to shut me out by building a wall to protect herself from ever being hurt again.

It has taken three long years for me to accept that Keegan and I are over. I never heard another word from her. It still hurts today as much as it did the last time I saw her at the hospital.

During this time, Annie has been here for me, and it's easy to slip into the old routines of past behaviors. On the evenings I'm off, we have dinner together as a family and then hang out until Sean goes to bed.

Bob is retiring, and I'm being promoted to fill his position as Battalion Chief.

It's Friday night, and Annie has made arrangements for Sean to spend the weekend with my parents at their house. We decide to take advantage of the evening and go out for a celebratory dinner to a nice restaurant. When I take Annie back home, she invites me in for a beer. One beer turns into many as we reminisce about old times and get drunk.

"God this feels good. I can't believe we've come full circle. You and I are meant to be together," Annie says to me.

"You think so?"

She giggles. "Yeah, I think so. Move back in. You practically live here anyway."

"Nah, I like having my own place. Never going to give that up again. Never." I drain my bottle and go for another. "Hey, Annie, you good or want another one?"

"I'm good. It's sad you're letting *her* have that kind of power over you."

"I don't want to talk about it." I slam back my beer.

She looks at me with sadness in her eyes.

"Annie, I don't understand why you haven't found someone yet. Why is that? Am I screwing that up for you by being here all the time? Hell, if that's the case, just tell me."

"No. You're not keeping me from seeing anyone else. I just haven't met anybody I want to date."

"That's too bad. You are a beautiful woman. I should know. I've seen you naked."

She laughs. "I think someone is drunk. You are in no condition to drive. How about crashing on the couch tonight?"

In my wasted state, I joke, "The couch? Hell, you used to let me share your bed."

Annie says nothing, collecting our empty beer bottles and tossing them into the trash. I watch her walk over to the stairs leading to the bedrooms. Standing on the first step of the stairs, she unbuttons her blouse, exposing herself to me in a thin see-through lace bra, and informs me, "You can share my bed with me tonight. Do you want me, Jack?"

Her invitation excites me, and I become aroused, looking at her breasts in that next-to-nothing thing she calls a bra, visualizing her naked.

Desperately missing the touch and feel of a woman's body, I go to the stairs and start lightly kissing her neck. "Yeah, if you're offering..."

It isn't long before we are naked, in her bed, taking care of each other's sexual needs. It feels good as I enjoy every damn inch of her body many times over, releasing my pent-up frustrations from the past three years.

33

Keegan

A warm fall breeze whips a few golden leaves around the door of the shop. It's mid-September when the days are warm enough to wear shorts and a sweater, or a light jacket is needed to take the chill off the evening air. Once my favorite time of year, it's now a season of melancholy filled with memories of past heartaches.

It took me almost a year to get both my body and mind healthy. I was in the hospital for not quite three weeks and continued on an outpatient basis for a short time afterward. My doctor then referred me to a therapist, Dr. Lowe, to continue my sessions. She's helped me work through issues using various methods, including critical incident stress management, personal strategic planning, and lifestyle changes.

I opened a pottery studio during this time, similar to the one I had visited prior to my surgery. I hired Marcy as the manager and a small staff along with a full-time roster of instructors to teach classes. The pottery studio was opened for a little over a year when the space next door became available. I leased the space to open up my next entrepreneur's venture, One of a Kind. The shop features original works of art, such as paintings, pottery, photography, and repurposed furniture pieces. The best thing is, both are located in the same strip mall as my favorite coffee shop.

Today, as I set up the studio for classes, I keep thinking back to my session with Dr. Lowe yesterday where the topic of the day was forgiveness.

At the end of the session, she asked, "How can one ask and expect forgiveness from another, if they don't feel worthy enough to forgive themselves for their own transgressions?"

I can't stop thinking about her question and how it relates to my life.

Though I might have gone through the infamous five stages of grief, there is not an ounce of forgiveness in my heart for Will. His letters set off a chain of events that no one had been prepared for, and it still upsets me to this day.

Dr. Lowe's question has me now looking at the letters from a different perspective. Unsure if Will ever understood why he wrote them, I begin to see this was his way of dealing with the past in the event of an untimely death. He didn't want to take the chance of me hearing about it from anyone but him, especially not from a newspaper or lawyers in a courtroom.

Months after Will's death, a large number of drug dealers were arrested. They were all members of a drug cartel along the Eastern seaboard. According to the media, Will's undercover work and death were connected to them. His letters had prevented me from being blindsided by this news. It was one of the few times that I was grateful he had written them.

I still remember Will's apology to me the last time we saw each other on my parents' dock. At the time, I was clueless as to its scope and the full meaning behind it.

And then there is Jack. Oh my God, I treated him so badly the day of my breakdown. I shudder, remembering hitting and screaming all those horrible things at him. Even during my angriest moments with Will, I never struck out at him. Jack loved me unconditionally and was there for me during my darkest days after my accident and surgery.

Why did I lash out at him in such an awful manner?

I knew exactly why. Our love was built on a foundation of trust and was strong enough for us to see each other at our worst. We hid nothing. During my time with Jack, I thought Annie was the enemy and would be the one to break us. It was quite the epiphany to discover I was the one who did it, all by myself.

Now, what do I do with this revelation?

It's been three years since I last saw Jack at the hospital. I was embarrassed by my behavior and couldn't handle the kindness or the love he was offering. It was emotional overload and unfair to expect him to wait until I could process it all.

During my first week of hospitalization, my paranoia subsided, and I could see things more clearly. Between my surgery and breakdown, I saw myself as damaged goods and knew Jack would feel obligated to never leave me. I hated the thought of that and was determined to give him an out from our relationship and my mental instability. On the other hand, deep down inside, I believed his words. I soon found out Jack wouldn't wait, and he checked out on us.

The week has blown by, and already, it's Saturday. I stop by the office to pick up the past week's receipts, so I can catch up on the books later today at home. Sitting at my desk, out of sight from the students in the studio, I freeze when I hear Annie's voice.

"I'm telling you, Caroline, Jack is going to ask me to marry him. I found the ring in his bedside stand the other day. I'm sure he's going to ask me any day. I'm so excited!"

I've heard enough, and I escape through the back door of the studio. I am heartbroken. Jack didn't wait for me and went back to her. *How could he after all she did to us?*

Later in the day, I get a text from Seth.

> *Seth: Marcy's no more fun since she's become a mama. Go out with me.*

> *Me: I don't know.*

> *Seth: Come on. You need a night out.*

> *Me: When?*

> *Seth: Friday?*

> *Me: Can we make it Thursday? I have plans to head to the lake on Friday.*

> *Seth: K. Pick you up at 7.*

> *Me: K.*

All of the colleges on Kyle's list of possibilities for the next fall are only an hour or two away from home, and we went on our first campus tour on Sunday. It's times like these when I feel the loneliest. Both Jack and Will are gone from my life, and I have no one to share the excitement of special times like these.

After this past weekend, I'm glad Thursday night is here and that I'm spending it with Seth at Donnelly's. It's packed due to a big celebration by a large group in the middle of the bar. Seth is getting us Black and Tans while I head to an open high-top in the back corner. I no sooner sit down than Cameron, a flash from the past, startles me by coming up and giving me a hug. We haven't spoken or seen each other since his call years ago when we broke up.

"Long time no see. May I?" he asks, motioning to one of the open stools.

I nod. "By all means."

Cameron continues, "I've been hoping to run into you, and today seems to be my lucky day."

"Why?" I ask.

He replies, "Because I never got to properly apologize for the jackass thing that I did. Keegan, I was falling hard for you. When I ran into Shelby, I…I…hell, I don't know what I was thinking."

"Oh, I do. You were thinking with your dick." I snicker.

Cameron laughs. "I guess I kind of deserved that one. I see you're still the same smart-ass I remember. Listen, I want to say I'm sorry. I really screwed up, and I wanted to properly apologize. I also heard about Will. Are you and Kyle okay?"

"Yeah, it's taken a while, but we're good."

I have a weird sensation that someone is staring at me. Looking across the room, I see Jack is watching me with a frown.

Cameron turns and sees him, too. "Someone you know?"

"Yeah, we had a pretty serious thing once. I haven't seen him for three years. I said some awful things, and I owe him an apology."

"Well, there's no time like the present," Cameron tells me.

I get up and start over to the bar.

I tap Jack on the shoulder and say, "Hi."

He turns to me, smiles and gives me a quick hug. "Hey, look at you. Your hair has grown back. How are you?"

I keep smiling until my face is hurting. "Great!"

"Kyle, your parents…how are they all doing?"

"Great. Everyone is doing—"

Jack interrupts with almost a scowl on his face, "Yeah, I know, great."

"So, how are you?" I inquire.

"Great."

"What's the big celebration over there?"

Jack says proudly, "Oh, nothing much. Only my recent promotion to Battalion Chief and an engagement."

Oh my God! He's already asked Annie to marry him.
I can't let him see my hurt.

"Congratulations! When's the big day?"

"What?"

"The big day?"

"Bob's last day was today. I start on Monday."

"No, I mean, for the wedding."

"Hell if I know." He shrugs his shoulders.

"Well, congratulations! I'm truly happy for you, and I wish you the best. I'm glad everything is going so well for you…for both of us," I say awkwardly. I can't do this anymore, and I need to get away from him. "Guess I'll be seeing you around." I can't get back to my table fast enough.

When I return to the table, Seth is back with our drinks, and says, "I saw you over at the bar talking to Jack. How did that go?"

"He got a promotion and is now engaged to Annie. I went over to apologize to him, but his good news sort of hijacked the conversation."

Cameron nudges me. "He's leaving. Better go after him if you still want to apologize. Fuck his good news."

I look at Cameron and nod. "You're right. Fuck his good news."

I run out of the bar and see Jack walking to his vehicle in the parking lot.

I yell out, "Jack!"

He stops to face me.

After reaching him, I say, "I wanted to apologize to you."

"What?"

"I wanted to apologize to you for the horrible things I said the last few times I saw you. I'm really sorry," I say to him.

"Continue."

"Huh?" Then, I remember how we used to talk things out.

"Continue," he repeats.

"I'm sorry it took so long for me to do this. I'm really sorry for how we ended."

"Anything else?"

I look at him and shake my head.

"That's just great! Have a nice life, Keegan!" He jumps up into his SUV and squeals his tires, exiting the parking lot.

I start walking back to the bar as I replay our conversation in my head. The more I think about it, the madder I get. He left with an attitude when it should have been me pissed off at him. Jack had promised to wait for me and ended up going back to that bitch.

Of all the women he could have picked, why Annie? I am going to find out why.

I text Seth.

Me: Taking a cab home. Talk to you later.

Seth: Everything okay?

Me: Going to find out some answers. Will touch base with you tomorrow.

Seth: K. Be careful.

Once home, it occurs to me that Jack and Annie might be living together. I pull up social media and see pictures of the happy couple plastered all over his page. I notice the latest one was taken at his townhouse, only a few days ago. It looks like they aren't living together because there are picture posts at her house, too. Thinking this is all the confirmation needed, I grab the keys to my new off-road, soft-top SUV and make the short trip over to Jack's.

I'm soon on his front step, ringing the doorbell and pounding on the door. I'm starting to think he's not home when the door flies open. There, standing in front of me, is Jack, bare-chested with the snap of his jeans undone.

"What the fu—Keegan?"

Before losing my nerve and not skipping a beat, I start tearing into him, "Why, Jack? Why her? You told me you'd be here for me. Well, I'm sorry it's taken me three damn years of hard work to get my shit together. I trusted you, Jack. I believed in you, in us. I was fighting to get back. I could always count on your honesty, even when it hurt to hear it. I never took you for a coward. And for what? Her? After all the pain she brought into our lives, why did it have to be Annie?"

Walking up behind Jack, Annie is standing in the foyer with her eyes as big as bottle caps, and a few of the top buttons of her see-through blouse are undone.

I've not only humiliated myself in front of Jack, but now, I've discovered that his fiancée got to see the show.

"Ah, shit! Just forget it. I'm done." I turn and leave.

With Kyle at his grandmother's and not expected home until next Wednesday, I stop by my townhouse to pick up the newest member of our family, Kirby, that we rescued from the local animal shelter. He's an adorable mixed terrier with long sandy-blond fur. With Kirby, I don't feel so alone, especially when he snuggles up next to me at night. Once Kirby is loaded in my SUV, I am Pennsylvania-bound to my lake house to leave all the bullshit behind me.

Once I get there, I text Seth, saying I am at the lake and will talk to him when I come back on Monday. Beyond physically and emotionally exhausted, I hop in the shower and get ready for bed. Once snuggled in bed with Kirby, I check my phone one last time. There are a list of texts and one missed call from Jack.

> *Jack: I'm sorry.*

> *Jack: Where are you?*

> *Jack: Call me.*

> *Jack: We need to talk.*

> *Jack: Please, Keegan, call me.*

The texts remind me of the ones Cameron sent to me after the Internet incident with Centerfold Chick's announcement about their relationship status.
Been there, done that, and got the T-shirt.

Seeing Jack's texts brings back all the humiliation of tonight's encounter. Being too embarrassed to return his call, I choose to silence my phone, turn off the light, and try to get some sleep.

Friday morning turns out to be a great day to put on some grubby clothes and whitewash the ugly brick fireplace in the kitchen. The split-foyer house has become my way of escaping in more ways than one. I love coming up to the lake, cranking up the music, and getting lost while doing little DIY projects around the house. The yard work has been contracted out to a local landscaping company. I have a large cement patio and dock by the water's edge with a slide and oversize lounger waiting for my next cigarette break.

As I whitewash the brick, I think back to last night's texts from Jack. We do have to talk but not by phone or text. A proper closure is needed, and the only way to do it is in person. When I return home, I'll call him to arrange a time and place to meet. It's going to be a hard conversation to have with him, especially since he's now engaged to Annie. Never once during the whole time we were together did I ever think he had feelings for her, and now, they're getting married. It doesn't make sense. The only logical explanation I can come up with is that his guilt over Sean is the driving force behind it.

Lunch is fast approaching, and all of my hard work has made me hungry. I'm craving pizza, and I decide to order one for delivery. There isn't much of the fireplace left to do, so I go back to my whitewashing until the pizza arrives.

34

Jack

After three years, that was all Keegan had for me? A bunch of damn greatness and a miserable *I'm sorry*? She couldn't even throw me a bone and say it was good to see me. I was so pissed off at all of her greatness and her being there with another guy that I exited the bar, leaving behind a party that was being thrown in my honor.

The doorbell rings minutes after I arrive home, and there stands Annie, wearing a see-through blouse with a matching lace bra, looking hotter than hell.

Without saying a word, she walks in and starts kissing me as I close the door behind us. I eagerly return her advances as we make our way to the living room couch. Annie takes off my shirt and unsnaps my jeans, while I start to unbutton her blouse. Just as Annie starts fumbling with my fly to unzip it, the doorbell rings.

Who in the hell is at the door now?

I start to get up, and Annie pulls me back down. "Don't answer it. They'll leave," she tells me between our kisses.

I try my best to ignore it, but the person is now pounding on the door and laying into the doorbell. Storming over to the door, I yank it open to come face-to-face with Keegan.

Could this night get any worse?

As I stand there, half-naked and praying to God she doesn't discover Annie is the one responsible for my state of undress, Keegan starts ripping into me. I can't believe she has the nerve to say these things to me, but at the same time, her words cut through me to the core.

Just when I didn't think things could get any worse, Annie lets her presence be known to Keegan.

What in the hell have I done in my life to deserve this?

Keegan takes one look at Annie, ends her rant, and leaves. Forgetting about Annie, I watch Keegan disappear down the street while trying to grasp what just happened.

"Well, that certainly was embarrassing! I'm glad she left before humiliating herself any further," Annie says, reminding me that she's still standing there.

I shut the door, rest my forehead against it. "Go home, Annie."

She comes up behind me and puts her arms around me. "Come on, baby. Let's go upstairs and finish what we started."

I face Annie. "Go home. Whatever little bit of fun we almost had is over."

Dropping her arms from around my waist, she takes a step back from me. "What? Jack, don't do this. We've been back together for almost a year, and you're telling me to go home after some psycho bitch's rant?" Annie asks, now standing with her hands on her hips, outraged by my rejection.

"Back together? We haven't been back together! What the hell are you talking about?"

"What about last Friday night?"

"We got drunk one night and fucked. That's all it was, and tonight would have been no different. Do you want to hear what Keegan and I did? We made love. I never fucked Keegan. There's a big difference between the two. Please leave before I say any more hateful shit to you."

"But the ring…you have a ring. I saw it. I know you have it," Annie says tearfully.

"What ring?"

"The one I found in your nightstand."

"What? Keegan's ring? I was going to ask her to marry me the night Will was killed. Keegan is the only woman I've ever wanted to marry, and now, I'm pretty sure she's walked out of my life for good. Just leave, Annie."

Annie grabs her purse and sticks her finger in my face. "Don't you ever come crawling back to me with your pathetic tail between your legs the next time you get dumped! I deserve better than you."

Annie's parting words sting as she leaves the townhouse, slamming the door behind her.

I fall back in one of my living room chairs, running my hands through my hair, as I wonder what the hell I am going to do. I dig my phone out of my pants pocket and call Keegan, but she doesn't answer. I follow up with numerous text, but still no response back from her. I need to go to bed and hopefully in the morning think of a way to salvage things with her.

The next morning, I head out to the Fitzgeralds', hoping Keegan hasn't left for the day. When there is no answer at the front door, I jog down to the dock, thinking she might be taking a cigarette break this morning. There is no sign of Keegan, only a chair along with an old ceramic pot filled with sand and a few cigarette butts. She's gone back to smoking since I wasn't there to hold her when she needed to talk things through. My next thought is to call Mitch to see if he knows where Keegan might be this morning.

"Hello?" Mitch answers in his gruff voice.

"Hey, Mitch. It's Jack. I'm at your house, and Keegan's not here. Do you have any idea where she might be?"

"Well, it's about damn time you showed up, boy. You do realize, it's been three years. Hell, she moved out a couple of years ago. She's probably at her studio or store."

How stupid of me.

Of course Keegan is working and has moved out. It has been her main focus in life since moving back in with her parents.

Mitch tells me the location of her businesses and townhouse.

I pull up in front of the studio and can't help but think back to our first date. I see a friendly face looking at me when I enter—or at least I think it is friendly.

"Hi, Marcy!"

She stares at me for a few seconds. "Well, I'll be damned. Look what the cat dragged in."

"Yeah, long time no see. I need to find Keegan. Is she here?"

"No, I manage the shop. Keegan only stops by occasionally to pick up receipts and other accounting stuff, like invoices and payroll. Does Annie know you're here?"

"No. I don't answer to Annie."

"Sure about that? According to her, your engagement is going to happen any day."

"What?"

"Yeah, she was in here the other day for a class, bragging about how she found the ring," adds Marcy.

"Listen, I'm not getting engaged to Annie. She found the ring for—never mind. I don't have time to get into all of this now. Do you think Keegan is at her townhouse?"

"Nah, she's at the lake."

"No, she isn't. I just left there. Mitch said she would be here or at her townhouse."

"Not that lake. Her house up at the lake in Pennsylvania."

Now, my head is really spinning. In less than twenty-four hours, I have found out Keegan now runs two businesses, owns a townhouse, and has a lake house. She's been very busy during the last three years.

"Can you give me the address?"

"Not sure if I should. First, tell me why you want it."

"To go up and do some serious begging with a little groveling thrown in for good measure."

"About damn time," Marcy mumbles under her breath.

She gives me the address along with directions, and I find it's a short forty-five-minute drive from the studio.

Starting Monday morning, I work eight-hour days with weekends off in my new position as Battalion Chief. I call the station and take leave until Monday, hoping it will be enough time to convince Keegan to take one more chance on us. I stop by my place to pack a bag, and then I head north, determined to get her back.

Once at the lake, I pull into the driveway at the address Marcy gave me. The property is gorgeous. The house sits on top of a slight incline at the end of a cove off of the main lake.

I look in my rearview mirror, and see a pizza delivery guy pulling up behind me. After paying for the pizza, I stand at her front door with the box in my hand, ringing the doorbell.

The next few minutes will determine my fate. If I can get her to let me in, I might have a fighting chance.

35

Keegan

I open my front door, and there stands Jack, holding my pizza. I'm speechless.

He asks, "Just going to stand there with your mouth hanging open, or are you going to invite me in?"

I step aside, allowing him to come in. "New job?"

"You still got that sass, don't you? I thought they would have fixed that while you were in the hospital."

"Watch it! You're skating on thin ice," I quip back at him.

Kirby is jumping up and down on me, whining, as the aroma of the pizza fills the air.

"What the hell is that?" Jack asks, looking down, gesturing with his head toward my dog.

"That's my new boyfriend, Kirby, and he hates pizza delivery guys," I answer back with a straight face.

"This box is hot! Where the hell am I taking the pizza?"

"Straight ahead, up the stairs. The kitchen is through the door at the top."

As he reaches the kitchen and scopes out the main living area, he comments, "Nice. Very nice."

"Thanks. Now, tell me why you're here. I'm sure your fiancée wouldn't be very happy with you right now."

"Why in the hell does everyone think I'm engaged to Annie?" he asks.

"Well, let's see, after her announcement the other day at the studio about finding the ring, which I personally heard myself, and—"

Jack interrupts me with a pained look, "Ouch. You did?"

"Yeah, I did. If that wasn't bad enough, you rubbed my nose in it last night, saying you were celebrating your promotion *and* engagement, and then I found you both half-undressed."

"What I said was, we were celebrating my promotion and *an* engagement," Jack clarifies.

"Oh. Who got engaged?" My surprise and curiosity sidetrack me for a moment.

"Nancy." Jack grins back at me.

"No way! Is she marrying that loser?"

"Nah, after seeing our match-up, she set up her own page and found a really nice guy."

I playfully slap Jack's arm. "Get out of here. Really?"

He laughs. "Yeah, really. I kid you not."

"Answer the question, Jack. Why are you here?"

"We need to talk. Would you like some pizza?" He opens the box as if it were his to offer.

On second thought, I guess it is his since he paid the delivery guy.

It appears our talk is going to be now, and I set us up on the floor in front of the kitchen's fireplace.

"First, how did you find me?"

"Mitch and Marcy."

"That easy, huh? And it only took three years to do it. Interesting."

"Wait a second. You were the one who had to do this fucking thing by yourself and told me not to wait, so don't you dare lay that bullshit at my doorstep. I begged you to let me be there for you. I was waiting for you to give some indication for me to come back into your life. You, at the bar last night with that guy, telling me how fucking great everything was, followed by your sorry-ass excuse of an apology, was not the kind of indication I was looking for. Christ, the first thing I saw when I walked into the bar was you hugging that asshole."

"Wow, do you kiss your mother with that mouth?"

Jack stares at me, waiting for an explanation.

Then, I say, "Okay, I'll try to explain things. Just a warning, sometimes, I still have problems clearly expressing my thoughts, as you got to see firsthand last night. Remember, everything I'm about to tell you happened a little over a month after my surgery.

"My brain was still healing, and I was on a lot of meds. I wasn't processing information in the most rational of ways. It was the perfect storm for what happened next."

"Stop stalling. I want to know everything. Don't leave anything out," Jack instructs me in a stern voice.

I start by going into detail about the reading of the will, my private meeting with the lawyer, and the contents of the folder and the letters it contained.

After telling him the specifics of the first letter, I go on by saying, "The second letter simply said, *'My dearest Keegan, I'm sorry. I love you with all my heart. Be happy. Will.'* Funny, to this day, I still remember the second letter word for word."

I tell Jack about Will's instructions and try to explain my behavior the afternoon of my breakdown. "After reading everything, I was feeling paranoid with a little bit of schizoid thrown in for good measure. Between the accident, my surgery, Will's death, and the letters, it became all too much for me to deal with. You got to see my mental breakdown up close and personal.

"During the first week in the hospital, I was in a bad way and didn't want you to see me like that. God, it took all the energy I had to keep my shit together during the visit with you that day. Looking back, somewhere deep down, I thought our love was strong enough to survive it all, and I thought you would always be there for me."

I take a sip of my soda and watch as he processes all the information I just shared with him.

"Anything else?" he asks.

Surprised he has nothing more to say, especially after my last comment, I add, "When I heard Annie talk about getting engaged, I knew, at the very least, you had gone back to her. I needed to know, after all she had done to us, why her? And then you opened the door last night, half-dressed, with her by your side. The why no longer matters to me. It is what it is."

Jack stares at me for a few more moments before speaking, "Let me get this straight. Will gave you two letters, professing his love and telling you all the unforgivable crap he did through the years, with the instructions not to tell anyone."

"Yes."

"Then, you went apeshit crazy on me."

"Yes."

"The last time we saw each other, you told me some sort of crap about doing it alone and for me not to wait. Is that close to what you've said?"

"I think there was a little bit more to it than that, but, yeah, pretty much."

"Okay, answer this for me. Did you cut Kyle and your parents out of your life during this time? I mean, you love them and care about them, right?"

Oh, no, I do not like where this is heading.

"Well, yeah, but they're different."

"How? Explain to me how your love for them is different."

"Well…they're family."

"Did Kyle do any therapy with you?"

"Yes."

"Did Mitch and Sandy talk with the doctors? Visit and see you?"

"Yes."

"So, let me ask you one final question. Who abandoned whom, Keegan?"

I don't know how to respond, so I say nothing.

"You did. And how did you abandon me?" he asks.

I can no longer find my voice.

"You did it by building a damn wall to shut me out—not Kyle or your parents, but me. Why?"

I drop my head, slightly shaking it back and forth, while looking down at the floor. "I honestly don't know."

"Well, let me give you a clue...Will's letters."

I look up at Jack, understanding where he is going with this.

Jack continues, "You said it yourself the day of your breakdown. He reached up from the grave and pulled you down inside with him. What was the date of the first letter?"

"Right after we separated for the second time."

"What's the date of the second letter?"

"The same day I saw him for the last time, and he kissed me on the dock."

"There is one thing you don't know. I was going to propose to you the evening Will was killed. Before that night, I met with Will to tell him my plans. Guess when that was?"

"When?"

"The day before he kissed you and wrote the second letter, which you still remember word for word. Will knew if anything happened to him, everything would come out in the trials and news. Both of those letters were nothing but a load of bullshit. God, you want to talk about Annie manipulating me? Christ, that man has been manipulating you from his grave. If he couldn't have you, he made

285

damn sure no one else would, even after his death. So, you can stop playing the little woe-is-me-brain-surgery-pain-med victim and face reality. Get a clue, Keegan, or you will never find happiness!"

Jack gets up and stomps down the stairs and out the front door, slamming it behind him. I just sit there, letting everything sink in.

I wonder what my answer would have been if Jack had proposed that night. *Did Will kiss me and say what he did to confuse me just enough so that I would have said no to Jack?*

That son of a bitch!

Kirby is scratching at the door to be let out. Opening the door for him, I notice Jack is sitting down at the dock. I walk down with Kirby following.

"Hey, I thought you left," I say to him once I reach the dock.

"Nah, I needed a cigarette break." Glancing over his shoulder at the ceramic pot filled with sand and butts, he says, "Between here and your parents' dock, I see you've been having a lot of cigarette breaks."

"You've been at my parents' dock?"

"First place I went to look for you today. Do you run a special on these butt containers at the studio?"

"Nah, I sell them at my store next door."

"So, One of a Kind is your store? Mom and Annie are always talking about that place."

Plopping next to him on the dock, I decide to rip the scab off. "So, you and Annie are back together."

"I never said that."

"Jack, a girl doesn't think a guy is going to propose unless she's in a pretty serious relationship with him. From what I saw last night, you two are a hell of a lot more than friends."

Jack sighs. "These past years have been hard on me. I would go over to see Sean, and it was easy to fall back into old routines. We talked and got beyond all the crap between us, more for Sean's sake than ours. I'd go over for dinner on my nights off, spend the evening there until Sean's bedtime, and then go home. Well, except for last Friday night."

"That's okay, Jack. You can spare me the details."

"You need to know because Annie is so pissed off at me right now that she's going to make sure you hear her version of what happened that night."

I ask in my best hillbilly twang, "What? You gonna be her next baby's daddy?"

He looks over and chuckles. "No, I learned my lesson over nine years ago to make sure to wrap it up at all times."

"So, let's hear your version of the story of what happened with Annie."

"I fucked her. In fact, we fucked all night."

"Wow, don't sugarcoat it or anything."

"Sorry. We got drunk while celebrating my promotion. One thing led to another, and it happened. I'm not proud of what I did. I totally used her, but, God, it felt good. After being faithful to you for three years, I just couldn't get enough once we started."

"What about last night?"

"We were well on our way to doing it again when you started pounding on the door."

"Why? You were sober when you left Donnelly's, so you can't blame it on being drunk."

"It felt like you had kicked me to the curb. Annie came over, looking hot as hell and asking for it. I was pissed off at you and figured, *What the hell?* So, we started going at it. After you left, I told her to go home."

Nodding, looking out over the water, I respond, "Hmm, I'm finding this all very interesting. You know, Will had a go-to girl. Her name was Brittany. He was dating her when we met in college. After our first divorce, he went back to her. It wouldn't surprise me to hear they hooked up again after our second divorce. Now, I'm finding out you're doing the same thing with Annie. Again, why Annie? And why did Will go back to Brittany?"

"You want to know the truth?"

I nod my head, indicating for him to go on.

"I can't speak for Will. For me, Annie is an attractive, hot woman who knows how I like it, and there's none of that awkward first-time bullshit. I know she's a sure thing."

Stunned by Jack's response, I wonder what happened to the sweet man I once loved and if it was my fault he turned into such a jerk.

Thinking two can play this game, I lean over and say breathlessly in his ear, "Hey, I totally get it. You know Cameron, the guy I was with last night? He has one hot, rock-hard body. Guess you could call him a sure thing, too. God, sex with him is awesome."

Bull's-eye!

From Jack's expression and the tightness of his jaw, I see I hit my target dead center. It was childish of me, playing tit for tat with him, and I hate that I allowed myself to be lowered to his standard of revenge. It was definitely unfair to Cameron since we haven't been together since before I met Jack.

I get up and head back to the house with Kirby following, not caring if Jack and I ever speak again. Jack wanted to hurt me for shutting him out, and he succeeded. And I also showed him that I could be just as cruel.

36

Jack

I return to the house and find Keegan upstairs, cleaning up in the kitchen. I can tell she's furious by the way things are being banged around.

"Hey, think I might have worn out my welcome, so I'm heading to a hotel. I was hoping we could hang out tomorrow."

She comes up to me and gets in my face. "I'm not the same woman I was three years ago. I own two businesses and properties, and I'm doing just fine on my own. I will not be disrespected by any man, especially you. If you can't live in the here and now, I suggest you go back home to your sure thing, who knows every which way you like it, and take your silly-ass games with you!"

"Keegan, I'm sorry for what just happened. I was a dick to say those things to you. I wish things could be different because, at the end of the day, I still love you. I'll just head out. If you want to talk later, you know how to reach me. Bye."

I get as far as the front door when I hear Keegan say from the top of the stairs, "Jack."

I stop and turn, looking up at her. "Yeah?"

Keegan stands there, looking as though she's debating on what to do next. "There's a guest bedroom downstairs if you want to stick around this weekend, but there's one condition," she says to me, leaning against the railing with her arms crossed.

"What's that?"

"No more childish games. We talk things out like adults. Deal?"

"Deal."

Later that evening, Keegan fixes us a simple meal of cream of crab soup, salad, and wine. We have dinner out on the deck with limited polite conversation about mundane things, like the weather and the colors of the leaves. Every once in a while, Keegan directs her conversation to the hairball she calls a dog, as if he understands what she's saying and he's capable of answering.

I help her with the dishes and then say, "Good night," before heading downstairs to the guest bedroom. It feels strange, spending the evening with Keegan and having no physical contact.

Crawling under the covers, I think of all that has happened in twenty-four short hours. I threw some real hurtful shit at Keegan today, and she took it all without a tear. The Keegan I remembered would have fallen apart at some of the crap I said. She has changed. I didn't think my love for her could become any stronger than it already was, but damn, her newfound confidence is sexy as hell.

I hear my door creak open.

Keegan walks up to my bed and holds out her hand. "Come with me."

We go to her bedroom.

I stop at the doorway and say, "Keegan, no. After what happened today, I don't think we're ready for this."

She faces me. "I don't want to make love or fuck or whatever it is you do these days. I can't fall asleep, knowing you're downstairs, not sharing my bed. I only want you to hold me, nothing more."

"Christ, I'm only human. I'm not sure I can do only the holding thing."

Keegan smiles. "Sure you can. Kirby's on duty tonight. I gave him strict orders not to let anything happen."

"You think I'm sleeping with that hairball?" I point to Kirby stretched out in the middle of the bed.

"If you want to be with me, you'd better get used to that hairball." She leans over the dog and starts rubbing behind his ears while kissing him. "Isn't that right, baby?"

Damn lucky dog.

"Well, no worries now. There's no way in hell I would kiss you after seeing your mouth all over him!"

She slowly approaches. "Wanna make a bet?"

I pull my head back. "No way, not until you brush your teeth and wash your face."

The next thing I know, Keegan gently caresses me through my boxers with her hand, making me hard, as she lightly kisses my neck. She hits the spot at the base of my ear, which drives me crazy.

A few moments later, our tongues are getting reacquainted with each other after three very long years.

Keegan abruptly breaks the kiss off and walks to her side of the bed. "Told you. Now, get your ass in bed."

"What? You're going to just cut me off like that with a bad case of blue balls?"

"Yep, pretty much."

I reach out to grab her to have my way when Kirby starts barking at me, daring me to make another move.

"See? I told you nothing was going to happen." Keegan smiles sweetly at me.

We climb in bed and spoon with my front to Keegan's back as she holds Kirby nestled against her chest under the covers.

Damn lucky dog!

The next morning, I wake up to find Kirby on my side of the bed, sitting and looking at me. I glance over at Keegan and see she is still asleep. I look back at Kirby. He hasn't altered his guard dog stance as he continues to watch every move I make.

I poke Keegan and wake her up. "Your dog is staring at me."

She yawns and stretches. "Yeah, he does that when he wants to E-A-T, go O-U-T, or go for a W-A-L-K."

"Seriously, did you just spell, so he wouldn't know what you were saying?"

"Yep, sure did. He tells time, too. He has his W-A-L-K look," she says.

"What? He has different looks?"

She giggles and nods her head. "Just don't say any of those words I spelled out loud."

"Why?"

"Because he goes nutso until he gets what he wants."

I look at the hairball and say, "Hey, Kirby, you want to go for a walk?"

He starts jumping all over us, barking and going crazy.

Keegan is laughing. "Told you. Now, you have to get up and take him for a walk."

Soon, both of us are up, taking the dog for a walk around the neighborhood. Well, the word *walk* is a slight exaggeration to describe what we're doing. It is more a tour of mailboxes, and Kirby has to christen every single one of them.

Later in the day, we pack an assortment of items onto Keegan's pontoon boat. I'm told the items are required to spend an afternoon on the lake. Once everything is loaded, including Kirby, she pulls away from her dock.

I ask, "Why a pontoon boat and not a speedboat for water skiing or tubing?"

She gives me a sexy little smile. "Mom and Dad's lake is a better place to ski. This is a good place to float."

After enjoying a good part of the afternoon, floating with her, I totally get what she meant. The front of the boat has two sunbathing couches with a table in between them. Keegan is stretched out on one, and I'm on the other as we float while sipping on some cold ones from the boat's built-in cooler.

Keegan looks over at me. "It's occurred to me. I don't know much about your pre-Annie days. Have you ever been in any other serious relationships?"

"I dated off and on. I lived with one other person before Annie, but she wanted to get married, and it just wasn't in the cards."

"So, who was she?"

"Huh?"

"Name. What's her name in case I ever run into her?"

"Chelsey."

"Chelsey? No last name?"

"Her last name isn't important. Our relationship was good and then bad, and then it ended." By Jack's tone, he is finished with discussing all things Chelsey.

"But you were going to propose to me. What made me different?"

"You're my paradigm shift. You made me rethink what I wanted in life. Question for you, what would have been your answer?"

"The person I was back then? Got to be honest, I'm not sure."

"What about the person sitting here with me today?"

"My answer would probably have been yes."

"That's good information to know." I wink at her.

"Please, don't tell me you're going to whip out the ring, fall down on one knee, and do the deed?"

"Nah, not today, but if I ever do decide to propose, you'll never see it coming."

We both break out laughing.

Keegan gets a serious look and kills me with her next question. "Why do guys keep leaving me to go back to their former loves?"

"Don't lump me in with Will. I never got back together with Annie. I slept with her once, and I'm not very proud of myself for doing it."

"It just wasn't Will. Alex and Cameron left me to go back to their exes, too."

After she explains what happened in her past relationships, everything makes sense about her viewpoint on marriage and her pounding on my door the other night. Keegan does a good job at hiding the pain these idiots caused her. I need to make sure she always feels cherished and rebuild the trust we once shared.

"So, what's happening here, Keegan? Are we back together? Friends? What?"

"My focus for the past three years was getting well and providing a livelihood for Kyle and me. Thanks to Will, I could think outside the box and start over. I used his money for the studio and my townhouse. My second store and this lake property are the results of my hard work. Now, I'm ready to focus on other parts of my life. I miss us, but we aren't the same people we were three years ago. I would call us a work in progress. Let's take it day by day and see where it goes. Does that work for you?"

Little does she know, I will take her on any terms she is willing to offer.

"Sounds perfect to me."

After we get back up to the house, Keegan suggests, while still in our swimsuits, that we take a couple of beers downstairs to the hot tub. The patio where the tub is located is off of the study beside the bedroom I'm staying in. As Keegan takes me through the study and out its sliding glass doors, I notice the mug and repaired plate we made on our first date are displayed on the bookshelf.

This patio is covered above by the upstairs of the house and has lattice on one side and rolled down screens on the others, giving the space total privacy from neighbors. We climb in the tub and sit with the jets beating on our backs while sipping ice-cold beer.

Life is sweet.

"So, tell me how Kyle is doing."

"Fabulous," Keegan answers. "I was really worried about him when I was in the hospital, recovering from my breakdown. After Will died, the news coverage seemed never-ending. I wasn't there, and you were gone."

"I wasn't gone."

"What?"

"I wasn't gone. I would never abandon him. I was there until you came home. You wanted nothing to do with me, so I spent my free time with him, and when you came home, I stopped coming over."

"Why didn't anyone tell me?"

"Because no one wanted to upset you and ruin the progress you were making. I was one of your triggers, and we decided it would be best if I didn't come around anymore."

"We? Who in the hell is *we*?"

"Your parents…Ryan…Kyle. A few nights before your release from the hospital, everyone was at the house. We talked and came to the consensus that it needed to be your decision to reach out to me. The night before you came home was pretty rough. There were a lot of tears and hugging. Never in my wildest dreams did I think it would be three years until I saw you. It killed me when you came up to the bar at Donnelly's, looking as if you were never sick, full of smiles, and saying everything was great. It was as if we or our love had never existed."

"Oh my God!" Keegan shrieks as she sets her bottle down on the edge of the hot tub. She scurries over to sit on my lap and kisses me. "I'm so sorry, babe. I was never told. I thought you saw me as damaged goods and didn't want to be around me."

I grab her face and pull it away, so she will stop kissing me. "What? Damaged goods? I was the one telling you I'd wait. I was the one pleading with you to let me be a part of things. How in the hell does that turn into not wanting to be with you because you're damaged goods?"

"I never got one card, letter, or note from you saying you missed me. Once I told you I had to do it by myself, you left. You never even contacted me to see how I was doing. I thought you didn't care enough to find out if I was okay," Keegan explains.

"But I did what you asked me to do," I say, pleading my case.

Keegan looks as if she's in pain. "I was a confused mess. I thought, when you witnessed my breakdown, you felt an obligation to stay. I had to come up with a way to let you off the hook. When I told you not to wait, you had the out you needed to walk away. I never heard from you while I was in the hospital, and once home, you didn't stop by, not even using Kyle or my parents as an excuse to visit."

"What the hell?" I shout. "Because I did *exactly* what you asked me to do, I find out three years later that all this bullshit didn't need to happen?"

I push Keegan off of me and climb out of the hot tub, going straight to the guest room and slamming the door behind me. After drying off and then slipping back into my shorts, I lie on the bed, thinking about the time we wasted.

I hear water running, and I assume, from the sound of it, Keegan is taking a shower. My thoughts shift to the showers we would take together after making love. It's times like those, ones of our shared intimate moments, that I've missed the most during our time apart. The water turns off, and a short time later, there is a soft tapping at my door.

"Jack, may I come in?" Keegan asks through the door.

"Not sure if it's a good time."

"Please, I have something to say to you."

"Come on in."

Keegan walks in, wearing her IrishEyes football jersey that comes to the middle of her thighs. My guess is she's wearing nothing underneath it.

She sits on the edge of the bed, and says, "Last week, my therapist asked the question, 'How can one ask and expect forgiveness from another, if they don't feel worthy enough to forgive themselves for their own transgressions?' I was confused by her question because, how do you apologize to yourself? I thought looking up the definition of *forgiveness* might help. I know, kind of silly, huh? I learned forgiveness is giving up resentment or anger against someone and to stop wanting to punish them. I also looked up its synonyms and found *understanding* as one.

"Then, it all clicked for me. I had to be the one to let go of my anger and stop punishing myself before forgiveness and real healing could begin. Talk about your paradigm shifts. My perspective of everything in my life completely changed. My new ink, an Easter lily, is my reminder to never forget to forgive myself. The how and why is only important to reach understanding. The here and now is what matters. We have to let go of the anger and frustrations of the past, so we can move forward to the future. Do you understand what I'm trying to say?"

"Who are you?" I ask.

"It's me, Keegan, the woman who loves and needs you in her life…and to rock her world again," Keegan answers with a wicked smile and a wink.

She pulls the jersey over her head, and I was right. There's nothing underneath. The first things I notice are two new tattoos.

To the average eye, the collection of Celtic artwork marking her body is in celebration of her Irish heritage. The first time we made love, I asked the significance of each one, and she told me the beautiful Irish folklore tales associated with them. The odd cross on her left front hip is called a Brigid's cross, honoring St. Brigid and her middle name. I later found it was associated with rebirth and the warding off of evil. In the middle of her lower back is a very cool three-legged spiral design called a triskele. She gave me some line about it representing her family. After looking it up, I learned it symbolized moving forward, and I found the placement of it in the area where tats were referred to as tramp stamps very intriguing. The piercing of her navel of a loop with a blood-red stone was done after her second divorce. Her latest two were of a harp and an Easter lily. I know the harp represents the day the music stopped in Ireland, and the lily is for peace and hope for the future. Yes, each is a beautiful design unto itself of her Irish heritage, but collectively, they represent her battle scars of love.

I promised her dad years ago, when Keegan and I first started dating, that I would never cause her to put another mark on her body. Here I am, staring at her new ink, and it's killing me.

An idea flashes through my head, and I ask her, "Who does your ink?"

"The tattoo parlor located in the same strip mall as the studio and store."

"Boy, how convenient. Your coffee shop and tattoo parlor are only steps away from work."

She giggles. "Why do you think I lease there?"

I pull her down and position ourselves, so I can kiss each of her new tattoos. I look up and see tears glistening in her eyes. After all that's happened between us this weekend, my kissing her new tats is what brings her to tears.

As I wipe her tears away, I tell her, "Baby, don't cry. I love you, and I want us to move forward with no more regrets."

We hungrily kiss each other, and we become reacquainted with each other's bodies.

Our lovemaking is frantic as if we fear this is a cruel dream that could end at any moment. It has been three long years, and I'm anxious to reclaim every inch of her body.

Pulling her beneath me, it feels as if I've come home as I sink into her. Soon we both are moaning God's and each other's names as our orgasms rip through us.

As we lie together afterward, Keegan announces, "I'm hungry. Let's go upstairs and raid the refrigerator."

Picking up her jersey on the way out of the bedroom, Keegan waits until we're in the kitchen before slipping it back on. I chuckle to myself, thinking she's still the same old Keegan.

We sit at the breakfast bar, feasting on cheese, grapes, crackers, and hummus.

"So, bring me up-to-date on Kyle," I say to her with my mouthful of food.

"Kyle is a junior this year and is planning to be a political science major in college with hopes of going to law school one day. He's a starter on the high school soccer team. There's a game this week, and I know he would love to see you."

"Great! I'd love to see him play. As Battalion Chief, my work schedule changes to working days and having nights and weekends off, but I'm still on call. Depending on the time of the game, I could bring Sean, too."

"That would be awesome. I know Kyle would love to see Sean, too. I wonder if we would even recognize him," she says.

"Sean turned nine this year. He's growing like a weed and putting me in the poorhouse with buying him clothes.

He still loves all things connected with the firehouse and sports."

"You mentioned your schedule as a Battalion Chief is going to change. What exactly does a Battalion Chief do?"

"I oversee the fourth battalion that is made up of seven stations. My biggest adjustment is the split stations of paid and volunteers since I have always been at a career station."

"Boy, a lot has happened to both of us in the last three years. It's almost too much to take it all in," Keegan says quietly.

"I know, but isn't it a good sign? I mean, no matter how much we missed being together, isn't it good that we kept moving forward with our lives?"

Keegan stretches and yawns. "Yeah, I guess. Hey, I'm beat from all this talk. Let's head to bed."

With Kirby tagging along after us, the three of us get in bed, assume our positions from the previous night, and fall asleep.

37

Keegan

I wake up in the middle of the night from a dream that felt so real it scares me. Will was holding me and saying never to forget him, an obvious manifestation from Jack's words yesterday in regard to Will manipulating me from the grave. Goose bumps send shivers down my spine, and I need a cigarette break.

Trying not to wake Jack, I get up and slip on my robe and slippers while grabbing a quilt off of a nearby chair. I leave the bedroom through French doors that go directly out onto a deck spanning the back of the house. The full moon is shining bright enough to light the way down to the dock for me. Once reaching my destination, I snuggle under the quilt and stretch out on the lounger.

Looking up at the sky, I'm fascinated by the harvest moon's colors this year. Its deep orange hue is in sharp contrast to the clear night sky filled with stars. Folklore is full of tales about the moon's magical powers, and I can't help but wonder if it's responsible for Jack and me finding our way back to each other. Becoming so lost in thought, I don't hear Jack until Kirby startles me, jumping up in my lap.

"Cigarette break?" Jack asks.

"Kind of. I had a bad dream."

"Scoot over," Jack tells me, lifting up the quilt.

I scoot back, giving him room to join me. I lay my head on his chest and sigh contently because being in his arms is my safe haven.

Making sure we're both covered, Jack pulls me closer. "Talk to me."

Snuggling further into his chest, I tell him, "Not much to talk about. All I can remember of the stupid dream is Will holding me in his arms, telling me never to forget him. Then, your words about him manipulating me from the grave came to mind. It was all a little too creepy for me."

"Are you feeling better?"

"I'm always better when you're holding me in your arms. I feel safe, right here, listening to your heartbeat. I've missed this...us."

Jack says nothing at first, and then he heaves out a sigh. "I feel the same way, babe. You complete me, is the only way I know how to put it into words. I felt lost these past three years, as if a part of me was missing."

"Yeah, I know what you mean. Whenever something special happened, my first thought would be to share it with you." I think back to the prior weekend's college tour and the emptiness I felt from not being able to share it with Jack.

A couple of minutes of silence pass between us.

Then, Jack says, "Come on, let's head back to bed. It's getting chilly down here."

As we walk up through the yard, hand in hand, I ask, "So, you start your new job on Monday?"

"Yeah, I need to go home tomorrow. Sean has a soccer game in the afternoon, and I promised I'd be there. When are you going back?"

"Early Monday morning. I need to drop Kirby off at the house and then stop by the store and studio before doing some grocery shopping."

We reach the bedroom and get settled back in bed with me back in Jack's arms.

"So, where do we go from here?" Jack inquires.

"You tell me."

"This weekend has been unbelievable. I don't want it to end."

"So, what are you saying?" I ask.

"Keegan, we've done the living apart and taking it slow. We both know how we feel. Let's just throw caution to the wind and move in together."

I bolt up in bed and stare at Jack as I shout, "Are you nuts?"

Kirby jumps up and starts barking at the two of us.

As I shush Kirby, Jack answers, "No, I'm not nuts. Three years have been unnecessarily wasted, and we will never get them back. I think we have psychoanalyzed the living shit out of the how, when, and why of things. Neither of our feelings or what we want has changed. Hell, even you said, out on the boat, if I asked you to marry me, you would say yes. So, my question to you is, why not?"

"Number one, we haven't even been back together for forty-eight hours. Number two, you have a son at a very impressionable age. Number three, we've changed during the past three years. Although we might still be in love, there's the possibility we might not like each other anymore."

"In regard to number one, screw how long we've been back together. You and I know we would be married now if Will hadn't been killed. Number two, Sean spent his first four years with me shacking up with his mother. Number three is total bullshit and an excuse to put off the inevitable. Yes, some of our viewpoints might have changed a little, but deep down, we're the same people. Keegan, promise me you will at least think about it."

The next morning, I take Jack to a local diner that is famous for its hearty breakfasts.

We return to my house, and Jack helps me with a few odd jobs before it's time for him to leave.

Once he has everything packed up, we walk out together through the garage to his SUV parked in the driveway. He stops for a moment, looking at the two vehicles in my garage—a black sports convertible and a dark charcoal soft-top, off-road SUV, exactly like his.

"Sweet rides. They look right, sitting there together. Admit it, you missed me, didn't you?" he asks.

I couldn't deny it. "Yeah, I did."

"So, move in with me."

"I'll give it some serious thought, and we can talk about it later." I lean up and give him a good-bye kiss he'll have a hard time forgetting.

On my ride back home the next day, as scary as it sounds, I find myself agreeing with Jack's logic. It feels as if we have picked up from where we left off. Knowing we will end up spending all our free time together, it does make sense.

The million-dollar questions are, whose house, and how do we merge the two households together?

There are a lot of logistical issues to address before the move can ever actually happen.

Back at the studio on Monday, I notice it is my time to exit because Annie's weekly pottery class is about to start. My routine is to keep my distance and leave the studio during her class to avoid running into her. Sometimes, I use this time to run errands, or I do paperwork at the coffee shop a few doors down. Today, I am going next door to One of a Kind to catch up on some invoices and see if anything happened over the weekend that might need my attention.

Losing track of time, I look up when the bells above the door jingle to see Annie walking in with a friend.

About the same time, Marcy comes up behind me saying, "Oops, too late."

I glare back at Marcy. "Ya think? Never mind. It was bound to happen. I've got it."

The store's manager, Carly, greets them as they enter and start to browse. Marcy decides to stick around for the show and be there for moral support.

Annie sees me.

I say to myself, "Let the games begin."

"Hi, Keegan. It's funny to run into you here."

"Why? I own the place."

"Really? I had no idea."

"Yeah. I own the studio, too."

"Well, you never cease to amaze me," Annie says cattily.

I tell Carly, "Good-bye." Then, I politely lie to Annie, "It was nice seeing you. Enjoy the shop."

My hopes of making a quick exit vanish when Annie makes it known that she isn't quite finished with our conversation.

"Before you leave, I want to apologize for the whole embarrassing incident at Jack's on Thursday night."

"No need to apologize," I reply, trying to put an end to our conversation.

"I just assumed you knew Jack and I were back together. Anyway, I hope your weekend wasn't totally ruined by what had happened the other night," she says, trying to act like she cares.

"Nope, it wasn't ruined at all. In fact, it was pretty damn spectacular. I spent the entire weekend with my boyfriend," I tell her.

Annie lights up, as if she's won the lottery. "You have a boyfriend? Do I know him?"

Oh, I should be ashamed of myself for what I am about to do, but Annie has been asking for it. I glance over to Marcy, who is now grinning from ear to ear, ready to bust out laughing.

"Aw, buttercup, I'm not surprised you don't know because we only got back together on Friday. Yes, you do know him and will probably hear all about it the next time he comes over to see Sean, especially since we're moving in together."

Finally, Annie is speechless.

But I should have known it was too good to be true for it to last for more than a few moments.

"Liar! Jack came running back to me the day you got locked up in the loony bin. In fact, we went out to dinner the other Friday—"

I hold up my hand, signaling for her to stop. "Excuse me for interrupting, but I frankly don't care. The only thing that's important to me is where Jack will be spending his time from now on. If you'll excuse me, I've got places to go and people to see. Peace out. Bye-bye!"

Marcy walks out with me.

I give her a high five. "God, that felt good!"

"I bet it did, girlfriend. I bet it did," she says, laughing.

$\mathcal{38}$

Jack

Monday evening, on my way home from work, I swing by Annie's to drop off a video game I promised to give to Sean. She knew I was stopping by, so I am surprised to find Sean is playing at his friend's house.

"Why isn't Sean here? You knew I was stopping by to drop off his video game."

"Well, I guess you have your new girlfriend to thank for that, buttercup!" Annie answers in a sarcastically sweet tone.

"Buttercup?"

"Yeah, I guess it's Keegan's new pet name for me. She verbally attacked me today in front of store staff and my best friend. All I did was say hello and try to make a little friendly conversation with her. She got all up in my face about you two spending the weekend together. I did nothing to provoke the attack, and I was totally humiliated."

I am taken aback by this news since Keegan mentioned nothing about it in our texts today, even after I told her I'd be dropping off the video game. I try to remain calm. "I'm sorry, Annie, but you haven't answered my question. Why isn't Sean here?"

"I want to talk to you in private about what happened. It's pretty obvious from her behavior today that Keegan is still having mental issues. If you two are actually back together, I'm not comfortable with Sean being around her."

Carefully choosing my next words to avoid throwing any more gas on a fire already burning out of control, I say, "Annie, I will make it clear to Keegan what is at risk. What would make you feel comfortable enough to allow Sean to be around her?"

"Well, first, an apology from Keegan. In the future, I expect respect from her at all times. This is the second time she has gone off on me. I let the first time slide because of her accident and surgery. If it happens again, I will be forced to take legal action to change our current agreement to me being present during all visitations with Sean. Keegan will be banned from being around him, and I'm giving it some serious thought to have a protective order served on her."

And there it is—the ultimate threat.

Trying to keep it together and not lose it, I respond, "I hope it doesn't come to that and that we find some common ground between the three of us."

"Me, too, since I understand the two of you are moving in together."

I head straight home after leaving Annie's because I need to cool down before seeing Keegan. Annie is forcing me not only to spend more time with her, but she's also making me choose between my son and Keegan. Annie knows there is no way I am giving up time with my son. I'm also upset with Keegan for giving Annie the ammunition to make this ultimatum. It isn't long after I arrive home when Keegan calls me.

"Yeah?" I snap at her.

"Hello to you, too! Rough day?" she asks.

"You could say that."

"Want to talk about it?"

"Nope."

"Was Sean happy to get his game?"

"Don't know. He wasn't home."

"Okay, Jack, just tell me why you're in such a pissy-ass mood, so we can stop the game of Twenty Questions."

"If you think real hard, you probably already know."

"Shit! Annie told you about this morning. She probably boohooed on your shoulder about mean old Keegan. Did I come close?"

"Sure did, buttercup!"

"And you're mad at me? Of course you are because this is all my fault, and poor little Annie had nothing to do with it."

"That's pretty much how Annie is seeing it. In fact, she's expecting an apology from you. If it happens again, Sean won't be allowed to be around you, and I will have to spend all of my visitations with Annie present because she fears you're mentally off. She's even considering getting a protective order against you."

"What the hell? She causes a scene in *my* store with her bullshit and then tries to pull this crap? Are you serious?"

"You need to come to terms with Annie. I'm not losing my son because two women can't get their shit together when they're in the same room."

"Excuse me? I don't know what the hell she told you, but thanks for the vote of confidence and for giving me a chance to tell my side of the story."

"Go ahead and tell me your side."

"I've got an even better idea. Go ask Marcy what happened. She saw and heard it all, word for word. If you still think I'm in the wrong, then you can forget about moving in together. Yeah, I can make ultimatums, too!"

The next thing I hear is dead air.

I'm invited over to the Bennetts' after calling Marcy about today's incident. Come to find out, she taped the whole thing on her phone, and I can see firsthand what actually occurred.

When I arrive, Marcy is putting Aaron down for the night. He's now three and getting unbelievably big.

As Roger gets me a beer, I ask, "What the hell are you feeding that kid?"

Roger laughs and agrees that Aaron is growing up way too fast for his liking. Marcy returns as Roger is picking up toys from the evening's playtime. I can't help but notice one of them is the fire truck I gave Aaron on the day of his birth.

Marcy motions to the couch and tells me to get comfy as she pulls out her phone. "This has been a long time coming, Jack. Keegan leaves the studio every time Annie is there to avoid exactly what happened today. When I saw Annie walking to the store after class, I went to warn Keegan, but I was too late. I taped it to show Roger. Here, you can watch for yourself."

I watch in disbelief as Annie announces that we're back together and comments about Keegan being "locked up in the loony bin."

Keegan knew the truth and could've have ignored Annie's comments. It wasn't Keegan's place to tell Annie we were back together. I was planning on talking to her this evening about everything. I'm also irritated with Keegan because she told Annie we were moving in together. I think I should have been the first to hear that news, not Annie.

After leaving Marcy and Roger's, I drive over to Keegan's to discuss things with her.

After letting me in her townhouse while walking ahead of me, the first words out of Keegan's mouth are, "Are you ready to apologize?"

"Well, no, I'm not."

She stops dead in her tracks and turns to me. "What?"

"I saw Marcy's tape of the whole thing."

"She taped it? I love that girl. She always has my back! So, you saw it all?" Keegan smiles, as if she's won a prize.

"Yeah, I saw it all. I saw Annie trying to bait you. You were more than too glad to take it, and now, I have a mess to clean up, so I can still see my son without Annie always being there. Keegan, you really put me in a bad place."

"You have got to be kidding! After all that's happened between us, you come down on the side of Annie. Unbelievable! I think you should leave before I say things I will regret or won't be able to take back," Keegan says in a defensive tone.

"No, not until you hear me out. Annie wanted you to think I was back together her. We know the truth, so there was no need for you to get into it with her. It was my place to tell Annie about us, not yours. And if you decided to move in with me, I should have been the first to know, not Annie. I could have broken the news to her in a more acceptable way rather than you rubbing her nose in it. Your shenanigans are now threatening my relationship with my son, and I won't tolerate it. Sean is my life, and neither you nor Annie is going to screw around with it. Got it?" My voice slowly gets louder and louder until I find myself almost shouting the last words.

Keegan stares at me, mulling over my words. I'm starting to get a little nervous because this could go either way. She goes in the kitchen and grabs a bottle of water out of the refrigerator. I notice she's not offering me any. Not a good sign. She still hasn't said anything. She's just drinking her water, staring at me. The whole time, Kirby is sitting in a chair, looking back and forth between us.

She then says to me, "You're absolutely right, Jack. I should have been the bigger person and not taken the bait. Yes, I know the truth about us, and you should have been the first one to hear I *was* going to move in with you. Annie should have heard all of this from you, not me."

I knew she would see it my way.

Wait. Did she say, was going to move in?

Shit, this is not the direction I thought this conversation would go. I was sure she would say I was right, she was sorry, and then we'd have hot make-up sex.

"But I will not apologize for my *shenanigans* of being human and reacting to her constant taunting. I've been overly considerate of that woman by leaving the studio when she's there for class. I was pleasant to her and tried to leave the shop. She was the one who insisted on continuing the conversation. As I've said before, I'm not the same person I was three years ago. If you think for one minute that I'm going to let Annie walk all over me, forget it. If we're going to take our relationship to the next step, then Annie has to accept and respect it. I'm sorry she's threatening to take you to court over your agreement, but that could happen anytime—with or without me in your life. You brought that crazy into your life the day you knocked her up, so I suggest you suck it up, buttercup! You know your way out. Good night. Come on, Kirby. Let's go to bed."

After Keegan and the hairball go upstairs to bed, I stand there for a couple of minutes, dumbfounded by her little speech. I was dismissed.

What happened to us promising to always talk things out?

I quickly follow her upstairs, enter her bedroom, and find her half-undressed.

"Excuse me!" Keegan shouts as I enter the room.

"You're not going to lay me out and then dismiss me. We talk things out. That's the way we roll, and it's not stopping tonight because you have your panties in a twist! Is Kyle home?" I ask.

"No, he's staying with Joyce this week, doing some yard work for her."

I notice Keegan is in a lace bra and silk sleep shorts, so I strip down to my boxers.

"What the hell do you think you're doing?" she asks.

"Leveling the playing field. You're at an unfair advantage over me with you being half-naked."

Over the weekend, I noticed the hairball would suck up to anyone who scratched him, especially his belly.

I lean over and start rubbing Kirby behind his ears. "Hey, buddy."

He immediately rolls onto his back and lets me give him a good belly rub. I then pull down the duvet and crawl under with Kirby flopping down beside me.

Keegan gives Kirby the evil eye. "Traitor!"

"Get in bed, and let's talk it out, Keegan," I order her.

She pulls a T-shirt over her head and throws mine back at me. "Now, I'm leveling the playing field. Put it back on."

Keegan gets under the cover and stays way over on her side of the bed with her arms crossed over her chest. "Start talking."

I begin by saying, "You and I need to come to an agreement about some rules when it comes to Annie."

Keegan nods. "Continue."

This is a good sign, so I immediately take advantage of it. "Rule number one, I break all news pertaining to our relationship to Annie."

"Agreed."

"Rule number two, you stop taking her bait. No matter what she says, just smile and leave through the nearest exit."

"I can't promise, but I'll try."

"Rule number three, if you break rule number two, you need to tell me immediately, so I'm not blindsided, and I can be prepared for Annie's crazy."

"Okay, I can do that," Keegan agrees.

"You have any rules?" I ask.

"You have to stop coming to Annie's defense all the time. First, at the very minimum, hear my side of the story before jumping down my throat. Stop looking at me like that! You're Pavlov's dog when it comes to Annie. She whines about something, and off you go to coddle her to make things all better. Her neediness is your bell. Today was like a bad memory from the past."

"I don't do that," I defensively respond back.

"Name one time during an Annie crisis when you haven't done exactly what I just described. When have you ever come to my defense first? Been in my corner, so to speak?"

"The night of the dinner when she lied about what had happened after the funeral. I told her to leave. I don't remember any coddling. By the way, I don't coddle."

"God, you sure have selective memory. You went to her house the next day to set her straight, she boohooed, and you ended up hugging it out. To make matters worse, you took her to the arcade with Sean and posted several family selfies of you all yukking it up. Every time you do shit like that, it reinforces her bad behavior. Right now...here in *my* bed...this whole discussion is about how to make Annie's boo-boo all better. Totally not cool, Jack!"

"It's the only way I can keep seeing Sean. I have to keep her happy."

"And that's where you're wrong. You have the court system to fight for your rights as a father. Keeping her happy has nothing to do with it. So what if Annie gets pissed off and becomes unreasonable because she doesn't get her way? Take her to court, and fight for your rights instead of feeding into her manipulative ways."

"I did not hug it out with her today. In fact, I kept things short and sweet. I told Annie we, meaning you and me, would discuss the situation and hopefully find some common ground for all of us to coexist."

Keegan gave me a small golf clap. "I'm proud of you. And what was her response?"

"Don't be too proud. It didn't get her to back down from her ultimatum," I point out to her.

"Annie's ultimatum was her upping the voltage of the electric shock."

"What?"

"Electric shock was another type of stimuli Pavlov used on his dogs."

"Whatever. That's when I left and came home."

"I'm sure that is exactly when she started to sing, *Keegan's in trouble*, and did a little happy dance."

I frowned at her. "Annie doesn't do happy dances."

"Oh, yeah, she does and often. Annie knows you'll be back tomorrow. She'll make sure Sean gets to say hi, and then she'll scoot him off to his bedroom. Knowing Sean is upstairs and could possibly hear, you begin to talk softly to Annie. She tearfully confesses her sins and apologizes. By the time you leave, you guys hug it out, and all is right once again in Annie's world. No matter how small it is, she still owns a piece of you."

I just stare at Keegan. "What the hell am I supposed to do?"

"Stop spending your time with Sean at Annie's. I know it's easier, and it has become second nature to do your visitations on school nights there, but it sends the wrong message to her. Don't go any further than the front steps of the house when picking him up or dropping off. He's a big boy. Have him walk to and from the car by himself. If you don't go inside, she can't hook you into any of her nonsense."

I'm stunned, listening to Keegan rattling all of this off. The sad thing is...she's right.

My pride won't let me admit it, so instead, I say, "Noted."

"Sorry, we got a little sidetracked. You were telling me about all the times you'd come to my defense and been in my corner. Go ahead. I interrupted you. My apologies. Please continue with your *long* list." Keegan smiles and bats her eyelashes at me.

"When she posted the picture of her and Sean in my recliner, I was fighting for us."

"Um, no...you were trying to save your own ass. Please correct me if I'm wrong, but when I got to the station, the happy family was playing on the fire truck. I was the one who asked Nancy to remove Sean from the area, so we could get down to the nitty-gritty. So, nope, doesn't count. Go ahead and tell me another time."

I've got nothing but silence.

Keegan says, "Jack, our past has been a series of Annie crises. I get pissed off and run away to sulk, you chase me, we talk it out, and then we have hot make-up sex. It was a vicious cycle with us ending up right back where we'd started each time. For us to move forward, this pattern of behavior has got to stop tonight."

We continue to hash things out until arriving at a plan for us to meet with Annie at the coffee shop. Keegan will apologize and have a letter from her therapist, stating she's of sound mind. I will also explain the new routine for my visitations with Sean.

We meet the following Saturday with Annie, and our plan seems to work. During our meeting, Annie finds out there is a video of her encounter with Keegan, and it would be used in court if she pursues changing our current agreement. She seems even more agreeable to our terms after hearing this news.

Annie calls the next day with some excuse for me to stop by after work. "Sorry, I'm busy after work. I can talk now over the phone. What's up?"

She makes up some bogus excuse for calling, and our conversation quickly ends.

After a few weeks, a new routine with Sean has been established, and more importantly, there have been no more run-ins with Annie.

39

Keegan

After I agreed to live under the same roof with Jack, it took us almost two months to coordinate and make the official move. We decide the logical thing to do is for Jack to move in with me because, out of the two of us, I'm the only one who lives in Kyle's school district. I have space for Jack's office and man cave in my empty finished basement. There is even room for his favorite recliner. I insist he puts the rest of his furniture in storage because it seems like a practical thing to do. Jack feels as if I'm setting us up for failure, but he begrudgingly does it and rents out his townhouse.

Four months later, Jack's biggest adjustment with us living together is Kirby, who he still fondly refers to as hairball. He is learning to spell out certain words when Kirby is present.

One day, Jack walked into our bedroom, finding me sitting in the middle of our bed, cross-legged, flipping through a magazine, while Kirby was snuggled up against my inner thighs in the middle of the opening. I heard him mumbling something about a damn lucky dog. Since that day, Jack now has a new term of endearment for Kirby—Crotch Critter. His new favorite pastime is to have Kirby chase after the red dot on the floor from the laser pen pointer Jack uses during meetings.

St. Patrick's Day falls on a Saturday this year, and Jack tells me not to make any plans for the day. He also informs me that Kyle is spending the weekend at Ryan and Liz's house, just in case some recovery time is needed. No details are being shared, and I'm told to trust him.

I wake up the morning of St. Patrick's Day to see Jack propped up on one elbow, wearing a tall green-and-white-striped hat that I wore once several years ago.

He asks me, "Are you ready to have some fun?"

"And what kind of fun do you have in mind?"

Jack throws the hat across the bedroom and removes my T-shirt and sleep shorts, and he begins kissing each of my tattoos. "These are the closest things I have to the Blarney Stone today."

His mouth eventually finds its way to the inside of my upper thighs, and in no time, I am coming undone. I want to return the favor, but he denies me by covering my body with his, making sweet, gentle love to me. With each thrust, he whispers how much he loves and cherishes me. It doesn't take long before our orgasms surge through us.

What a great way to kick off St. Patrick's Day!

We eventually shower, and he takes me to my favorite place for coffee and scones.

As we lazily sit, enjoying what is left of the morning, I comment to Jack, "Pretty tame St. Paddy's Day, if you ask me."

Jack laughs. Then his lighthearted expression turns into a mischievous one when he asks, "Do you trust me?" He pulls a green scarf out of his jacket's pocket. "I mean, really trust me. To take total control of the day, and you'll have no idea where we're going or what might happen along the way?"

I nod. I've never been blindfolded like this before or given myself entirely over to someone. I feel a little uneasy, but at the same time, I find myself getting excited.

Once I'm blindfolded, Jack whispers in my left ear, "Can you see anything?"

I shake my head.

Then, in the right ear, he whispers, "I'm going to hold your hand and guide you. Do you promise to do everything I ask?"

I nod.

"Good. Let's get started."

I know we are leaving the coffee shop because I hear the bells over the door, and I feel a cool spring breeze. I expect to be taken to his SUV, but instead, we turn right and start walking in the direction of the studio and shop. We stop to step into another place. The smell of sandalwood fills the air, and the background noises are all too familiar to me.

Jack whispers in my ear, "Do you know where we are?"

"The tattoo parlor," I reply with confidence.

Jack takes off the blindfold, and we're at the counter of the place where I go for all of my tats. I'm confused, and I look at him for an explanation.

"Look, I know each of your tattoos represents a bad time in your life. You have them in places where they are hidden from the world most of the time. I've decided it's time to get a tat in honor of the good in your life for the whole world to see. What better time to do it than on St. Patrick's Day? I have arranged for us to have matching Celtic love knots tattooed on the inside of our left wrists in celebration of us and our love. I had three designs drawn up, and I want you to choose which one we'll share."

Drew, one of the tattoo artists, shows me the designs.

"They're all so beautiful, but I think this one is my favorite. Is that good for you?"

"Good choice. It's my favorite, too."

We walk down the hallway to the rooms of the tattoo artists, Drew and Josh, only to pass both and continue to a larger one in the back. There are two stations set up side by side, so two clients can face and sit next to each other while getting tattooed.

Jack shrugs his shoulders. "It's my first time, and the guys at the station said it could be kind of painful. I want you holding my free hand. This way, we can talk, and you can help take my mind off of the pain. I only ask one thing."

"What's that?" I ask.

"All cell phones are turned off. I don't want you posting any pictures of me fainting."

We turn off our cells, lay them on a table nearby, and let the artists begin their work. We talk, laugh, and share our story with them. Before I know it, the tattoos are finished, ointment and bandages are applied, and the artists leave to get care instructions for us to take home.

Jack takes my hand and says, "Keegan we've been through some pretty rough times. Life tried its best to get in the way and break us once, but ultimately, we found our way back to each other. Like these tattoos, the love we share is continuous and never-ending."

Jack drops to one knee and pulls a ring from his pocket. "Keegan, I love you with my whole heart and soul. I want to continue our journey together as man and wife. Keegan Brigid Fitzgerald Henderson, will you please do me the honor of becoming my wife and marry me?"

I stare at him, then at the beautiful ring he is offering me, and then back at him. I find my voice and scream, "Yes!"

I jump into his arms and kiss him while repeating over and over how much I love him.

Josh and Drew knock on the door, asking if it is safe to come back in. I show them my engagement ring with tiny round cut diamonds set around the shoulders of a band filled in the middle with a beautiful Celtic knot design, highlighting a round cut diamond in its center. It's simply exquisite.

Retrieving his phone from the table, Jack turns it back on, puts his arm around me. "Show them your ring, baby."

He takes a selfie of us kissing with me holding my ring up for the world to see. He then posts it with the caption, *She said yes!*

Once my phone is turned back on, a small feeling of disappointment comes over me, seeing no congratulatory messages from Marcy, Seth, or my family.

Jack tells me it's time for the blindfold to go back on. I think to myself that there is no way he can top this unless he is taking me to some luxurious hotel suite to celebrate.

This time, he has me get into his SUV, and it seems as if we drive forever. I have no idea where we are because there have been so many turns. I do notice there isn't as much traffic noise, so I know we're in a rural area. Maybe instead of a luxurious hotel suite, he's taking me to a quaint bed-and-breakfast. We make one last turn and stop.

He helps me out of the vehicle and carefully guides me up some stairs and through a door. I think I heard a giggle. Jack asks if I know where I am, and I shake my head.

He quickly takes off the scarf, and I discover we're at my parents' house with everyone I love yelling, "Congratulations!"

My mother has the house all decked out in St. Patrick's Day finery. Someone turns on the Irish music and starts pouring the Black and Tans.

Once all the congratulatory kissing and hugging ends and things settle down a bit, Jack looks at me with a devilish grin. "See? I told you."

"Told me what?"

"You would never see it coming."

"You're right. I had no idea. I have one question. Why did you have us turn off our phones? You do know I would have so grabbed my phone and taken pictures to post if you had passed out."

"The last time I tried to propose, those damn things interrupted and almost ended us. I wasn't taking any chances this time. I knew everyone was here, waiting for us. Nothing else mattered until I got my girl to say yes. By the way, take your ring off and read the inscription," Jack tells me.

I slide it off and see the inscription.

GRA GO DEO

I look at Jack.

He translates, "It's Celtic for *love forever*."

"It's perfect! I love you, Jack Grady."

"I love you, too, the future Keegan Grady."

After personally greeting all the guests, I watch along with Marcy as Roger follows Aaron, who is on the go nonstop and gets into everything.

It dawns on me that no one is tending to the stores. "Uh, Marcy, I'm thrilled you're here, but who's at the stores?"

"We're closed for the holiday." She laughs, giving me a big hug.

The party goes on forever. Jack has made sure all our family and friends are there to celebrate this moment with us. It is the best damn St. Patrick's Day ever.

Ryan comes up and asks if he can speak with me in private. I follow him outside to the front porch swing.

"What's up?" I ask, sitting down beside him.

"I wanted to tell you how damn proud I am of you. You've been through hell and back. I don't know if I could have handled what you've been through. Jack's a good guy. I know you'll be happy. You want to know why?"

I nod to him.

"Because he reminds me of Dad, and you can't get any better than him."

"Thanks, Ryan. I love you." I give him a hug.

"I love you, too, sis. Remember, I've always got your back."

"As I do you," I reply back to him.

When I come back in, Jack asks, "Is everything all right?"

With a smile, I tell him, "Everything is perfect."

By the end of the night, Jack and I are feeling no pain between the shots of Irish whiskey and Black and Tans.

Since we're in no condition to drive, Jack and I spend the night at my parents' house in my old bedroom. We wake up the next morning to the smell of greasy bacon, and I barely reach the toilet in time.

Jack stumbles in. "Are you okay, babe?"

I finish brushing my teeth and splash cold water on my face. "Yeah, I'm fine."

We both pop some pain relievers to ease the pounding in our heads.

Fortunately, Jack had the forethought to pack an overnight bag for each of us. After a shower and a change of clean clothes, we feel almost human.

Mom has giant mugs of coffee waiting for us on the breakfast bar.

While Jack and I are sipping our coffees and nibbling on some toast, Mom asks, "Have you given any thought to the wedding?"

Even though it's been three years since my surgery, I still experience overload when it comes to processing my thoughts. With the combination of my hangover and still wrapping my head around becoming engaged, it is way too soon to have this conversation.

I need to shut her down, so I can take a breath. "Please, not now, Mom."

"But, Keegan, we have to get started. It can take up to a year to plan, depending on the size of the wedding. Do you even know, at least, what season you want to get married?"

I look at Jack and then back at Mom and say, "Sorry, I can't do this now." I jump down from the stool and leave through the sliding glass doors to head down to the dock.

I am looking out over the water when I feel Jack's arms come around me. He nuzzles my neck. "Start talking."

"I don't need her on my back about a wedding five minutes after we've gotten engaged. I need a moment to breathe and adjust to the whole idea of it."

Jack's body stiffens behind me. "Are you having second thoughts? Are you starting to regret saying yes?"

I turn to face him. "God, no! I want to marry you. There are no second thoughts or regrets. I can't wait to become Keegan Grady. It's hearing my mom mention the word *wedding* that's causing my head to spin. We haven't even had a chance to talk about what we want, much less get into it with her. This is our wedding, and it's up to us to plan. The only thing I can tell you right now is what I don't want."

"Continue."

"I don't want a big church wedding. I know it's probably something you would like with it being your first time getting married, but I've done it, and I hated how all the preparations ruined the day. It went way too fast, and I never got to enjoy it."

"Continue."

"I don't want a civil ceremony at the courthouse either. It was awful when Will and I did it the last time."

"So, I guess no Vegas wedding, huh?" Jack chuckles.

I playfully smack his arm. "What about you? This is your first time. What do you want?"

With one of his shrugs, Jack responds, "I haven't given it much thought. I guess what I want the most is to enjoy the day, for it to be special and reflect who we are as a couple."

"How do we make it a day about us?" I ask him.

"I don't know. If I did a word association to describe us, I would say *cigarette breaks*, *coffee*, *family*, *lake*, *tattoos*, and even throw *Kirby* in the mix."

"I would add *simple* and *easy*. By the way, thanks for making arrangements for Kirby to be here today."

"It wouldn't have been the same without the little hairball." Jack laughs.

"God, this place—the dock—has witnessed every part of us. All those memories come flooding back when I stand here. The beginning, our cigarette breaks, our laughter and tears. I feel a connection to you whenever I'm down here," I explain.

Jack nods and adds, "It's the first place I look when searching for you. Maybe this is where we should get married."

"But I don't want a big outdoor wedding with white tents and all that stuff."

"Then, we won't have them. We can have it here and keep it simple. I think we've proven that rules don't mean a whole lot to us. If we have our wedding down here, how would you do it to reflect us?" Jack asks.

"Oh, I don't know. We would be standing on the dock with some sort of an officiate, maybe the fire department's chaplain. It would be just our immediate families, including Marcy, Roger, Seth, Bob—you know, the people that were here yesterday. We would do our own ceremony and use our own words to say what's in our hearts. I would be in a simple sundress, and you would be in khakis and a button-down shirt. You know…nothing over the top."

"Then, that's what we'll do. I hate to ruin the moment, but there's something you need to know," Jack says cautiously.

"What?"

"I did a dumb thing yesterday."

"Excuse me?" I shriek.

"No, not that...well, it kind of involves when I proposed." Jack shrugs.

Oh no, not the shrug.

"Why do I think this is possibly going to ruin everything?" I ask.

"Because what I have to tell you is not going to make you happy, and I hope you understand how it happened," Jack answers.

"Don't tell me. It has something to do with Annie." By the look on Jack's face, my comment hit the nail on the proverbial head. "She's heard about the engagement. Out with it. What happened?"

"First, I take full responsibility for everything. I didn't tell her in advance about proposing to you, fearing she would spoil the surprise with some of her drama. In all the excitement yesterday and without thinking it through, I posted the selfie of us, so everyone waiting here would know you said yes."

"And she saw the post and is having a meltdown. So, what's the problem?"

"Annie has been blowing up my phone ever since I posted the picture. I have to go over and talk to her," Jack tells me.

"No, you don't. People get engaged every day without having heart-to-hearts with their exes. Annie will stomp her feet and pout, but she will get over it like a bad cold. You running over there will be taking a gazillion steps backward with her. You are not going over there and feeding into her little tantrum."

"Yes, I am going over there to talk to her. I've already made arrangements to meet with her at her house. Sean is still with my parents and won't be coming home until later this evening. I'll be home as soon as things are squared away between us."

I shake my head. "Unbelievable. She's even managed to ruin one of the most special days of my life. I have a question for you, Jack. If I blow up your phone and have a little hissy fit over this, will you stay with me and not go running over to Annie's?"

"That's unfair, and you know it. I have to do this because of—"

I cut him off, "Yeah, I know, Sean. Because of him, you will always be at her beck and call. Well, doesn't my future look rosy? Tell you what I'm going to do, Jack. I'm returning this ring to you. When you can make me your number one priority along with our sons, then come talk to me about getting married. Until that day comes—which I'm not sure it ever will—we'll just keep things as they are with us being roomies. Oh, by the way, while you're over there, talking to Annie, I'll be moving your stuff down to the man cave. Yeah, I can have temper tantrums, too."

Jack is furious. "Seriously? You're throwing my ring back in my face because I need to apologize to her for the post. The plan was to tell her today, but instead, she got blindsided by my post before we had a chance to talk. You're getting off easy because Will's dead. Like it or not, Annie's going to be in our lives. If you can't handle it, maybe you need to think real hard about accepting this ring, if I ever offer it to you again."

"Go to hell," I say through my tears before I run up to the house.

As I enter the kitchen, I call for Kirby, grab my purse, and tell my parents, "The engagement is off."

Mom tries to say something, but I interrupt her. "Dad, can you drive me home?"

On the way home, Dad asks, "You want to tell me what happened?"

"It's what always happens. Annie pushes Jack's buttons. She makes him feel guilty and uses Sean against him. He runs over there to smooth things over with her. Jack never takes into consideration how it makes me feel like a doormat every time he does it. I was Will's doormat, and I'll be damned if I'm going to be Jack's."

Dad doesn't say another word until we pull up to the curb. "Do me a favor. Don't do anything stupid. Jack will figure this out."

"That's the problem, Dad. I've given him so many opportunities to figure it out. I don't understand why Annie is still even a consideration in our lives. I just can't do it anymore." I give Dad a kiss and thank him for the ride home.

As I walk into the house, I read Jack's text.

Jack: Will be home soon.

Then my phone rings with FFCap52 flashing across the screen. I don't answer and send it to voicemail.

Jack sends me another text.

Jack: Talk to me. Please answer your phone.

When my phone rings again, I turn it off and decide to deal with things when he gets home.

The only problem with my plan is, he doesn't come home, and I'm devastated.

40

Jack

I know things are bad when I see Keegan leave with her dad and Kirby. Sandy steps out on the deck and starts down to the dock.

Once she reaches me, Sandy says, "Mitch is taking Keegan and Kirby home." Her tone becomes stern as she continues, "I know it's none of my business, but you are about to lose the best damn thing in your life. I suggest you fix this. The sooner, the better!"

After I think things through, I realize that Keegan is right. There is no need for me to run over to Annie's and discuss my engagement. I dig out my phone and call Annie to inform her I'm not coming over.

After I hang up with Annie, I text and call Keegan to let her know I am coming home, hoping we can get this misunderstanding behind us. She doesn't respond to my texts or answer my calls.

Mitch pulls up as I'm about to get into my vehicle. I wait for him to get out of his truck, so I can check on Keegan.

Before I can get a word out, he looks in my direction and barks at me, "You. In my study. Now."

I waste no time in going back into the house and taking a seat on the study's leather couch.

Mitch sits in his oversize desk chair with his feet propped up on the desk as he begins lecturing me, "Boy, you really fucked up this time."

He picks up his decanter of Irish whiskey and starts pouring.

After that, it's all a blur of him telling me what I need to do and me saying, "Yes, sir," over and over.

I wake up on the couch in Mitch's study with a pounding headache and a bad case of cotton mouth. I've got to stop doing this because my liver will never survive. I try to remember how I got here, and it all comes painfully back to me.

Damn it! If I had only handled things differently with Annie, all of this could have been avoided. Instead, I have my ring back in my pocket.

I go out to my SUV to get the duffel bag with my spare uniform in case I'm called into work while away from home. Keegan is always teasing me that it's my Superman bag and threatens to get an S emblem decal to stick on it. I go downstairs to use the bathroom off of Keegan's old bedroom and get ready for work.

Still feeling like shit, I load up our overnight bags and leave for work. Being over an hour early, I decide to crash in an open bunk and try to get a little bit more sleep.

Instead of calling or texting Keegan from work today, I decide to wait until I get home this evening to clear the air between us.

About an hour before it's time for me to leave for the day, I hear a ping from my phone, signifying an incoming text.

> *Keegan: I've boxed up and moved your things downstairs. I will be out, so you can get what you need for tonight. Let me know how you want to handle the move of everything else. I don't want to be here while you move out.*

>> *Me: What the hell? I'm not moving out. You might not want my ring, but I'll be damned if I'm moving out without us at least talking.*

> *Keegan: No need to talk. You said it all when you didn't come home last night from Annie's. Let me know when you're done tonight, so Kyle and I can come back home. Please don't take too long because it's a school night.*

Shit! She thinks I was with Annie all night.

>> *Me: I never went to Annie's. Mitch got me stinking drunk, and I passed out on the couch in his study. Ask him if you don't believe me.*

I hear nothing back from Keegan for the longest time, and then there's another ping.

> *Keegan: Come home…the sooner, the better.*

When I walk into the townhouse, as usual, Kirby comes running up to greet me. Hearing music coming from upstairs, I head to our bedroom, finding it lit in soft candlelight. Keegan is naked, lying across our bed on her stomach, propped up on her elbows with her hair cascading down, looking like a centerfold model.

333

"Welcome home," she greets me.

While unbuttoning my shirt and pulling it out from the waistband of my pants, I walk over to the bed and reply, "It's good to be welcomed back home. You had me worried today."

She sits up, kneeling back on her heels at the end of the bed, giving me a full view of her. "I apologize for jumping to conclusions. I just assumed you were with Annie. I never thought of myself as being insecure, but I found out differently today."

"Did you really think I slept with her? If you did, we have a real problem here."

"I didn't think you went to bed with her. I totally trust you, Jack. But you are a kind and caring man who would never leave anyone until they were safe and okay. I thought you cared more about her feelings than mine, and it hurt."

"After you left, I called her to say I wouldn't be coming over. I apologized for my post and said her feelings would be considered in future posts. I was leaving to come home when Mitch pulled up. He took me to his study, and I don't remember much after that."

Keegan giggles, leaning up on her knees to help pull my shirt down off my body, letting it fall to the floor. She puts her arms around my neck. "I know. I talked to Dad and gave him hell for getting you drunk. Um…I think you have something that belongs to me, and I would like it back."

"I'm not sure if I want to give it back."

Dropping back on her heels with her hands falling to her lap, she looks hurt but says nothing.

I pull her engagement ring out of my pocket, holding it up between us. "Keegan, when I gave you this ring, I expected it always to be on your finger along with your wedding band. This ring isn't to be randomly taken on and off whenever you get pissed off at me. I'm upset that you threw it back in my face during our first disagreement as an engaged couple. Living in fear of you ending things every time we disagree is not the kind of marriage I want for us. Couples use that kind of fear to manipulate and justify their lies to each other. I suggest you take a couple of days to decide if you're in this for the long haul and can handle what might be facing us down the road."

Keegan sits there with tears running down her face. "I'm sorry," she apologizes while getting up from the bed. She puts on her robe, turns on a bedside lamp, turns off the music, and blows out the candles. As Keegan leaves the bedroom, she tells Kirby it's time to go out and goes downstairs.

I finish undressing and put my sweats on. I check Kyle's room to see if he's home. Keegan must have made arrangements for him to be gone this evening, so we could have the townhouse to ourselves.

Keegan hasn't returned, so I go downstairs to check on her. I notice the sliding glass door is cracked open. When I get closer to it, I hear her sniffling. I find Keegan outside on the lounger, holding her knees to her chest quietly crying. Sitting behind her with my legs on each side of the lounger, I wrap my arms around her.

Through her tears, she begins to speak in a soft, contrite voice, "All I want is for you to think about me before Annie. I know it sounds selfish and small of me, but it kills me that you care so much about her feelings. It's also one of the many reasons I love you. I don't know what to say or how to make things right between us. I've lived the marriage you described, one full of lies that eventually destroy everything you worked so hard to build. I love you and want the same kind of marriage as you do."

I pull her back, so we are lying on the lounger with her head on my chest. "Please know your needs and feelings will always be number one with me. Try to understand that Annie has given me such a gift in Sean. He needs both of us at our best for him to be his best. When she's falling apart and focusing her energies on me, then he suffers. Does that make any sense to you?"

Keegan nods and says, "Yeah, it does."

"I think there are times Annie fears losing Sean to you."

"Jack, I would never do that to her."

"Maybe not intentionally, but sometimes, special bonds just happen. I understand her fears and need for reassurance. I admit, there are times when I overreact to Annie's meltdowns. Old habits are hard to break, and I'm asking for a little patience from you while I learn new ways to deal with her. All of this has been tough on her. When the day comes when she brings another man into Sean's life, I might do a little acting out myself."

"I'll be there to help you through it."

"You promise?"

"I promise."

I look down at Kirby, and the little hairball is doing his staring thing at us. "Come on, I think someone is ready for bed."

Once we get settled in bed, I pull Keegan into my arms. "You are the love of my life, the person I want to be with until my last breath. Will you, Keegan Brigid Fitzgerald Henderson, please marry me?"

"Absolutely." She smiles as I place the engagement ring back on her finger.

Epilogue

The Wedding
Jack

On this beautiful day in May, I stand with my best man—my son, Sean Grady—at the dock, waiting for my bride. We are a handsome pair in our khakis, white button-down shirts, green plaid bow ties, and deck shoes.

The county fire department's chaplain stands to the right of us.

I look out over the sea of family and friends that are seated in five rows of white chairs. There is an aisle parting the chairs that Keegan will follow to where the land meets the dock and me.

Off to the side, standing in the cool shade of a grouping of trees is Mitch's wedding gift to Keegan—an Irish ensemble.

As they begin to play an old Irish wedding march, I watch Marcy step out of the lower-level door. She's in a green printed sundress, and she's guiding Kirby on a leash. He's wearing a small green plaid bow tie, too.

Following Marcy, Kyle escorts his mother—my bride—down to the dock to me.

She has on a pale muted green sundress with her auburn hair cascading down. As she walks, the light spring breeze catches the hem of her dress, making it appear as if she is floating, like an angel. She carries in her hands two long-stemmed white lilies, representing each of our children.

Keegan is simply stunning, and I can't take my eyes off her as she finally reaches the dock.

The chaplain waits for the music to stop and begins the ceremony. "Dearly beloved, we come together in the presence of God to witness and bless the joining together of this man and this woman in holy matrimony. Who gives this woman in marriage?"

Without hesitation, Kyle speaks up, "I'm sorry, but I refuse to give my mother away because she is far too precious to me."

You can hear everyone's shock over Kyle's statement.

He turns to me. "Jack, I will be more than happy to share her with you and Sean, so we can become one family. I'm trusting that you will love and cherish her, as I do, and always see her for the incredible woman that she is."

Overwhelmed by Kyle's words, I respond, "Thank you, Kyle, and you're right. She is far too precious of a gift to give away. And, yes, I promise you that I will always love and cherish her." I shake Kyle's hand, followed by a man hug.

Kyle turns to a tearful Keegan, hugging her, and I hear him say quietly to her, "I love you, Mom."

I take Keegan's hands into mine and whisper in her ear so that no one else can hear, "God, you're beautiful." Then, I kiss her cheek.

The chaplain then asks us, "Do you, Keegan and Jack, take each other as man and wife to live together in the covenant of marriage? Will you love, comfort, honor, and keep each other in sickness and in health and forsake all others, being faithful to each other, for as long as you both shall live?"

We both answer in unison, "We will."

Then, the chaplain addresses our family and friends, "Will all of you witnessing these promises do all in your power to uphold these two persons in their marriage?"

They respond, "We will."

Seth steps to the front of the gathering where a guitar sits in a stand. He puts the strap around him and serenades the gathering with our favorite love song.

At the conclusion of the song, the chaplain says to our guests, "Keegan and Jack wanted their vows to be in their words and no one else's, so I now turn this ceremony over to them. Jack?"

I face my beautiful bride, my soul mate, as I take her hand in mine. "When I walked into the coffee shop on that cold winter day four and a half years ago, I never thought it would turn into this incredible journey we are on now. I've said it before, and I will say it now. Thank God for coworkers and friends with good intentions.

"You've taught me all about cigarette breaks, tattoo parlors, and paradigm shifts. When we were separated, you were always in my thoughts and my heart. I knew, someday, we would find our way back to each other. During our time apart, I found out that you completed me and that I was a better man with you by my side.

"The tattoos we wear on our left wrists will serve as a reminder of our promises today, so we never lose our way again. Keegan, come be by my side forever on this wild ride called life. In the name of the Father, I, John Patrick Grady, take you, Keegan Brigid Fitzpatrick Henderson, to be my wife. From this day forward, know I will always remain true and honest to you. I promise that you and our sons will always be my first priority in life. I will be by your and our children's sides through both the good and bad times. And, above all, I will always respect, love, and cherish you until we are parted by death. This is my solemn vow to you and Kyle."

Keegan

It takes a second for me to catch my breath after hearing Jack's vows. I look into his eyes and say, "When you came into my life, I was lost. I had no sense of who I was or where I was heading. When I was broken, you were this shining beacon of light leading me out of the fog. You've taught me how honesty builds trust in a relationship.

"When I thought I was finally finding my way, the rug was pulled out from under me, and I went spiraling down, thinking I'd lost you forever. But there you were one day, delivering pizza to my front door, with a side of reality to help me find my way back to you.

"I, Keegan Brigid Fitzpatrick Henderson, am honored to have you as my husband, John Patrick Grady, to have and to hold from this day forward. I will share in the joy of our good times together and be your beacon of light when you are struggling to find your way out of the fog. I promise to build our marriage on a foundation of honesty, respect, and trust. But, above all, I will love and cherish you until death. This is my solemn vow to you and Sean."

The chaplain then blesses our rings. Jack and I place our wedding bands on each other's ring fingers as a symbol of our vows. Mine is a band with tiny round diamonds that complements the ones on my engagement ring. Jack's is a platinum band with a continued Celtic knot design that matches the one in the middle of my engagement ring.

The chaplain pronounces us man and wife, telling Jack he may kiss me—his bride.

Jack takes me in his arms and then passionately kisses me. Our guests applaud with a few wolf whistles in the mix.

As we come up for air, Jack says, "I love you, Mrs. Grady."

"I love you beyond the stars and back, Mr. Grady."

Keegan and Jack continue their story in
Revealing You
Coming in 2017

Acknowledgments

This book has been a labor of love, and I have so many people to acknowledge who helped make it a reality.

First, kudos goes out to Sarah Hansen of Okay Creations for a beautiful book cover. Jovana Shirley of Unforeseen Editing for her editing, proofing, and formatting talents. All first-time authors should be blessed to work with such gifted ladies. They held my hand through the process of getting my first novel published, and I am truly grateful.

On a more personal note, I would like to acknowledge my daughter, Kate, who encouraged me to write this book. In dealing with her own personal struggles, Kate has taught me not to fear challenges but to face them head-on.

My son, Michael, a high school computer graphics/photography teacher, served as my art adviser. He's responsible for my headshot on the About the Author page. Michael is constantly teaching me about good design. He has been an awesome sounding board when it came to making decisions pertaining to the artwork for this book.

My husband, Mike, never once complained about the long days and nights I spent writing my book. During this time, he made sure our home continued to run smoothly and that Kirby got fed. Yes, there really is a Kirby. He is exactly as portrayed in the book, down to our need to spell out words and his ability to tell time.

To my beta readers—Girls, you are the best! I picked three amazing women with versatile backgrounds and told them to go at it with a red pen. Their input was invaluable and gave me much food for thought. Thank you, ladies!

Thank you Susan, my FB bud, who is always there to double-check my postings for me.

A special shout-out to Lois, who is not only a dear friend, but also my editorial sounding board. We had numerous discussions about book titles, taglines, grammar, and storyline. Her honesty was not only refreshing, but also made me a better writer.

Finally, I give thanks for my father's family, the Tinneys, who hail from County Donegal, Ireland. My great-grandfather, Patrick Tinney, came to America to start a new life in 1865. My life has been enriched by my Irish heritage, and I feel truly blessed to be one of the many who have green running through their veins.

"May St. Patrick guard you wherever you go,
And guide you in whatever you do—
And may his loving protection be a blessing to you always."

About the Author

S.T. Heller was born and raised in Maryland. She now lives on a lake in southern Pennsylvania with her husband and dog. Retired from a local school system, she has two children and five grandchildren. Along with enjoying fun times on the lake with family and friends, her other pastimes include quilting and making pottery. She  loves the sound of her grandchildren's laughter, daydreaming on a beach by the water's edge, getting lost in a good book, and floating on the lake at sunset.

The second book of this series, *Revealing You*, will be released in 2017.

Please follow S.T. Heller.

Website: www.shellerauthor.com

Facebook:
www.facebook.com/stheller2016

Twitter: https://twitter.com/@stheller16

More on Meningioma

My daughter was diagnosed and treated for a meningioma in 2014. The following is information that I have learned during the past two years.

A meningioma is a slow-growing growth on the meninges—or the tissues of the membrane—that cover the brain. The majority of the time, they are benign and are found more often in women than men. A meningioma might be monitored over a period of time with no treatment, if there are no significant symptoms. The tumor might reach a large size before becoming symptomatic and interfering with the normal functions of the brain.

Symptoms include, but are not limited to, headache, seizures, weakness in arms or legs, personality changes, and problems with vision. When the tumor becomes symptomatic, surgery and/or radiation might be required.

The most important thing I have learned through my daughter's illness is that you need to be your own advocate in your treatment. Be informed, be persistent, and ask questions.

I like to end with an excerpt from an email from a friend, who is also a meningioma survivor.

> *"I would like those who first hear the words,* You have a brain tumor, *to know that there is hope. The meningioma diagnosis is not a death sentence."*

Websites for More Information on Meningioma

Support Group

Meningioma Mommas

http://meningiomamommas.org/

Non-Profit Organizations

Brain Science Foundation

http://www.brainsciencefoundation.org/
bUnderstandbPrimaryBrainTumors/
Meningioma/MeningiomaSymptoms
Diagnosis/tabid/189/Default.aspx

The National Brain Tumor Society

http://braintumor.org/brain-tumor-
information/brain-tumor-facts/

The Race for Hope in DC Funds the National Brain Tumor Society

http://www.braintumorcommunity.org/
site/TR?fr_id=2360&pg=entry

The American Brain Tumor Association (ABTA)

http://www.abta.org/brain-tumor-
information/types-of-
tumors/meningioma.html

Hospital Websites

Johns Hopkins

http://www.hopkinsmedicine.org/
neurology_neurosurgery/centers_clinics/
brain_tumor/center/meningioma/menin
gioma-brain-tumor.html

Bringham and Women's Hospital in Boston: Meningioma Center of Excellence

http://www.brighamandwomens.org/
departments_and_services/neurosurgery/
meningioma/meningiomafacts.aspx

Made in the USA
Middletown, DE
03 July 2017